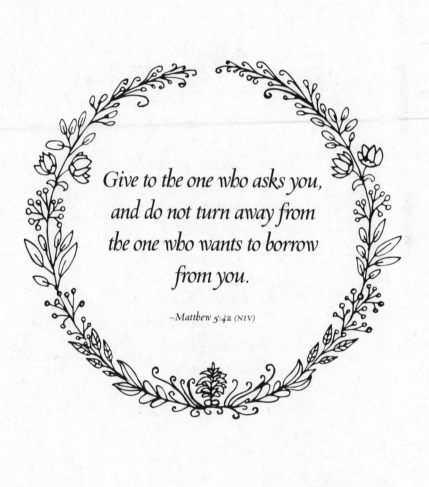

Give to the one who asks you,
and do not turn away from
the one who wants to borrow
from you.

–*Matthew 5:42 (NIV)*

MYSTERIES *of* LANCASTER COUNTY

BEG, BORROW, OR STEAL

MYSTERIES *of* LANCASTER COUNTY

Anne Marie Rodgers

Guideposts
Danbury, Connecticut

BEG, BORROW,
OR STEAL

CHAPTER ONE

Sunlight streamed through the tall, east-facing windows of the Mount Zion Mennonite Church's fellowship hall, and birdsong drifted in through the open sashes, weaving a charming counterpoint to the chattering crowd. It was an unusually warm, mild April day in Lancaster County, Pennsylvania, and Elizabeth Classen felt the pull of spring. Some of the women in more contemporary garb had traded wool and warmth for lighter fabrics, and the tables around the room sported vases of sunny daffodils.

The fellowship time during the short reception between Sunday school and church was always well attended, but today was Palm Sunday, and there were even more people than usual at the traditional morning service.

Several pots of hyacinths had been set on the long table where baked goods and drinks were located, and Elizabeth could smell their sweet scent, though she stood some distance away with her sister Martha and several of their friends in the congregation. The bright colors of the spring flowers were echoed by the lighter, brighter colors many of the women in the congregation wore. Everyone seemed happy that spring had arrived, and the bluster of March had finally given way to warmer spring temperatures across Lancaster County.

Elizabeth wore a blue and yellow flowered skirt with a pale yellow twinset, relatively new wardrobe pieces she'd chosen because she loved the colors. She felt a bit self-conscious. Sometimes she still felt as if she was calling attention to herself with her new style of dress, even as modest a change as it was.

As she listened to Martha discuss a recipe for Paska Easter bread—a slightly sweet Slovak egg bread made in round loaves with dough crosses—with a friend, Elizabeth's gaze roamed the assembled people. Dozens were seated at the tables provided, enjoying snacks from the refreshment stand at the far end of the room. Mary was in front of the stand, exchanging a few words and a smile with the woman who was refilling drink cups. Ever casual, even on Palm Sunday, she wore a slim pair of jeans beneath a flowing pink and blue paisley blouse with a scalloped hem and bell sleeves. It was a slight departure from the oversized painter's shirts she often wore, but not drastic.

Elizabeth smiled, watching a young mother who appeared to be trying to dissuade her toddler from grabbing a handful of cookies from the dozens of baked goods. Words apparently were not working, because the child began to wail loudly. The mother, looking mortified, quickly snatched him up and carried him through the double doors into the hallway beyond. As the doors slowly closed, the sound of his tantrum diminished in volume.

At the far end of the refreshment table sat several bowls holding fruit. A slender teenager placed an apple from one of the fruit bowls into the pocket of her oversized tan jacket. The teen's back was to the room, and all Elizabeth could see was shoulder-length, rather curly and wild-looking black hair and a pair of faded jeans with a ripped-out pocket and frayed hems that were significantly less dressy than most of the other young people in the room wore. The girl at the table stood out because of the shabbiness of her clothes.

The teen picked up a banana and stuffed it into another pocket. Then Elizabeth saw her take another apple. What on earth...?

It appeared someone else had noticed the unusual behavior. Geraldine Goertz, a large woman who wore a conservative plain blue dress with a small lace prayer cover affixed to her hair, stepped up to the table and addressed the girl. Elizabeth saw the slender figure startle, but she apparently responded, and Geraldine said something else. Then, before Elizabeth could even process what had happened, the girl turned sharply, took several almost running strides, and slipped through the exit leaving a trail of crumbs behind. Perhaps she had some cookies in her pocket as well. Geraldine frowned after the girl for a moment, shrugged her shoulders, and then meandered along the table and picked up a cookie.

"Did you see that girl?" Elizabeth turned to her sister Martha, lovely in a soft lavender sweater set and a matching flowered skirt that swished around her calves. Her middle sister was a beauty, Elizabeth thought, admiring Martha's brown hair and the light in her blue eyes as she chatted animatedly with a fellow chef in the crowd.

But Martha was still talking recipes with Essie Baldwin. Both women looked at her as one. "What girl?" they asked in unison.

Elizabeth shook her head, smiling. "Never mind."

Mary approached. "That's good lemonade," she said. "Would you like me to get you some?"

"No, thank you," Elizabeth said. "Did you happen to notice the girl who was standing near you in the oversized jacket?"

Mary glanced around the room. "No. What girl?"

Elizabeth gestured. "She was at the other end of the table from you. It was really odd. She was filling her pockets with fruit."

"That is sort of strange." Then Mary shrugged. "Or maybe not. Kids do weird stuff all the time. Maybe she was taking some for friends."

"It certainly caught my attention," Elizabeth said. "She didn't eat any, just started loading her pockets with apples and bananas. She had plenty of room in that big jacket she was wearing. And then she left abruptly."

"Where'd she go?" Mary looked around as if she might be able to spot the teen.

"She ran outside."

When Mary's eyebrows shot up, Elizabeth elaborated. "Geraldine Goertz noticed what she was doing too. Geraldine walked over to speak with her. And about six seconds later, the girl bolted out the exit just behind the end of the table."

Mary's eyebrows rose even higher. "What on earth…? Seems like if she was doing something innocent, she wouldn't have run away like that. What do you suppose Geraldine said to her?"

"To who?" Martha had finished speaking with Essie, who was turning to greet someone else. She raised her eyebrows inquiringly.

Elizabeth repeated what she'd told Mary. "I'd give a lot to know what Geraldine said that made that child take off like that," she concluded.

"Well, why don't you just ask her about it?" That was Martha, always sensible.

"I think I will," Elizabeth said.

But before she could look around and locate Geraldine, Mary tapped the face of her watch. "It's time for church."

Elizabeth followed her sisters to the sanctuary, promising herself she would catch Geraldine later.

Entering the sanctuary, they were greeted by the usher teams for that Sunday and given bulletins with the order of the service and the coming week's relevant announcements. As they made their way into their pew, they exchanged greetings with the familiar families who sat around them.

Shortly after the sisters took their seats in the pew the Classen family had been sitting in since the sisters' grandparents first attended Mount Zion, the prelude began. When it ended, the organist began to play a lovely piece of music composed by Jean Baptiste Faure that had been a staple of the church's Palm Sunday celebration since Elizabeth's own childhood. One by one, the children of the congregation carried palms to the front of the church, where they were received by the elders and the pastor and piled before the altar. As the refrain began, Elizabeth felt her throat grow tight and tears sting her eyes. She and her sisters had been among those children many years before.

> *Join all and sing, His name declare,*
> *Let ev'ry voice resound with acclamation,*
> *Hosanna! Praised be the Lord!*
> *Bless Him who cometh to bring us salvation!*

The final word was drawn out into roughly seven syllables.

For the past several years, the "palms" had consisted of plentiful local grasses scythed in the fall and stored throughout the winter, as members of the congregation had become more aware that ordering palms from Central American countries, where they were harvested with little regard for the damage done to the ecosystems of the surrounding forests, was not an environmentally friendly practice.

As the choir and congregation sang, and the grasses piled up, Elizabeth continued to feel moved by the beauty of the moment. It was a lovely ritual, made even more poignant when she contemplated Jesus' entry into Jerusalem. Palm Sunday preceded a week of somber reflection on His tragic death less than a week later. Throughout the coming week, they would mourn. But today, Christ had made a triumphal entry into the Holy City accompanied by an enthusiastic crowd. She felt herself relaxing into the joy of the moment.

A bit later, she listened attentively to Pastor Nagle's message, which focused on his vision for ministry in the community and on his anticipation of his eventual face-to-face meeting with his Lord. How would each member of the congregation react when Christ asked for an accounting of how they had responded to those who asked for assistance, whether in monetary form or otherwise? Would assistance have been conditional, based on a personal decision about how worthy they had judged the need to be? As he moved on to discuss Christ's knowledge of what He was about to face after the celebratory crowd embraced Him, expecting salvation from their overlords, Elizabeth's attention strayed, caught by the question.

How would she have reacted earlier if she had been the one to speak with the girl in the tan jacket who had been stuffing her pockets with fruit? She had an uncomfortable feeling her first question would have been along the lines of why the girl needed all that fruit, and she wondered if that was what Geraldine had said.

Surreptitiously, she looked around the congregation. The girl did not appear to be among her fellow worshippers. It was possible she hadn't stayed for church or was helping out with the youngest children in the church nursery. But Elizabeth couldn't recall ever having seen that particular girl before. Was she a church member at all? And if not, what on earth could have led her to attend the social time between Sunday school and church? Surely she hadn't come only to pick up some fruit and possibly some cookies. That was just too strange to contemplate.

After the service Elizabeth and her sisters filed out of the sanctuary, speaking to friends along the way. She blinked as she, Martha, and Mary stepped out into the bright sunshine. Scanning the sidewalk, she located Geraldine Goertz chatting with several members of her extended family a short distance away. She hadn't forgotten her desire to ask Geraldine about the conversation she'd had with the teen.

Elizabeth smiled warmly as she approached the other woman. "Good morning, Geraldine."

"Good morning, Elizabeth. Blessings to you on this Palm Sunday." Geraldine smiled.

"Thank you. And to you." Elizabeth cleared her throat. "I saw you speaking to a young girl during the fellowship time. I didn't recognize her, and I wondered who she was. Did you know her?"

Geraldine snorted in a good-natured way. "There wasn't much speaking going on. I saw her putting fruit and crackers in her pockets. Did you notice that?"

Elizabeth nodded. "I noticed the fruit. Did she say what she was going to do with it?"

"She didn't say. I mentioned that the fruit was a much better snack than cookies, and she agreed with me." Geraldine's eyebrows rose. "And then she asked if I had twenty dollars she could borrow! Can you imagine such a thing? She said she'd pay me back when she was able."

Elizabeth felt a shock of surprise. "What did you say to her?"

Geraldine shrugged. "I didn't know what to say, to tell you the truth. I asked her to tell me her name and why she needed twenty dollars. And the next thing I knew, she turned around and hurried out the door like a pack of wild dogs was on her tail."

Elizabeth had to chuckle at Geraldine's description. But concern niggled at the corners of her mind. The girl had appeared slender. Was she hungry? "What did she look like?" Elizabeth asked. "I could only see long, curly, kind of wild dark hair from the back. Is she a member of the congregation?"

Geraldine shook her head. "I'd never seen her before. I'd remember those eyes."

"What about her eyes?"

"She's got a thin little face," Geraldine said. "But she has these great big eyes of a very light color. Not blue. Perhaps greenish. The color is not what struck me. It was more that her eyes are the most memorable feature of her face."

"I don't believe I've ever seen her before either," Elizabeth said. The two women fell silent for a moment.

Then Geraldine shrugged. "I guess it's just going to be a little Palm Sunday mystery."

"I guess it is." Elizabeth chatted a little bit more before returning to her sisters. They had stopped to speak with others on the way to the parking lot. After joining the group, Elizabeth recounted the incident with the unknown girl, sharing Geraldine's close-up description of the girl's memorable eyes. "Does that sound like anyone you might know?" she asked the group in general.

Rella Wiens, who had overseen the guest book for today's services, cocked her head to one side. "I don't recall any young person coming in who fits that description exactly, but it could be Tammy McClain's daughter, Brittany. She has long dark hair, and she's in the youth group. I'm not sure I'd describe her hair as wild, but that's sort of a subjective term, isn't it? She hardly ever comes to church, but I believe she came in the side door with her mother today."

"You know," Mary said, "there's a girl with shoulder-length black hair who plays the guitar at the evening service. She looks like an older teen to me, and her hair's definitely what I'd call wild. In fact, it often has a streak of some color or other in it."

Elizabeth almost never attended the evening service. She couldn't bring the guitar player to mind at all. The girl she'd seen today hadn't had any noticeable color in her hair, but a streak could have gone unnoticed, especially from a distance. "Do you know her name?"

"Sorry." Mary shook her head regretfully. "I've never actually met her."

"That's Sheila Canner," said someone behind Elizabeth. She turned to find Minerva Helman, the head librarian at the Bird-in-Hand Free Library, standing at her left shoulder. "Sheila's a bit of a wild child." Minerva smiled to take the sting from her words, shaking her head fondly. "It would not surprise me to find Sheila sneaking off with her pockets filled with goodies."

"But it was fruit and crackers, not cookies," Elizabeth said. "I think I'd understand it more if it had been goodies."

"Well, nothing would surprise me," Louise Schott said. Her mouth pursed. "That child has been poorly supervised her entire life. I remember when she was just a toddler, she yanked on one of the table legs and pulled an entire table of salads over at a potluck dinner. And I've seen her sneaking handfuls of extra cookies from the dessert tables any number of times. I wouldn't be surprised if that's who you saw."

But why had she asked Geraldine for money, Elizabeth wondered, if that was who it had been? Twenty dollars wasn't insignificant. She hadn't mentioned the monetary request to the group, and she wasn't inclined to after hearing Louise's pronouncements. She resolved to try never to be so judgmental, no matter how old she got.

Mary tugged at Elizabeth's elbow. "Are you ready to go? Don't forget I have to be home to take that puppy this afternoon. I want to have time to grab some lunch."

Mary had volunteered to foster a beagle puppy for a rescue. The young dog was a new intake, and the foster family that was going to care for him couldn't take him until they returned from vacation next week. Mary, after checking with her sisters, had felt that for such a short period, she could handle the extra work that caring for a puppy would require.

Elizabeth snapped her fingers. "Sorry, I forgot. Yes, I'm ready."

"Elizabeth?" A voice behind her stopped her as she began to move toward the car. Mary and Martha went on ahead.

"Good morning, Frannie," Elizabeth said, stopping to speak with the woman who had hailed her.

Frannie Bartel was a church member who volunteered at a food pantry along Route 30. "There's a girl who stops into the food pantry that fits your description, although I didn't see her here today, and I don't know that they've ever attended church. Her name is Ellie Pearce." She hesitated. "I don't want to be known as a gossip, but there are things you should know if Ellie turns out to be the girl you saw."

"I won't pass on anything you share with me in confidence," Elizabeth promised. "Well, I might discuss it with my sisters," she added honestly, "but none of us will spread it around. I was concerned when I saw the girl taking fruit from church today, and I suppose I felt led to offer help if she needs it."

Frannie looked relieved. "The Pearce family is known to be in what my mother used to call 'reduced circumstances.' The father lost his job, and I don't believe he's found another one yet. Ellie's mother works two jobs to keep food on the table. People suspect her husband beats her when she doesn't bring home enough in tips from waitressing. The mother comes into the food pantry sometimes, and once she had a black eye. I've heard he drinks a great deal."

Elizabeth made a sympathetic murmur. "That's sad for all of them."

"That's not really gossip," Frannie said. "It's a pretty well-established fact, and I'm only telling you because I'm a little concerned for your safety if that's the family you become involved with."

"I understand." Although Elizabeth didn't expect to be doing anything that would put herself in danger.

"The girl is very quiet," Frannie added, "but if she's the one you saw, she could be trying to protect the mother by bringing food home."

"Thank you. If it was Ellie Pearce, perhaps I can find a way to help the family that isn't obvious," Elizabeth said. "Have a good week, Frannie."

"You too," Frannie said as Elizabeth hurried off to join her sisters for the drive home.

She was almost to the car when she saw Pastor Abraham Nagle and his wife heading for their own vehicle. "Pastor?" She hailed him.

"Hello, Elizabeth." Pastor Nagle was a pleasant man who was fitting in well in his new position, having come to Mount Zion not quite a year ago. "How can I help you?"

"I just have a quick question." She mentioned the Pearce family, and Ellie in particular.

The pastor shook his head. "I'm not familiar with the family, I'm afraid, and I was not introduced to anyone by that name today. But Palm Sunday and Easter are services that draw a lot of unfamiliar faces, and they could have been in attendance today without my knowledge."

Or the girl could have slipped into the fellowship time expressly for the purpose of foraging, Elizabeth thought. Aloud, she said, "That's true. Oh, by the way, do you and Maida have plans for Easter dinner? Because if you don't, my sisters and I would love to have you join us."

"That's very kind of you," Pastor Nagle said. "We're going to be taking communion to some of our members who live at Morningside Nursing Home after church. We'd love to eat with you if we won't hold up your meal too much."

"Not at all," Elizabeth said. "Shall we say two o'clock? Will that give you enough time for your visits?"

"I think that would work nicely," the pastor said. "Thank you for the invitation."

Finally, Elizabeth climbed into Mary's car. The engine was already running, and they pulled out immediately.

"Sorry to rush you," Mary said. "I just don't want to be still having lunch when the rescue person arrives with the dog. I told her to come between twelve thirty and one."

"I'm the one who's sorry," Elizabeth said. "But I stopped to invite the Nagles to have Easter dinner with us next Sunday."

"Oh, what a nice idea," Mary said. "Are they able to come?"

"Yes, after they take communion to the church members at Morningside who can't attend the Easter Sunday service. I told him two o'clock, and he said that would work."

"That was a very thoughtful thing to do," Martha said. "Oh boy, a bigger group to cook for! What shall I serve?"

"Ham," Mary said immediately. "We always have ham for Easter. Why would you even think of doing anything differently?"

"I didn't mean I wouldn't serve ham," Martha said with a chuckle. "Relax. I was just thinking about what dishes I should serve with it."

"Some kind of potatoes, some kind of vegetable, and rolls," Mary replied promptly.

Martha rolled her eyes and sighed. "Mary, you're a food philistine."

"No, I'm not," Mary said. "I'm neither hostile nor indifferent to your cooking and baking, which is what I'd be if I were a philistine. I only know that whatever you serve will be so scrumptious, I won't care what it is."

Martha laughed. "Oh, well done. Compliment me so I can't insult you anymore. Elizabeth, do you have any opinions on side dishes for Easter?"

From the back seat Elizabeth said, "I really love those four-cheese scalloped potatoes you make. Would they go well with ham?"

"Oh yes," Mary said. "They'd be perfect. Good idea."

"What else, Elizabeth?" Martha asked.

"What? Oh, I don't know." Elizabeth's mind had already wandered back to the mystery girl.

"What's on your mind?" Martha asked. "Since it's clearly not on Easter dinner."

"There was something about that girl I saw during fellowship time today," Elizabeth said. "The one I saw hiding fruit in her coat. She really caught my attention. It seemed like such a strange thing to do, and it's equally odd to me that hardly anyone noticed her. Even weirder, I think, not a single person recognized her."

Mary signaled a left turn. "Definitely odd. So Pastor Nagle didn't know her either?"

"Well, he didn't see the girl when I did," Elizabeth admitted, "so we didn't really discuss that. I asked him if he knew Ellie Pearce or her family."

"Who's Ellie Pearce?" Martha wanted to know.

"A girl Frannie Bartel mentioned. Her family goes to the food pantry. That's where Frannie knows her from. And she fits the description of the girl I saw today."

"A slender teenage girl with long dark hair," Martha said with a chuckle. "That only describes about two-thirds of the teen girls in Bird-in-Hand."

Elizabeth sat back with a sigh. She knew what Martha said was true. There were scores of teenage girls in town who had long dark hair and who were perfectly fine. But Elizabeth knew in her heart she had to find this one. This one needed her help.

CHAPTER TWO

After a few moments of silence Martha asked, "Does Pastor Nagle know Ellie Pierce?"

Elizabeth shook her head, and then realized her sisters in the front seat couldn't see her. "No. He didn't recognize the name, and he didn't think he was introduced to the Pierce family today."

"So he wouldn't be of any help. Did Frannie give any particular reason for thinking that it could have been this Ellie person you saw?"

Elizabeth hesitated. "In confidence, yes. Her family situation is difficult, and Frannie thought it was possible the girl, Ellie Pearce, could have been trying to help feed her family."

"Oh." Mary's soft heart was evident in the single syllable.

"But I have no evidence that it actually was her," Elizabeth hastened to add. "You heard how many other people volunteered the names of girls within our church that fit the description. Let's see." She counted on her fingers. "Including Ellie, there were four teenage girls mentioned."

Martha turned her head and looked at Elizabeth. "You do realize she could have been doing nothing more sinister than loading her pockets for her friends, right?"

Elizabeth smiled. "Yes. But then why would she have asked for money?"

"Good point," Martha conceded.

"And *sinister* isn't quite the word I'd use." Elizabeth hesitated. "I read an article about intuition the other day, about how we've been conditioned to ignore that little voice inside that sometimes warns us something's not right. That's how this feels to me. Like there was a significant reason she was taking the fruit, that perhaps she needs help."

"Some people might say that's God whispering in your ear," Mary said cheerfully. "I'm happy to do whatever I can to help."

"First, I have to find her and see if God really was whispering in my ear," Elizabeth said.

"And how are you going to do that?"

"I suppose I'll try to speak with each girl whose name was mentioned to me. I got a pretty good look at the fruit-taker's hair and physique, and I have Geraldine's description of her face, so I think I'll know her if I come across her."

"And we really can't help with that since neither of us noticed her," Mary said. "All right. Let us know if you need any assistance."

Elizabeth smiled. "Absolutely. Thanks."

After a short silence, Martha said, "Mary, tell us more about this dog you're going to be fostering."

"I don't know much more than what I've already told you," Mary said.

Mary turned onto their lane, which led up a rise past Secondhand Blessings, the thrift and consignment store the three sisters operated out of a restored barn at the bottom of the lane. Slowing, she steered around a pothole they needed to have filled in now that winter had ended. The lovely old Victorian, painted in soft shades of cream with green and lavender trim, stood on a bit of a hill past the shop near the road.

"He's from Safe Harbor Beagle Rescue, which saves beagles from puppy mills. His name is Bolt. The woman who is fostering him is taking her family to Niagara Falls over spring break. They didn't want to take Bolt along, so Safe Harbor needed a temporary foster for him."

"We should be able to handle a week," Martha said.

"Right," Mary agreed. "I figured that would be a perfect introduction to foster work." Safe Harbor was a village about half an hour southwest of Conestoga Township, down near the junction where the Conestoga River met the much larger Susquehanna.

"And you said he's a puppy." Elizabeth knew Mary had a soft spot for warm, cuddly puppies.

"Technically, he is." Mary hesitated. "I actually assumed he was a very young one, but last night the foster told me he's about eleven months old."

"That's almost a year," Elizabeth said, startled. "He'll be dog-size, not puppy-size!"

"Yes, but hopefully he'll have outgrown some of the more undesirable puppy behaviors. And it's only for a week," Martha repeated.

"And they provide a crate," Mary added. She pulled the car to a halt in front of the garage.

"That's good." Martha opened her door. "Let's have lunch. I'm starving!"

In the kitchen, Martha piled Lebanon bologna, lettuce, tomato, red onion, and tasty sharp cheddar cheese on large potato rolls while Elizabeth filled glasses with ice and water, and Mary ladled fruit salad made with canned cherries that Martha had put up last summer into bowls.

As soon as they'd said the blessing and began to eat, Mary said, "I forgot to mention it at breakfast, but I think we might be missing a hen."

"'Missing a hen'?" Elizabeth echoed. "What do you mean?"

"I couldn't find Barnie this morning," Mary told her, referring to a newer addition to their flock.

The Barnevelder was a handsome bird with striking black-on-reddish-brown laced feathers that made her look as if she wore scallops or tiny chevrons all over. She usually produced four chocolatey-brown eggs each week, with a few light speckles over them.

"Are you sure she wasn't just hiding?" Martha asked. Hens were notorious for going to roost early outside in trees or the woodpile or other unlikely places.

Mary shook her head. "I looked everywhere. And I distinctly remember putting her in the coop last night, because she was the last one in the yard, and I had to get stern with her."

Elizabeth chuckled. "How does one get stern with a hen?"

"One stamps one's foot and points to the ramp leading up to the door," Mary said, grinning. "And the hen gets the message and moves her little feathered fanny inside."

Elizabeth felt her smile fade as real concern filled her. "And she wasn't just malingering in the coop this morning?"

Mary shook her head. "No. I looked around after all the others came out, and she definitely wasn't in there. I need to check the coop more closely and make sure there's no place she could have gotten out."

"Oh, I hope not," Martha said. "You didn't have the easiest time finding a Barnevelder, did you?"

"No. They're becoming more popular, but they're certainly not common," Mary told her. "Besides, I don't want another one. I want my Barnie back. She's a sweet little girl and a very reliable layer."

"Maybe she'll be back tonight," Martha said, but Elizabeth could hear the doubt in her voice.

Privately, Elizabeth feared there might be another reason for the big hen's absence. But since neither of her sisters appeared ready to recognize it yet, she held her peace. Her sisters had lived with their families in the suburbs of cities for much of their adult life. They may have forgotten about the realities of rural life. Elizabeth had remained closer to her parents and the farm, and she had her suspicions about what might have happened to the Barnevelder.

The sisters had barely finished their meal when they heard car tires crunching on gravel.

"I bet that's our puppy," Mary said.

Elizabeth helped Martha clean up the remains of the meal while Mary went ahead onto the porch. Then they followed their younger sister outside.

Mary was standing beside the open rear hatch of a Nissan crossover in an eye-popping shade of orange. A woman was leaning into the vehicle, and Elizabeth could see a leash in her hand as the woman opened the door of a plastic airline dog crate taking up about half the space.

A moment later, a small dog with soulful brown eyes and adorably floppy ears hopped nimbly down from the back of the SUV. He bore a distinct black saddle over his back extending to most of his tail, with light sable across his rump and shoulders. His head and ears were light brown as well, while his muzzle and chest were white, and he looked like he was wearing white socks on his paws and lower legs. He stood beside the woman, his classic white-tipped tail flopping happily from side to side like a metronome as he surveyed his surroundings with what could only be described as a happy smile.

Mary introduced both of her sisters to the woman, Deb O'Hare, who turned out to be the foster coordinator for the organization. Deb wore jeans and a T-shirt that proclaimed: RESCUE IS MY FAVORITE BREED. She wore a woven straw hat with a long braid falling over one shoulder, and curly tendrils that had escaped waved around her freckled face.

"This is really good of you to volunteer," Deb said to Mary, who had knelt to stroke the dog. "We're filled to the gills with rescues right now, and he'd have had to go to a kennel for the week otherwise. I hate having them live in kennels when they're used to being in homes. Coming into rescue is tough enough for a dog without that kind of stress."

"Where did he come from?" Martha asked her. "How long has he been in your care?"

"Bolt is new to our rescue," Deb told them. "You'll be his first fosters. His owner passed away quite unexpectedly recently, and the daughter did not want him, so she took him to the humane society. We have an arrangement with them. Although we often get our dogs straight from puppy mill situations, anytime a purebred beagle is surrendered to the local shelters, we pull it. We just picked him up yesterday afternoon."

"Why?" Elizabeth was confused. "I mean, wouldn't he have gotten adopted from the shelter?"

"Probably," Deb said. "But the more we're able to take off their hands, the more kennel space they have free to take in others. Wonderful mixed-breed dogs often get overlooked when they have to compete with purebred puppies."

"Oh, I didn't think of that," Elizabeth said.

Mary made a soft sound of approval. "That's true."

"Also," Deb went on, "beagles are wonderful little dogs, but not everyone understands how strong their instincts to hunt are. We don't want any shelter to place a dog only to have it returned a month later because it heads for the hills following its nose the first time you let it out the door."

Martha chuckled. "Amen to that."

Deb grinned. "We like to work with our adopters to ensure that they understand the beagle has very strong sporting dog instincts so they know what they can and cannot expect."

Deb handed the lead to Mary and turned back to the vehicle, emerging with a large bag of dog food and a cloth bag with the rescue's logo printed on the side.

Martha stepped forward. "I can take those."

"All of his paperwork is in there," the foster coordinator said. "Including the vet we use and permission for treatment in an emergency. I'll need to have you sign the foster agreement.

We like you to call us first for authorization for medical issues, but we do recognize there could be a time when speed is of the essence. There also are toys, instructions for feeding, and a few other notes from the owner's daughter." She turned back to the vehicle. "Where would you like this crate?"

"I can take that," Elizabeth said, coming forward.

The crate wasn't enormous, just a bit unwieldy. She lifted it out of the back of the Nissan and carried it to the porch, where she set it beside the bag of dog food and the bag Martha had deposited there. They had discussed keeping the crate in the kitchen for the week. She would wait to move it there until one of her sisters could hold open the door for her.

Hands free again, Deb dropped to her knees. "Come here, Bolt."

The little dog pranced over, with Mary still holding his leash, and put his front paws up against Deb while she hugged him. "You're such a sweet boy," she said, snuggling him affectionately. "You're going to make some family very happy when we find you a forever home. Now you be good for Mary and her sisters, okay?"

Bolt lunged up and swiped his tongue across her face, and they all laughed.

After leading the way inside, Mary offered Deb a seat at the table and extracted the folder of foster paperwork from the bag she'd been given.

Deb reviewed the pertinent items with them all, and Mary signed the paperwork.

As Deb rose, Martha asked, "Would you like some cinnamon buns to take along? I made a fresh batch this morning."

"Cinnamon buns! Now that's an offer I can't refuse." Deb watched as Martha placed several of the sweet buns into a bag and sealed it before handing it to her. "Wow, thank you. These look amazing."

"They are," Martha said with a wink, making Deb laugh.

"Well, if you have no further questions, I guess I'll get going."

Mary ushered the foster coordinator out the door, and both Martha and Elizabeth followed them into the yard.

Deb knelt and gave the puppy a final pat, then rose and smiled at Elizabeth and her sisters. "Thanks again for caring for Bolt this week. I'll touch base on Friday and make arrangements to pick him up Saturday. Don't hesitate to contact me earlier if you have any questions or concerns about his health." Heading back to her car, she slipped into the driver's seat of the Nissan, reversed, and started down the lane toward the road. The little dog, tail wagging, strained against the leash as he watched the car get farther away.

"He's pretty adorable," Martha commented. "Hey, Bolt." She patted both palms against her thighs.

Mary also had been watching the Nissan leave, holding the leash in one hand. She must not have had a good grip, because the little dog lunged toward Martha, yanking the leash from Mary's clasp.

"Wha—?" Mary whirled, but she wasn't fast enough to grab the end of the lead. Elizabeth reacted as well, trying to snag it, but it whipped out of her hand.

"Ouch!" Her palm stung where the lead had whipped across it.

Bolt headed for Martha, but just before he came within reach, he veered sharply to the left and raced in a wild, exhilarated circle around the yard.

"Bolt, come here!"

"Here, boy, here, Bolt!"

"Bolt! Come!" Elizabeth knew her voice sounded exasperated.

The young dog raced in merry circles around them, just wide enough to be out of reach, while both Mary and Martha called the dog repeatedly. Then he took off in a straight line out through the yard, with all three sisters in hot pursuit that proved fruitless. He was just too fast.

Then, thinking of the dogs of her childhood, Elizabeth whistled sharply.

Bolt's ears pricked at the sound of the whistle, and he plowed to a halt. But a moment later, he was off again, dashing through the lovely display of blooming spring flowers along the far edge of the yard, leash snaking through the flowers in his wake.

"No!" Martha called sharply, clapping her hands as he approached the roses she so carefully tended.

Bolt veered again, circling back into the yard. Then he stopped, nose twitching, before lowering his head to the grass and sniffing as he trotted in a Byzantine path, following the scent he'd picked up. The white tip of his tail practically vibrated with excitement.

"Now we're in trouble." Mary groaned. "He's caught a scent. He could go for miles."

Elizabeth saw her chance. While the dog was busy casting around for the track he'd found, she slowly crept closer. When Bolt noticed her and took off, Elizabeth stomped firmly on the very end of the leash just within her stride. "Gotcha," she said with satisfaction, gathering up the excess leash as Bolt was jerked to a halt.

The little beagle didn't appear to mind. His tongue lolled as he trotted happily to her side. He looked so innocently delighted that Elizabeth didn't have the heart to scold him. After all, he was a hound dog. He'd only been doing what instinct demanded.

"Good catch." Mary sounded quite out of breath.

Martha surveyed the damaged tulips and daffodils with dismay. "Well, I guess we're going to have a vase of flowers on the table for dinner tonight."

"Now we know why they named him Bolt," Elizabeth said, rolling her eyes.

The next hour was less eventful with the new foster dog. Martha, looking through recipes for menus for the upcoming week, observed that Bolt seemed to have good house manners. He followed Tink's and Pal's example, trailing them around the house and lying near them when he could. He went and sat by the door when he needed to go out or stood in front of Mary and scratched at her leg. When she produced a chew toy from the bag of his belongings, he lay on the floor beside her and gnawed happily.

Midafternoon, Martha moved into the office to check her e-mail. Elizabeth was outside working on her annual restaining of the picnic table on the patio, and Mary was in the living room with a sketch pad, all three dogs sprawled comfortably on the floor and dog beds around her.

Taking a seat in front of her computer at the large old desk she shared with Elizabeth, Martha was delighted to see that she'd gotten e-mails from each of her children. After answering those, she moved on, deleting some junk before she came to an e-mail from a woman who belonged to the Friends of the Library. Martha had volunteered to work at the library's annual book sale, and she saw she was scheduled to work on Thursday from two until six. Well, she probably could make that work if their Amish neighbor, Rachel, was available to help at Secondhand Blessings.

Since it was Sunday, she knew Rachel would not get the message until tomorrow, but she called and left a voice mail for her friend and neighbor anyway.

She had just completed the call and started to review several other e-mails from people who wanted to consign items to Secondhand Blessings when her phone rang again.

She picked it up and accepted the call. "Hello?"

"Martha? This is Hilda Brunner."

Martha's internal radar went on high alert at the quavering tone in the woman's voice. Hilda was one of her fellow volunteers in the Friends of the Library group—the president, to be exact. Martha had been active in a similar group back in Hillsboro, Kansas, where she'd attended college and then settled down with her college sweetheart, Chuck. One of the first things she'd done after coming back to her childhood home here with her sisters was to seek out the library, and recently she'd begun volunteering with the Friends of the Library. "Hi, Hilda. Is everything all right?"

"I, uh, I have bad news."

"What's wrong?" Martha asked, bracing herself.

"Anya Presser had an emergency appendectomy, and she can't chair the book sale."

"Oh no. Poor Anya. One of my children had appendicitis. It's frightening."

"Yes. Well, we were hoping you'd take over," Hilda said in a rush, pushing the words out as if she'd lose her nerve if she didn't hurry.

"Oh, but I—"

"The planning's done, and almost all the books are sorted. There are only a few last-minute things to do, and everyone knows their jobs so well it won't be any work at all."

"If that's the case, why couldn't you do it?" Martha asked. "You're the president of the group."

"Oh, but I only took that because no one else would do it," Hilda protested. "I'm no good organizing and straightening out things that might come up. Please, Martha, you're so good at dealing with people."

Martha sighed. The book sale was this Thursday, Friday, and Saturday, right before Easter. It was true that most of the work was done. Even the volunteer schedule was in place. She wouldn't necessarily have to be there the whole time. It was really a matter of oversight. And she knew other members of the committee would help. It was simply that everyone seemed to be allergic to leadership. "All right," she said. "I guess I can do that, as long as you and the other committee members promise to help me with anything that comes up."

"Oh, absolutely! Thank you so much!" Hilda sounded as if the weight of the world had been lifted from her shoulders. "I'll let Anya know, and she can make arrangements to get you her notebook."

Martha concluded the call and was just about to turn back to her e-mail when she heard Mary shout, "Help!"

"Oh boy," she muttered to herself. "Now what?"

She rose and hurried to the door. Mary was no longer in the living room, and the back door stood ajar, although the screen door was closed.

Hurrying now, she rushed outside after pushing her feet into her sneakers. "What's wrong?" The very same words she'd uttered a few minutes ago, she realized.

Elizabeth had abandoned the paintbrush with which she'd been staining the picnic table, and she had both Pal and Tink with her. She inclined her head in the direction of the garden and the fields beyond. "The screen door wasn't latched, and Pal pushed it open. All three dogs got out. These two, of course, came when I called, but Bolt took off. Mary went after him."

Martha groaned. "I'd better go help. It's going to be a long week, I fear." She started jogging to the end of the yard.

"I'll help as soon as I put these guys in the house," Elizabeth said, leading the pair away.

Martha had to climb the fence that encircled the Fischers' pasture. She could see Mary running toward their neighbors' home, and she headed that way. Thank goodness she'd stopped to put her shoes on. There were already thistles galore in the pasture. Although they were mostly just starter plants on the ground and not tall enough to scratch arms and legs yet, they'd have been awful to step on.

She was out of breath by the time she approached Rachel's house. Mary was nowhere in sight. Several of Rachel's children were clustered near the pigsty, and she could hear their high-pitched voices squeaking in excitement, so she headed in that direction. Silas, Rachel's husband, came around the corner of the barn with a length of rope as Martha approached. He was frowning.

"Hello, Silas. I'm sorry to intrude on your Sunday. Have you seen Mary?"

"She is after that dog. He was chasing the piglets." He jerked a thumb in the direction of the sty.

"Oh no. I'm so sorry. We're keeping him for a week for someone," Martha said.

"He needs a leash," Silas replied, handing her the rope.

"He has one, but he sneaked out of the house and got away from us," Martha said. "Thank you. I promise we'll keep him away from your animals."

"Ah, well." Silas seemed to relent. "It is not the first time and it will not be the last that a dog causes a ruckus."

Mary came into view from the far side of the shed where the pigs were housed. She was disheveled and bent over, dragging Bolt beside her. Her fingers firmly gripped the light blue collar that bore the slogan ADOPT ME!

Martha knelt and tied the rope to Bolt's collar, noticing, as she did so, that he smelled disgustingly fragrant.

"Little *schnickelfritz*," Silas said, telling the panting dog he was a rascal. "You have had your fun. Home with you now."

"He didn't hurt the piglets," Mary said earnestly. "He was just excited. I'm so sorry, Silas. It won't happen again."

The two sisters were silent as they trudged homeward across the field. Bolt gamboled between them, happily oblivious to their mood. Every time he got close, Martha caught another whiff of pigsty.

Elizabeth met them halfway across the field. "Oh, mercy me," she said as she got a good look at the dog. "What did he do? Are we still on speaking terms with the Fischers?"

Mary snickered. "He got into the pigpen and chased the shoats around. Silas looked annoyed at first, but I think he was trying not to laugh by the time we left."

As they approached the house, Mary said, "Do you think we should put a hook and eye or a dead bolt on that screen door?"

"Not a bad idea," Martha said. "It would help us remember to check it when we have a situation like this. And if we put it up high, then when small grandchildren are visiting, they couldn't get out if we didn't want them to either."

"That's an excellent idea," Elizabeth said.

Mary smiled. "A dual-purpose solution." Then her smile died, and she wrinkled her nose. "This dog stinks."

"He was in the pig wallow," Martha pointed out, gesturing backward with one arm. "He's not going to smell like roses."

Bolt apparently took the wave as an invitation and promptly jumped up on her, smearing her with the disgusting mix of mud and other pig substances that covered him. Mary made an impulsive grab for the dog and succeeded in covering herself with the same foul mixture.

Elizabeth quickly danced backward, avoiding the beagle's happy leap. "Oh no you don't!"

Mary and Martha looked at each other ruefully. "Bath," they groaned in unison.

"And then showers for us," Mary said.

"I'll get out the hose, towels, and the dog shampoo," Elizabeth said. "But I think the two of you have this covered, so I'll leave you to it." She snickered. "Covered. Get it?"

Martha, soiled and smelly, advanced on her threateningly. "I think you'd like to join us, wouldn't you?"

"No!" Elizabeth turned and fled.

CHAPTER THREE

Bolt was not nearly as big a fan of soap and water as he had been of mud. When her sisters arrived home with the wandering beagle, Elizabeth had been both horrified by the odor and hard put to hide her amusement at their appearance. And she'd scrambled well out of range of the wild splashing that had ensued when they hosed him down, soaped him up, and hosed the lather off. She had consented to wrap the wriggling pup in a towel and carry him inside, where she'd rubbed him down, tried to dodge the water droplets that flew when he shook himself off, and put him in his crate to reflect on his adventures.

Now, after her sisters had taken much-needed showers, and they'd all thrown their wet and dirty clothes into the washer, they were off to a sixtieth anniversary party for elderly neighbors who lived on the next farm down from the Fischers. The couple, the Lauffers, had lived in the big farmhouse as long as Elizabeth could remember, and they knew the family well.

It was close to four o'clock and still pleasant enough to be outside, so the family had chosen to hold the gathering outdoors. The elderly couple were seated in rocking chairs at one side of an area set up with folding tables, and a line of newcomers was taking turns paying respects to them.

Elizabeth parked her car near others along the road, and the sisters walked past a number of buggies belonging to Amish neighbors to the picnic-style celebration, where they got in line and waited until they could congratulate Sam and Suzi Lauffer. Martha had brought a casserole to contribute to the celebration, and she took it off to the side tables covered with special dishes while Elizabeth and Mary chatted with neighbors and friends.

Rachel approached, moving slowly with her daughter-in-law Leah at her side. Leah would soon be having her first child.

"How are you feeling, Leah?" Elizabeth asked the young woman.

"Ready to become a mother." Leah grinned. "And it will be nice to be able to see my feet again."

"Not long now," Elizabeth consoled her.

As Rachel and Leah moved off to visit with others, someone else approached. It was Minerva Helman, with whom she'd spoken after church earlier that day. "Hello again," Minerva said. "I'm heading for the buffet. Care to join me?"

"I'm game," Elizabeth said. "All that good food looks delicious."

"Me too," Mary said. "Chasing that dog worked up my appetite."

Together, the three women moved toward the long table laden with food that all the families attending had contributed. Martha joined them as they started to fill their plates.

There were several kinds of soups, a ham and bean, chicken corn, and pepper cabbage. Next were slaws and relishes. Elizabeth chose some of Rachel's chow chow and a bit of coleslaw. A carving station took the center of the setup, and one of the Lauffers' sons placed thin slices of roast beef on her plate. Next she added creamed potatoes, buttered brown noodles, a teeny bit of fried fish, several spoonfuls of vegetables, and a sweet roll with a dollop of butter straight from the crock.

After filling their own plates with a variety of scrumptious foods, Elizabeth's sisters and Minerva followed her to seats at one of the long tables.

Mary surveyed their laden plates. "I don't think any one of us chose the same dishes."

"We'd have to take three plates to have room to try every-thing," Martha pointed out. "I'm going back for dessert. I had no room."

"We'll all go back for dessert," Elizabeth said. "I'm not missing that shoofly pie."

"I've been thinking about that girl you saw ever since you mentioned it at church," Minerva said. "Have you learned any-thing more?"

Elizabeth shook her head. "No. No one I talked to noticed her."

"Could it have been Jean Ann Brean? She has longish dark hair."

"Oh, I hadn't thought of her. Possibly? I haven't seen her in a long time," Elizabeth admitted. Jean Ann was a teen girl with intellectual disabilities whose parents attended Mount Zion. But Elizabeth hadn't seen Jean Ann in ages. Years, really, if she was honest. Elizabeth didn't usually interact with the youth, and as a result, she couldn't picture Jean Ann except as a much younger child who stood off to one side when the children per-formed and didn't really interact with her peers. And, like most children, she'd hung around the food tables anytime there was something set out to eat, Elizabeth recalled.

"Well, there's no lack of teenage girls with long brown hair around here," Minerva said with a chuckle.

"Why are we talking about girls with long brown hair?" Angie Rempel pulled out the chair beside Minerva. "Anyone sitting here?" Angie was a paraprofessional at the middle school, and she also attended Mount Zion.

"No. Please join us," Elizabeth said. She quickly recapped for Angie the odd incident she'd witnessed during the social hour that morning and explained Minerva's comment.

"I think I saw the girl you're talking about. If it was her, it wasn't Jean Ann."

"Jean Ann's put on a little weight since she hit adolescence," Minerva said. "I don't believe anyone would describe her as 'slender.'"

And that was exactly the word Elizabeth had used when she'd told Angie about the sighting.

"The girl I saw was sort of hanging around the fringes of the social hour at church," Angie volunteered. "She looked vaguely familiar, but I don't know her name."

"No one does," Elizabeth said glumly. Whoever would have thought it would be so hard to identify one teenager?

"There's a new girl in one of the eighth-grade classes, I think," Angie went on. "Maybe it's her, and that's where I've seen her before."

They were diverted from the topic when some Amish friends and neighbors stopped by to speak with them. Others followed. It was a pleasant get-together, combining good food, fine weather, and time well spent visiting with many friends and neighbors.

A group of Amish youngsters was playing croquet on a wide swath of lawn past the area where all the tables were set up. As they were organizing a new game, Mary got up from the table and approached them. She spoke, and all the children giggled.

Then one nodded and handed her a mallet, and a new game began.

"Uh-oh," Martha said. "Mary's got the blue mallet. They're setting her up."

"What do you mean?" Elizabeth asked.

Martha chuckled. "The blue mallet goes first. See the colors on the stake? Blue's at the top, which means the player with the blue mallet goes first. And then all the other players go. If you're first, your chances of having your ball knocked out of the right line of play increase a lot."

"Mary better be a good croquet player," remarked Minerva. "Those kids play all the time, and they're good."

The group at the table all stopped talking and focused on the croquet match.

Mary hit her blue ball a respectable distance. Unfortunately, she was followed immediately by a small girl in a lavender dress who stepped up, took aim, and with one deliberate swipe of her mallet, sent her red ball glancing off Mary's to knock it sideways far from the first wicket.

"Oh, she just 'roqueted' her," Minerva said, as the little girl went on to hit her own ball twice more before conceding play to the next player.

"That's not a word," Elizabeth said. "Is it?"

"Librarian," Martha said succinctly, pointing to Minerva. "Are you really going to doubt her word?"

"It's what happens when you strike another's ball with yours," Minerva said. "You receive two bonus strokes any time you strike another player's ball. You can use your bonus strokes to advance your ball, to hit the other ball, or to use your ball to knock the other farther out of play."

"Oh brother. She's sunk," Elizabeth muttered.

Everyone chuckled.

They watched as child after child sent his or her ball sailing through the wickets. Every time Mary's turn came around and she got through or near the first wicket, someone knocked her ball out of play. The Amish children jeered and clapped, but there was no malice in it, and Mary responded with good-natured mock sorrow, pretending to be crushed, which only heightened the children's amusement.

Rachel's youngest daughter, Dorcas, who was seven, came over to lean on the edge of their table. She was adorably shy.

Tucked under one arm was a large rag doll that Elizabeth suspected Rachel or Phoebe, Rachel's eldest daughter, had probably made. The doll wore a dress of cornflower blue that matched the one Dorcas was wearing, and its yarn hair was almost the exact same shade of wheat blond as the little girl's beneath the small white prayer caps that covered each of their heads.

Elizabeth leaned down. "Hello, Dorcas. Your doll is lovely. Does she have a name?"

Sky-blue eyes solemnly regarded her, and then the child nodded. One thumb crept toward her mouth.

"Can you tell it to me?" Elizabeth leaned lower. "You can whisper it in my ear if you like."

The child regarded her for a long moment, and Elizabeth didn't think she was going to comply. But finally, as Elizabeth remained quiet and still, the child stepped forward and put her little rosebud lips almost against her ear and whispered her answer.

"Oh, I see," Elizabeth said. "What a beautiful name! Is she named for your mother?"

Dorcas nodded.

"I have always loved the name Rachel," Elizabeth said.

The child beamed. Elizabeth had to smile at the expression on her face. Her eyes crinkled, and dimples popped up in her chubby cheeks.

Elizabeth patted her lap. "Do you think Rachel would like to sit here? You could sit here with her if you wanted."

The little girl's sky-blue eyes shot to Elizabeth's face, and then she smiled and nodded. Dorcas allowed her to pull her up onto her lap, arranging the doll beside her just so. Soon, Elizabeth and Martha were chatting about the croquet match with the little girl, and the child was nodding and pointing, shyness forgotten.

Out on the lawn, Mary was struggling along in the wake of the other croquet players, beginning to get more cutthroat now and aggressively whacking the children's balls out of play when she got a chance. The kids loved it, teasing her relentlessly, and they all were laughing and giggling, as were many of the adults watching the game.

Soon after the meal, cake was served, and Dorcas abandoned them for her mother's lap. As the anniversary celebration drew to a close, one of the Lauffers' daughters announced that her parents had requested a hymn sing. She began by leading the group in singing "Amazing Grace."

Everyone sang, and a number of people created beautiful harmonies. Next, someone started "There Is a Balm in Gilead." It was one of Elizabeth's personal favorites. After that, they sang others, including "The Old Rugged Cross," "Blest Be the Tie That Binds," "Just a Closer Walk with Thee," and one that always reminded her of her father because he had particularly loved it and wanted it sung at his funeral, "How Great Thou Art."

She felt her throat close up as she began to sing the familiar words, rendering her mute. Around her, voices swelled in the late afternoon sunlight:

O Lord my God, when I in awesome wonder,
Consider all the worlds Thy hands have made;
I see the stars, I hear the rolling thunder,
Thy power throughout the universe displayed.
Then sings my soul, my Savior God, to Thee,
How great Thou art, how great Thou art.
Then sings my soul, my Savior God, to Thee,
How great Thou art, how great Thou art!

As the second verse began, Elizabeth felt a hand creep into her own. Mary had returned to her seat beside her. Elizabeth glanced at her sister, seeing tears welling in Mary's eyes as they had in hers, and the siblings shared a smile. In those smiles were thousands of memories of their childhoods, moments spent in the love and security of those bygone days.

Elizabeth swallowed, realizing that shared grief eased the moment of pain a bit. Finding her voice, she joined in the final chorus of the song. "How great Thou art!"

Once she'd arrived home after six, Mary took Bolt for a short walk before dusk fell. Elizabeth put a final quick coat of polyurethane on the picnic table, and Martha headed to the kitchen, as usual. Bolt seemed as fresh as if he'd never run a mile across the fields that afternoon, pulling at the leash and dragging Mary if she wasn't watching every move he made. After recalling something she'd read online when she googled dog training, she began using the walk as an obedience exercise, calling him to her side and giving him treats from the little bag she'd attached to her belt loop to reinforce the appropriate behavior. She was mildly astonished when she began to see results, but it motivated her to even greater effort.

Each time the little dog ran out ahead of her, pulling the lead taut between them, Mary stopped and patiently called him back to her, reeling in the extra line as he drew near. At first, she gave him a tiny treat of cubed chicken just for returning to her.

It didn't take Bolt long to figure out the game. Pretty soon, he was wheeling and galloping back to her immediately before the leash between them could get pulled too taut. At that point, Mary asked him for a little more. "Bolt, sit," she said when he came back to her.

Bolt's tail wagged as he gazed up at her expectantly, looking for his chicken.

"Bolt, sit," Mary said again.

This time, her words penetrated, and the little dog's rear end sank to the ground. Mary gave him a treat immediately, along with a hefty dose of verbal praise, and for the next halfmile, they played the game that way.

Mary was longing to forge ahead with more advanced training. But she'd read that if she tried to do too much at once, Bolt would forget the basics. There was some formula of how many days to work on a skill before you moved on to a new one. It would ensure the first skill was cemented into the canine brain. She'd have to try to find that information again.

In the end, the only other thing they worked on that day was "heel." She found that as they turned and headed back home, Bolt was less distracted and more able to stay by her side, his gaze focused on her face in hopes that another bite of chicken was coming his way.

After returning to the house, Mary put the beagle inside and made sure the door was securely latched before she went out to put the chickens away.

The missing Barnevelder still wasn't anywhere in sight. After counting to be sure she'd put away every other chicken they owned, Mary checked the fences and nearby trees, just in case. But she knew it probably was a futile effort. Researching the breed before she'd bought, she'd learned that they did not fly well. Mary didn't clip the chickens' wings, but even so, it was unlikely that Barnie had flown any distance or gotten enough height to roost in a tree.

Besides, she was sure she'd put the bird away last night. She had trekked quite a distance along the fence line. The hen surely wouldn't have traveled any farther than this. Turning, Mary was about to retrace her steps when a distinctive feather on the ground caught her eye. She bent and picked it up.

Her heart sank as she noted the color and pattern on the feather. Barnevelder hens were stunningly gorgeous. Their brown feathers were laced with two black *Vs* that produced a bi-tone "arrowhead" effect. And Mary was holding one in her fingers.

It was the worst sign yet that something had gone very wrong. At first, she'd been sure Barnie had simply sneaked back outside. Maybe she'd even managed to roost in a tree, although that was unlikely. But this feather, so far from the safety of the coop and any trees, indicated that the pretty hen had probably met an unkind fate.

The light was fading. It was time to give up the search. Mary took one last look around as she began to head back to the house, holding the single feather. Just then, something moved at the far edge of her vision. She turned her head just in time to catch a glimpse of a dainty red fox picking its way along a far hedgerow. The sight confirmed her suspicions.

"Hey, you," Mary said sharply.

The fox froze, looking at her. Objectively speaking, it was a lovely creature, with its white blaze highlighting the breast, dark socks, and a bushy tail with a white tip.

Mary shook the feather at it, now almost certain she knew what had become of poor Barnie. "Stay away from my henhouse!"

Startled by her movement, the fox leaped across a broken fence rail and raced away, tail streaming behind it.

Mary walked back to the henhouse with indignant, angry strides. As she neared it, she saw Elizabeth coming toward her.

"Did you find the hen?" her sister called.

Mary held up the feather. "I'm pretty sure a fox must have killed her," she said. "I caught a glimpse of one just a few minutes ago right after I found this on the ground way out in the field."

"Oh, I'm sorry." Elizabeth's face registered chagrin. "I was afraid a fox or a hawk or something might have gotten her."

"I am absolutely positive I put her away last night, though," Mary said. "How could she have gotten out? I need to check around the exterior of the coop."

"You take one side, and I'll take the other," Elizabeth said.

They started at the door into the chicken coop, Elizabeth going left and Mary going right, studying the weathered boards as they went.

Mary found nothing along the right side. But as she rounded the corner to begin checking the back, something caught her eye. Bending, she saw a clump of red fur caught on a board that didn't quite meet the ground anymore. It was a very, very small hole, and Mary would never have suspected that a fox could squeeze through it. But perhaps she was wrong, and the fox was a lot more agile than she thought.

"Elizabeth?" she called, kneeling to examine the hole. "I think I found our problem."

Her sister came around from the other side and was kneeling next to her in a flash. She pulled the clump of red fur away from the ragged bottom of the board. "Well, how do you like that?" she murmured in disgust, rubbing the fur between her fingers. She studied the hole and reached up inside it. "How could a fox have fit through there?" she wondered.

"That's what I thought too," Mary agreed. "But he must have."

Elizabeth whistled. "Do you realize how lucky we were? He could have killed every hen in there. I can't believe he only killed one."

"Maybe the hen got out through this hole, and he didn't actually get in," Mary theorized, thinking about it from a different angle.

"How could that hen have squeezed out through that hole?" Elizabeth asked. "She's not exactly on the slim side."

Mary snorted. Barnevelders were robust birds, and Barnie definitely was not the smallest chicken in their flock, but... "You know what a determined hen can be like."

Now it was Elizabeth's turn to be amused. "True."

"That makes more sense. I bet she managed to squeeze through that hole." Mary ran her fingers along the edge of the hole. "And maybe the fox really doesn't fit, even though he tried. I bet that's what happened. She got out, he got her, and then he tried to get in to go after the rest." She shuddered.

"We need to get a board, hammer, and nails." Elizabeth indicated the hole. "We need to temporarily close this off until we can get it repaired. We should ask Bill to come out and check the whole thing for rotten boards and weak spots."

"Good idea." Mary jumped to her feet. "I'll be back in a minute."

She gathered the requisite supplies from the barn and returned to the chicken coop. Laying the flat edge of the board against the coop horizontally at ground level, she then secured one end with two nails before passing the hammer and two more nails to Elizabeth so she could do the same thing at the other end. It took them only minutes to nail a two-by-four securely across a wide section of the back of the little building, creating a secure barrier through which a bird couldn't get out and a predator couldn't get in.

"I'll sleep better tonight, knowing that hole is walled off," Elizabeth said as they replaced the hammer and nails in the toolbox they kept in the barn.

"You and me both," Mary said. "I only wish poor little Barnie hadn't gotten out before I discovered we had a problem."

CHAPTER FOUR

As Elizabeth washed up inside after helping Mary board up the hole in the chicken coop, she noted that Martha had kenneled Bolt.

Drying her hands, her thoughts wandered back to the odd scene she'd witnessed during the social hour that morning. Was she making a mountain out of a molehill, imagining drama where there was none? It was possible. Looking at it on the face of things, she could see that it was even probable that she'd overreacted.

But something told her she hadn't. There had been an air of desperation clinging to that young girl, some sense of urgency that Elizabeth had found unsettling. Geraldine Goertz was the one who had spoken to her. But thinking back over Geraldine's breezy recital of her encounter with the teen, Elizabeth had not gotten the impression that Geraldine had felt any special concern. Then again, Geraldine was not the person with whom Elizabeth would most associate intuitive discernment and tact.

Thinking of the odd behavior, Elizabeth wondered if there was any chance the girl had had run-ins with the police. She decided she'd call her friend John Marks and ask if he knew anything about such a person. It was a sensible thing to do, she told herself. And it had nothing to do with any attraction she might feel for the tall, blue-eyed officer.

She pulled out her cell phone and made the call.

"Hello, Elizabeth."

Her pulse sped up at the sound of John's deep, pleasant voice, and she admitted to herself that finding out about a troubled teen was only part of the reason she'd called him. "Hi, John," she said. "How are you?"

"Good," he said. "And you?"

"I'm well," Elizabeth said. "Is this a good time? I have a professional question for you."

"This is fine," he said. "What's up?"

Elizabeth related the story of the girl she'd seen. "I can't tell you quite why her behavior intrigued me," she said, "but I can't stop thinking about it. She was very…maybe *furtive* is the best word. And her behavior when Geraldine spoke to her was distinctly strange. Why would she run if she wasn't guilty of something?"

"Maybe she was scared."

"Of what? That concerns me too." Elizabeth sighed. "John, I just think that child may need help."

"And you want to know if I know her?"

"Well, not necessarily. I just wondered if you knew of any incidents of theft or strange behavior involving young teen girls matching her description."

The connection was silent for a moment. Then John said, "Honestly, I can't think of anything that might relate to your girl. We get shoplifting reports from the convenience stores, but that's often by kids working together. One or more will distract the cashier while the other sneaks out. Sometimes, they catch them by watching the surveillance video, but more often not. Are you sure she was alone?"

"I'm not positive," Elizabeth said, "but when she left, no one left with her. And there didn't appear to be any partner to distract people around her. She was just quietly picking up fruit and stashing it in her pockets."

"The fruit-nabber," John said. He sounded amused. "Sorry I'm not much help."

"Well, she did ask a fellow churchgoer for twenty dollars," Elizabeth added. "But when the woman asked her what it was for, the girl took off."

"Sounds even less like a thief," John commented. "They don't generally advertise their intentions. If she wanted to blend in, she sure didn't succeed."

"Oh well," Elizabeth said. "I can't stop thinking about her, so I thought I'd ask." She hesitated. "Do you have plans for Easter Sunday?"

"I'm working night shifts this week," John said. "Why?"

"We're going to have Easter dinner around two on Sunday. You and your children are welcome to join us. And of course, you're welcome to join me for Easter services at Mount Zion if you like."

"My kids are spending the weekend with Carol's parents. I'd better pass on church this time though, since I'll have worked all night. Maybe another time. Two o'clock should give me time to get some sleep before dinner."

Elizabeth chuckled. "We wouldn't want you to be sleep deprived."

A warm silence hummed between them.

"Great," John finally said. "Thanks for the invitation. I guess I'll see you Sunday at two."

Elizabeth was smiling as they said their goodbyes. She went into the living room, where both of her sisters were sitting. Martha, book in hand, had Tinkerbelle curled in her lap. Pal lay curled at Mary's feet while Mary's pencil flew over the sketch pad she held. Catching the glances Mary threw Martha's way, Elizabeth suspected her middle sister might be the subject of whatever had Mary so engrossed.

Then, as the sight of the dogs registered, Elizabeth blurted, "Oh goodness, the puppy's still kenneled!"

Mary waved a hand. "Bring him in here. We can keep an eye on him now."

Judging from each of her sisters' absorption in her respective endeavor, Elizabeth wasn't so sure about that. But she could watch him, so she went to the kitchen and opened the kennel door. Bolt trotted out and rolled on his back, encouraging her to rub his belly, and then he followed her into the living room. The moment she sat down on the couch, he hopped up beside her and curled up as if he'd been doing it for years.

Mary looked up from her drawing and chuckled. "Make yourself at home, Bolt." Then she shifted, likely so she could view the dog more easily, flipped a page in her sketchbook, and began to eye the dog, her pencil flying over the paper in quick, sure strokes.

Elizabeth opened the sewing basket she'd begun keeping beside "her" spot on the couch since she'd begun to quilt. She was piecing a log cabin quilt in shades of soft blues, teals, and greens. Half the pattern of each square was darker shades, and half was very pale shades in a similar color palette, and the squares were turning out beautifully. She could hardly wait to sew them together and begin quilting. Every time she finished another one, she would lay out the completed squares in various patterns, but she couldn't decide which she was going to like best.

Did she want to have a diamond center? Or simply stripes of light and dark? Probably not. She was looking for something more unique. One layout she liked turned the squares different ways so the effect was that of a star. But she'd need to piece some squares in only dark shades to set off the star effect, she realized. Still, that might be the one she liked best.

Looking up from her work, she saw that both her sisters were still engrossed in their respective hobbies. "I invited John and his children to Easter dinner," she said casually. "His kids are going to be at their grandparents' for the weekend, but he said yes."

"He won't be with his kids at Easter?" Mary asked.

"He said he's working night shifts this week." Elizabeth felt slightly defensive on John's behalf, but she forced herself to relax. "I wouldn't want a teenage daughter staying alone in my house if I had to work nights, would you? His son's at college, so I imagine he'll be joining them straight from school."

"That was kind of you to invite him." Martha looked up from her reading. "No one should be alone at Easter."

"He's working night shift, so he can't attend church, but he'll be here for dinner."

Mary looked over at her. "You asked him to come to church again?"

Elizabeth nodded, smiling. "I really think he might have come if he hadn't had to work."

Mary resumed sketching. "Progress," she said lightly, grinning.

"Anyone else we should invite?" Martha asked with an arch look at Mary.

Elizabeth eyed Mary, whose smile grew sheepish. "Maybe?"

Of course, Martha was probably thinking of Bill Richmond, their longtime family friend who they all knew wanted to be more than a friend to Mary. Oh, he wasn't obnoxious or obvious about it, and he'd respected her need to find out who she was as a single, independent woman who was more than just someone's wife and someone's mother...but Elizabeth and Martha were both certain that if Mary ever decided to take a good look at Bill and invite him into her life, she wouldn't be single for long.

"You don't have to decide now," Martha said. "Just let me know if you do invite Bill."

"I will," Mary told her sister.

Pleased that Martha had let the subject drop, Elizabeth let herself become absorbed in her quilting.

The moment her eyes opened the following morning, Elizabeth thought of the girl she'd witnessed hiding fruit in her pockets. Geraldine had said the girl asked her for twenty dollars. Why would she have done that? It was hard to imagine anyone, even a brash teenager, asking a perfect stranger for money without a very good reason. According to Geraldine, the girl had turned and run when asked why she needed it.

Shortly afterward, during the service, Pastor Nagle's sermon had discussed the way individuals in society treat beggars, and he'd asked how Jesus would have treated them. Suddenly, the theme seemed very applicable.

"Were you listening to yesterday's message?" she asked her sisters as the three of them sat down to breakfast.

Martha looked up. "Of course."

Mary grinned. She often admitted her mind wandered during sermons. "Mostly," she said. "I have a hard time with auditory processing, and I have to keep dragging my attention back. Why?"

"I can't stop thinking about that girl who took the fruit during the fellowship time." Elizabeth paused in the act of buttering some toast. "Geraldine said she asked her why she needed money, and that's when the girl ran. And as I think about it, if a young person asked me for money, I might have asked the very same question." She grimaced. "I may have been a bit more subtle about it, but I bet that's exactly what I'd have done."

Martha nodded. "So might I."

"I think it would be a natural question if someone asked me for money," Mary offered. "Most humans are wired to be curious."

"And yet," Elizabeth said, "Pastor Nagle spoke of how Jesus might have reacted, and it would have been very different, wouldn't it? He wouldn't have asked prying questions about how she planned to use it."

"It's a little different," Martha said dryly. "He would have known already, right?"

"But I see what you mean." Mary reached for the salt. "He would have encouraged us to give without putting conditions on the gift. Wow. That goes against all my natural instincts, I think. I'm nosy."

"Or maybe just naturally curious," Elizabeth said with a smile. "So yes, that's my point. Christ would have given freely just for the asking. He wouldn't have asked questions or offered advice, as I suspect most of us would have."

"You mean advice like, 'You could get a job babysitting to make money,'" Mary put in.

"Exactly," Elizabeth said.

"Oof. That puts me in my place," Martha said. "I can actually hear myself saying that, from my smug, superior adult point of view."

Elizabeth smiled. "I didn't bring this up to make either of you feel guilty. Or myself, for that matter. I'm just trying to explain this need I have to find this girl and help her. It's as if God is speaking directly to me. I feel compelled to find her and give her that twenty dollars she asked for. No questions asked."

"Maybe she needs the money for food," Mary said. "There are a lot of folks out there who don't make enough to feed their families properly. Or maybe she needs it to help a family member who needs special medication. Heaven knows that's ridiculously expensive these days."

"Or rent," Martha added. "Or gas or to pay the utility bills."

"I'm worried about that," Elizabeth said. "I keep fearing that she's starving. Or her family is. She looked like an awfully slender child."

"And here we are," Martha said with a wry smile, "assigning reasons to her need for money. The exact opposite of Christ's actions."

Elizabeth sighed, grinning and shaking her head. "It's part of the human condition, I fear. That old saying, 'Curiosity killed the cat,' was invented to admonish adults as well as children. I can't seem to stop wondering what's going on in that girl's life."

Shortly before ten, the sisters started down the lane toward Secondhand Blessings. The weather was cool but clear, and it was apparent that winter was truly behind them now. Forsythia gone wild added splashes of sunny color to the new greens along the fences, while crocuses and early species tulips in shades of pink, red, and lavender graced beds fronting the house and along the driveway. Masses of daffodils were just on the verge of an all-out show of spring, and Elizabeth calculated one more really sunny day would be all they needed.

She cast a doubtful look at Mary as they walked. "Are you sure you want to bring Bolt to the shop?" Their little foster companion pranced happily along, straining at his leash, practically dragging Mary in his wake. He sniffed here, zigzagged there, and generally made the walk a hazard for anyone trying not to trip over a beagle and his leash.

"Absolutely," Mary said. "Exposure is the key to getting dogs adopted. The more people who see him, the better."

"You're going to have to keep a close eye on him," Martha reminded her. "He's a slick one."

Mary chuckled ruefully. "He sure is. I brought several toys, a puzzle ball, and a bone to keep him busy. I'm planning to tether him so he can't do a disappearing act. I'll either attach him to a sturdy piece of furniture or loop the leash around my waist."

Elizabeth considered that. "Make sure you keep him far away from the baked goods."

Things went well as they began their workday. Mary took Bolt back to the stockroom with her while she sorted some new acquisitions. Elizabeth did the opening chores, and Martha set up their baked goods.

The first customers came and went, purchasing bed linens, a decorative wreath, a number of baking utensils, pots and pans, and a set of flatware. Bolt was doing really well, Elizabeth thought, watching him move along at Mary's side as she helped a customer near the rear of the store.

Close to eleven, two women arrived together. The older one held a toddler by the hand, the younger had a sleeping infant bound in a ring sling on her chest.

"Hello, Barbara," Martha said. Turning to Elizabeth, she introduced the younger woman. "Elizabeth, this is Barbara Epps. She's one of my fellow volunteers in the Friends of the Library group. Barbara, my sister Elizabeth."

"And this is my mother, Emily," Barbara said. "She lives in Lancaster and comes out here two days a week to help with the children."

"Snuggling my grandchildren is *such* a hardship," Emily said with a wink.

Martha chuckled. "I know the feeling. Our children think they are imposing, when in reality, we'd be devastated if they didn't need our help."

As Martha chatted with the women, Rella Wiens, one of the church members Elizabeth had queried about the teenager she'd observed during social hour, entered the shop.

"Hi, Elizabeth," she said. "Any luck identifying the mystery girl?"

Elizabeth shook her head. "Not so far. Several people volunteered the names of girls they thought it could be. I still want to know why she was filling her pockets with fruit."

At her last words, Barbara Epps turned around. She and her mother had been just about to move off, but she stopped, rocking and patting lightly as the sleeping baby squirmed and stirred. "Pardon me for interrupting. You saw a girl filling her pockets with fruit? Was it at the library?"

Elizabeth shook her head. "No, it was during the social period at our church yesterday. Why?"

"That rings a bell," Barbara said. "I saw a girl at the library story time last week putting apples in her pocket. I remember thinking it was really odd. What did yours look like?"

"Slender," Elizabeth said immediately. "Dark hair, longer than shoulder-length, and rather curly. Wearing an oversized light-colored jacket with big pockets."

Barbara's eyes widened. "The girl I saw had dark hair and wore a big jacket with pockets. That seems too coincidental, doesn't it?"

Elizabeth nodded. "It sure does. I don't suppose you got her name or any other information?"

Barbara shook her head. "I didn't. But why would she have been in that room at story time? Did she bring a child? I didn't notice, but I'd have to say that's likely. Story time is in the community room, so she probably wouldn't have been in there at all if she hadn't been there for the activity."

"Unless she knew they always set out goodies for story time," Mary said.

"Oh, true." Barbara looked rueful. "One of the librarians approached her, but I think the girl saw her coming. Before Fanny got to her, the girl turned and slipped through a group of moms and disappeared into the stacks. And then someone asked Fanny a question, so she couldn't follow her."

"So maybe she hadn't brought a child," Elizabeth mused. "Maybe you're right, and she just knew there would be food for story time." She thought for a minute. "You're sure she only took fruit?"

Barbara nodded. "Yes, because I thought it was odd. What kid eats fruit when there are cookies and crackers laid out?" She made a wry face. "But my little one started to fuss, and I got distracted and forgot about it, until you mentioned it just now."

"So you never saw her with a child, and she got away before anyone could speak with her," Elizabeth summarized.

Barbara nodded. "I can't believe you saw her too."

The toddler at Emily's side suddenly let out a loud protest as his grandmother tugged him away from a display of handmade baskets he had begun banging on. Both women turned and smiled absently, continuing their conversation through the howling.

"I—" But Elizabeth never got to finish her sentence. The distinctive baying of a beagle filled the store.

CHAPTER FIVE

B olt! Come!" That was Mary's voice from the back of the shop.

But the baying grew louder and more frantic, and suddenly the little dog came into view, dashing toward Barbara Epps, her mother, and the children. His ears flopped, his tail wagged frantically, and he had a maniacally excited gleam in his eye as he bayed. The toddler holding his grandmother's hand began to shriek, and she snatched him up just as Bolt arrived, leash trailing behind him.

Elizabeth and her sisters had grown up with dogs. Elizabeth recognized that the excitable puppy wasn't planning to take a bite out of anyone, but she understood that he could look quite menacing to anyone unfamiliar with dogs.

Bolt simply wanted attention. As he jumped up against Emily's legs, Elizabeth snagged his collar and dragged him back to sit.

"Oh my gracious, I am so sorry," she said.

Mary had dashed from the back of the store, red-faced and apologetic. She snatched up the leash. "I'm so sorry," she said, repeating Elizabeth's words. "I had him attached to a chair I was sitting on, and when I stood, he jerked the leash out from under the leg and raced up here to see what was going on."

Deprived of his freedom, Bolt barked several more times, straining at the end of the lead. The toddler shrieked and clutched his grandmother's neck, and the baby in Barbara's arms began to wail.

Elizabeth pointed at the door. "Get him out of here!" she whispered furiously to Mary. Annoyance made her voice tight. They worked so very hard to make shopping at Second-hand Blessings an inviting experience, and she could almost hear the whispers about "the scary dog" that was kept in the store.

Mary quickly moved toward the exit, dragging the pup by the leash that proclaimed ADOPT ME.

Fat chance of that happening any time soon, Elizabeth thought.

"I'll take him back to the house," Mary said.

"I'm calling an obedience trainer," Martha called after her. "We've got him for five more days. We need help."

"We can't just do that without permission," Mary said. "He's not ours, remember?"

Martha raised her eyebrows. "Do you really think if we say we'd like to consult an obedience trainer, and we'll pay for it, Safe Harbor is going to object?"

"They may have some opinions on which trainers we consult," Mary argued. "I'm not against getting some help, but we have to follow their rules."

"Fine," Martha said. "I'll see what I can find and then check with Safe Harbor to be sure they approve."

"Great idea," Elizabeth said. "Now take that dog home!"

"On my way," Mary called over her shoulder, as Bolt, barking forgotten in the joy of rushing outside, raced past her out into the sunshine.

The noise level abated the moment the dog disappeared.

Barbara had succeeded in soothing the baby, and her son's screams had dwindled to occasional hiccupping sobs, although he wouldn't let his grandmother set him down.

"We are so very sorry," Elizabeth said. "We took in a foster dog, and Mary thought bringing him to the store would be good socialization. But clearly, we're going to have to keep him at home in the future."

Barbara's lips twitched, and then she snickered, patting the baby's back. "Screaming children are definitely one form of socialization." She certainly didn't seem overly upset, but Elizabeth was taking no chances.

"We really do apologize," she said. "Would you like to select something from our bakery shelf on the house?"

Emily chuckled. "We're never going to turn that down, are we, Barbie? But please," she went on, "that little dog was just excited, and we understand. Don't punish him on our account."

"Oh, we won't," Elizabeth assured her.

Martha, over at the counter, looked up from the computer where she'd already started looking for dog obedience schools. "But I am serious about contacting a trainer to start working with Mary. One way or another," she said, "that little guy is going to learn some manners."

"When our golden retriever was a puppy, she was wild," Barbara said. "This was before we had kids, and my husband spoiled her stinking rotten. I finally told him either we train her, or she leaves, because we can't have children with a crazy dog that doesn't listen. We used an obedience instructor down in Soudersburg. She really helped us learn to manage Bella's behavior. Hold on. I'm pretty sure I still have her card." She dug in her bag and eventually fished a dog-eared business card from her wallet. "Manners and More."

The sisters examined the card. "That's not far," Elizabeth said to Martha.

"Oh, that's listed right here," Martha said, almost at the same moment. She pulled her phone from her apron pocket. "I'm calling the foster coordinator to give us the green light right now."

CHAPTER SIX

Elizabeth took a late lunch. Mary had eaten hers at the house when she'd taken the dog back, and Martha had brought her lunch. She'd set a chair in the sunshine out back while she'd taken a lunch break.

Elizabeth had brought a sandwich with her, and she ate it in the car as she drove to the Bird-in-Hand Free Library. She couldn't take long, but it wouldn't take much time to visit the library and speak with Fanny Fraser and Minerva Helman, the librarians. Perhaps one of them had noticed the girl at story hour. And she wanted to ask Minerva more about Sheila Canner anyway.

Although Lancaster County had a large library system, many local communities had small branch libraries, and Bird-in-Hand was no exception. The library was housed in a home that had been built well before the beginning of the twentieth century. In the early '40s it was bequeathed to the community by the single bachelor grandson of the original owners, with the stipulation that the house and all the books it contained become a public library.

The chat with Barbara earlier that day had been galvanizing for Elizabeth. Now she felt certain that the girl she'd seen hadn't simply been taking fruit for her friends. If she was taking it from other places, there had to be a more significant reason. It couldn't have been a silly spur-of-the-moment type of dare.

She turned into the alley beside the library and drove back to the parking lot. But as she got out of her car, she was astonished to see a familiar figure digging in the small dumpster next door. The dumpster belonged to a local sandwich shop, a tiny establishment largely overlooked by tourists but patronized faithfully by those who lived and worked in the area.

The girl wore the same oversized tan jacket Elizabeth had noticed at church with a wild spill of dark hair curling down the back of it. Her legs in faded jeans looked as slender as Elizabeth remembered. Was she starving?

Quietly, Elizabeth made her way across the parking lot and along the alley, watching her step so she didn't kick any stones or make other noises to alert the girl. Mentally rehearsing her words, she counseled herself to remember the pastor's message yesterday. As she walked, she carefully fished her wallet from her handbag.

"Hi," Elizabeth said when she was almost directly behind the girl.

Dark hair flew as the girl straightened and whirled around. She looked ready to flee, but before she could move, Elizabeth extended a twenty-dollar bill loosely held between her thumb and bent forefinger. "I saw you at church yesterday," she told the girl. "I thought you could use this. No questions asked."

Those memorable eyes—were they pale green or gray?—widened, and the girl slowly reached out and took the money. "Thank you," she said in a husky voice. "Thank you so much. It will make all the difference in the world."

"You're welcome." But the girl shoved the cash into a pocket and sprinted away in one smooth motion, and Elizabeth found herself speaking to empty space. Swiveling, she tracked the girl until she vanished up the alley and around the corner of the feedstore at the top of the hill.

"Well," she said aloud. "That was unexpected."

She wished she'd been able to speak with the girl more, to get her name. The air of seeming desperation that clouded the teen's petite features was palpable, as was the flash of relief that had appeared when she'd seen the money. Elizabeth suddenly realized she'd missed an opportunity. She knew the names of several girls who loosely fit the description of the girl she'd just seen. Why hadn't she called out a name, to see if the girl looked back as she was running off? If only she'd reacted faster, instead of having a great idea after the fact.

Slowly, she turned toward the flagstone path that led to the back entrance of the library through the little courtyard at the rear of the building. She felt even more compelled to help the mystery girl now. There had to be a way to identify the child and offer her longer-term assistance than just a stray donation here and there.

Fanny was at the desk, helping a patron learn to use the digital checkout machine, but Elizabeth could see Minerva in the office, so she detoured in that direction and waved when she caught the head librarian's eye.

"Hi, Elizabeth. Looking for something to read?" Minerva smiled over the top of her reading glasses.

"Always," Elizabeth replied with a grin. "But today I'm seeking information more than books."

Minerva removed the pencil from behind her ear and gestured toward the computer desks over in the reference section. "Need some help searching online?"

Elizabeth shook her head. "Not that kind of information. Remember the girl I saw yesterday that you said you thought could be Sheila Canner or Jean Ann Brean?"

"I sure do." Minerva nodded, sitting forward with an interested expression. "Did you track her down?"

"Not exactly," Elizabeth said. "She was digging through the dumpster behind the parking lot when I pulled in." She grimaced. "I wish I could have gotten a picture of her on my phone, but she skedaddled as soon as I began speaking to her."

"She was alone?"

Elizabeth nodded. She decided not to mention the fact that she'd given the girl money.

"Then I seriously doubt it was Jean Ann," Minerva said. "Her mother keeps her pretty close. She would not have been roaming around town by herself."

Elizabeth filed that bit of information away. It certainly dropped Jean Ann down a few places on her list of names that could match the girl she'd just given money to.

"How about the other girl you mentioned—Sheila?"

Minerva spread her hands. "Dark hair, shoulder-length or longer, but I think I told you that before. A little shorter than you are, perhaps. I don't know what color her eyes are."

"Would she be out and about without her mother?"

"Oh, absolutely." Minerva's tone was definite. "She comes in here on her own, and I've seen her walking with a boy sometimes. Older, kind of goth looking."

Elizabeth's interest ratcheted up. "I don't suppose you have a picture of her? I've seen you put up photo displays of teens visiting the library, using the computers and things."

Minerva paused for a moment, thinking, but then she shook her head. "Sorry, I don't think so. But the family's in the church directory, if you wanted to visit and meet her. Maybe she's your girl, and there's a reasonable explanation for what seems like sneaky behavior."

"Perhaps. That's a good idea. Here's something else I learned this morning. Do you know Barbara Epps?"

"Oh yes. Delightful woman. She brings her toddler to story time almost every week."

"Yes, I gathered that she attends story time. She says she saw the same girl I saw at church at story time, says she was taking apples from the table."

"You're kidding!"

"Well, that answers my next question," Elizabeth said. "Barbara told me one of the librarians started to approach her, and she fled. I guess it wasn't you, since you don't remember her."

"I'm pretty sure I'd remember that," Minerva agreed. "Fanny usually helps with story time. We can ask her as soon as she's done assisting that patron." Then Minerva frowned. "Don't you find it odd that she'd only be taking fruit again, just like at church? The moms bring a ton of cookies to story time. I'd have expected a teenager to go for the junk food, I suppose."

"I thought the same thing, but maybe she's a health-conscious teenager."

"I doubt a hungry one would be picky about what she could get her hands on. Do you think this kid is in need of regular meals?"

"I just don't know." Elizabeth sighed. "She does look really thin, but I can't say she was skeletal. Maybe that's just her natural build."

"Fanny?" Minerva raised her voice.

Fanny, the assistant librarian, had finished helping the patron with the digital checkout machine. A young woman with long braids, she looked more like one of the teen patrons than she did an employee, but Elizabeth knew she was highly qualified and capable. She came over, shaking her head and smiling. "I bet I've shown May Rook how to do that fifty times, but I always end up doing it for her."

Minerva chuckled. "And I've shown her at least fifty more. Oh well, people like May keep us employed, right?"

"Right," Fanny said. "What's up?"

"Elizabeth has a question about story time," Minerva told the younger woman.

"Sure thing." Fanny looked attentively in her direction.

Elizabeth explained the incident at church. She started to mention the incident that Barbara Epps had described, but Fanny's eyes had already lit up, and she was nodding. "I know exactly who you mean. It was pretty strange to see a big kid like that loading her pockets with apples." Fanny shrugged. "I'd have let her have more if she'd asked. None of the kids want to eat them."

"Did you speak with her at all?" Elizabeth asked.

Fanny shook her head definitively. "I headed in her direction, and the minute she saw me coming, she ran. She went that way"—

she pointed back into the stacks—"and I started to go after her to tell her she could have all of the apples, but then someone called my name, and I got sidetracked. I checked through the stacks later, hoping she was still around, but she was gone."

Elizabeth thought for a moment. "I wonder why she was at story time in the first place. Did she have a small child with her?"

"Not that I saw," Fanny replied. "And there weren't any unattended children wandering around when it ended."

"That's what Barbara said too" Still, it made Elizabeth wonder how the girl had found out that there was free food at story time. Just a good guess?

"Thanks for your time," Elizabeth said to both librarians. "If you see her again and are able to engage her in conversation and perhaps learn her name, I'd love to hear about it."

"Ooh, Minerva," said Fanny, "we get to play detective."

Minerva laughed. "I do that every day trying to figure out what books our patrons want to read."

She would take Minerva's suggestion, Elizabeth decided as she bade farewell to the librarians and headed back to the parking lot. No one was hanging around the dumpster this time, although she looked in every direction to see if the girl might still be in the vicinity. She would also look up Tammy McClain, whom Rella Wiens had mentioned, and see if her daughter Brittany was the girl she had just handed twenty dollars to.

Mary and Martha arrived at the house a few minutes after closing Secondhand Blessings for the day. The store had emptied out in the late afternoon, so they hadn't lingered a moment longer than they needed to.

Mary was anxious to let Bolt out and take him for a walk. She had felt terrible kenneling the little dog for the afternoon, but clearly he couldn't stay at the store. She had gone to the house again midafternoon and taken him out for a short walk, but she'd have to take him for a longer ramble tonight. He certainly seemed to have an inexhaustible energy supply. It was probably a good thing the trainer Martha had called had offered to come by around six. It would be nice to send Bolt on to his regular foster with some good routines and habits in place.

The sisters stepped up onto the porch and headed for the back door. Martha was slightly ahead of Mary, and she withdrew the key from her bag and began to open the door. But as she turned the knob, she peered through the window. "Good heavens," she said. "What on earth is that?"

Mary crowded close behind her, wondering what had elicited the exclamation. As Martha unlocked the door and stepped into the kitchen, Mary followed, only to halt just inside the doorway beside Martha, completely speechless.

"Mercy me. Oh, my sweet mercy me." Martha seemed incapable of coherent speech. She whispered the phrase several times.

Mary, looking around, felt similarly wordless. The kitchen floor was covered in white fluff of an indistinguishable content, so thickly laid in some places that it resembled a snowfall. Patches of white clung to the seats of the chairs, and random clumps dotted the table and the counters.

"Oh, Bolt," Mary said aloud. "Whatever have you done?" For there was no doubt in her mind that the culprit was the little foster beagle.

At the sound of her voice, a stirring came from the living room. A set of paws thumped down from some piece of furniture onto the floor, and other rustlings ensued. Canine nails clacked on the bare wood of the hall flooring. A moment later, Bolt rushed into the room, plowing through the white debris and sending bits and pieces flying into the air. Immediately, Mary realized how the table and counters had acquired the pieces of white.

Tinkerbelle and Pal, obviously far more cognizant of trouble, stopped in the doorway and regarded the humans with wary expressions.

"Bolt! I know I kenneled you," Mary said to the beagle. She held up both hands helplessly.

But the door to the kennel in the corner of the kitchen was ajar. "I must not have latched it properly," she concluded, turning to Martha apologetically. "I'm so sorry. He chewed up a couple of our throw pillows."

Martha bent and picked up a mangled, deflated piece of fabric that had once been a small pillow on the couch. The brown and rust pattern was ripped and torn and flapped limply from her hand. "At least the old ones Grandma Lois needlepointed were put away." She sighed. "What are we going to do with this dog?"

"It wouldn't have happened if I'd kenneled him properly," Mary pointed out, guilt swamping her.

"I know. He's just—too much," Martha moaned.

"I'll clean it up," Mary promised. "And get new pillows."

"Why don't you take him—all of them—outside, and I'll clean this up? The trainer should be arriving soon."

"Oh, but I should help," Mary protested. "I'm the one who had the brilliant idea to bring in a foster dog."

Martha managed a grim smile. "Believe me, getting him out of my sight right now will be helping."

Mary sighed. "Okay. C'mon, Bolt." She lifted his leash from the set of hooks inside the door, and the little beagle came toward her, the white tip emphasizing the happy wagging of his tail. Apparently, he'd already forgotten his transgression.

Martha grabbed a broom from the pantry and cleared a path across the floor, and the other dogs followed Bolt and Mary out the door. They both looked as guilty as if they'd committed some crime, until they got off the porch and realized they weren't in trouble.

As they walked along a narrow trail that wound through the meadow, Mary wondered who on earth was going to adopt a dog that seemed to attract mischief as diligently as had Tom Sawyer in Mark Twain's memorable novel. The path wound through grasses just beginning to green up in anticipation of the summer to come. Last year's stands of Queen Anne's lace, cornflowers, and bellflowers had been flattened beneath the weight of winter snows, but sturdy stalks of thistle still stood, leaves tattered and torn. New growth was already noticeable here and there.

As she walked, Mary couldn't help assessing the landscape with an artist's eye. In another month, there would be even more early flowers. She needed to get out here with her easel then, while swaths of spring color enlivened the landscape.

Accompanied by all three dogs, Mary rambled over the fields for nearly thirty minutes. She knew they'd be eating later tonight because Martha had arranged for the trainer—

Oh no! The dog obedience instructor was probably waiting for her! Picking up her pace, she made a beeline back toward the house, arriving just as a small blue car crested the top of the driveway and braked behind Martha's car. Bolt immediately began to bark and bay wildly, lunging at the end of his leash and straining to approach the car.

"Hello," Mary called as a woman in cargo pants, boots, and a tank top emerged from the vehicle. Pal and Tink trotted over and greeted her. Tink yapped twice, but as soon as the woman knelt, the little dachshund sidled over for a cuddle. Pal waited his turn for a greeting and a pat, and then both dogs turned away and calmly headed for the outdoor pump and their water bowl.

"Hi." The woman strode toward Mary. Her brown hair was confined in a long braid that hung down her back, and her complexion was bronzed and rosy. Mary was aware of keen green eyes assessing Bolt as they moved toward her. "I'm Ruth."

Bolt moved to leap on the trainer before Mary could stop him, but the woman smoothly hooked a thumb in his collar and prevented him from jumping up, just as Elizabeth had done in the store that morning. She knelt and stroked him, speaking softly. "Hi, buddy. Are you happy to see me? Looks like you've been on a hike. Need a drink before we get started?"

"He probably does. I'm Mary, and this is Bolt. Our problem child."

Ruth laughed as she indicated Pal and Tink, both of whom were lying placidly on the porch. "Your sister told me you needed help with a beagle, but I think I could have guessed." She fell into step beside Mary as she headed for the pump, beside which they had set an outdoor water bowl.

"I can hold him," the trainer offered, extending a hand for Bolt's leash.

Mary pumped the handle several times, and as cool, sweet water began to gush from the spigot, she refilled the water bowl. Bolt surged forward and buried his face in the bowl, slurping loudly. Mary pumped the handle a couple more times, washing her hands and cupping them so she also could take a drink.

"So I understand he's a foster," Ruth said. "God bless you. People who give animals a second chance are special souls."

"We don't have him long," Mary told her. "He was surrendered to a shelter after his owner died, taken by Safe Harbor Beagle Rescue, and we're helping until the weekend when a long-term foster family is available. But my sisters and I would like to get a head start on some training this week. He's pretty lively, to phrase it as positively as I can."

"He's a beagle," Ruth said, grinning. "Hunting dogs are still very much creatures of instinct. If there's a scent, he has to follow it."

"Unfortunately, that isn't so great for potential adopters," Mary said wryly. "And his house manners need some work."

"Is he housebroken?"

"Oh yes," Mary said. "That's one area we haven't had any trouble with. But he's a terrible scavenger. He gets into the trash, and he destroyed a couple of pillows just since he arrived. I'm afraid he's never going to get adopted if we don't get some of these misbehaviors under control."

"Trash cans are beagle heaven," Ruth said, rolling her eyes.

"It was my fault he ruined the pillows, because I didn't make sure his kennel was securely closed. But he barks at people and everything else. He pulls so hard while on lead he practically dislocates my arm, choking himself all the while, and then he doubles back and trips me with the leash. And he doesn't respond to any commands. Once he's off lead, he lives up to his name."

"Okay," Ruth said. Her eyes grew wide and serious, for which Mary was grateful. She'd feared the woman might laugh at their problems, and Bolt was quickly becoming no laughing matter. "So let's talk about some realistic goals for this boy. Off lead in an unfenced area is probably not an option. Not now, not ever, even for whoever adopts him. Beagles really are ruled by their noses, and the world is full of irresistible scents if you're Bolt. However, we can work on some basic obedience commands that should, if you practice faithfully, make him show better at adoption events *and* give you a bit more control in the house."

"He's usually not a terrible problem in the house," Mary said. "It's more a matter of training whoever he lives with not to leave temptation in his path or give him access to things like the trash."

"Well, that's an easy enough fix," Ruth said. "Just get one of those large metal cans that latch or put your garbage under the sink."

"We can put it in the pantry," Mary said. "And I'll add your recommendations to a list I'm going to give the new owners. Normally I kennel him when we're gone, but the latch didn't catch, and he got out. He did bark like crazy at one of our customer's children," she added, recalling his behavior at the store that morning.

"What triggered the barking?"

Mary related the incident with the child. "The louder the little boy cried, the more Bolt barked. It was awful." Then she added, "And to be honest, it's not just children. He wants to jump on everyone. Not to hurt them, just to inspect and greet them."

"The jumping is going to require more work, but it's also very fixable." Ruth took an electronic tablet out of the backpack she carried and held it up. "Let's sit on your porch and look at a training sequence. Then I'll try it with Bolt so you can watch me. After that, we'll work on some basic obedience commands. If you make time for several short practice sessions each day, you should start to see some improvement. And I'll give you a link to my website so you can refresh your memory on the training exercises and make sure you're performing them correctly."

Together, they moved onto the porch and watched the video, in which a handler and dog were approached by a stranger who had been coached to turn and walk away every time the dog jumped. Finally, after a number of repetitions, the dog waited, fanny wriggling impatiently, for the guest to greet him.

"I could do that at the store. We get a lot of regular customers, and I bet some of them would help." Mary was excited to take some positive steps. Then her anticipation faded. "But what about the barking?"

"We'll address that with a two-pronged approach," Ruth assured her. "First, we'll teach him the 'speak' and 'quiet' commands, and you can use the same approach you use with the jumping."

"Oh good." Mary was relieved. "I was hoping you weren't going to tell me to put him in one of those collars that makes a noise or gives a shock every time he barks."

Ruth grimaced. "Both of those methods are negative reinforcement. If you don't do this, a bad thing won't happen. I prefer a positive approach. If you do this, a good thing will happen. Reinforce only the behavior you want, and ignore everything else. It helps that he's largely barking because he wants attention, not because he's trying to warn people off, as a breed with more of a guarding instinct might do."

As Ruth was beginning to show Mary how to teach the "speak" and "quiet" commands, Elizabeth's car came crunching up the gravel lane. Bolt immediately went into his frenzy of barking. The trainer quickly took the lead from Mary, dug in the pouch at her waist, and produced a dog treat, which she laid in front of Bolt. The beagle stopped barking long enough to sniff the treat, and Ruth immediately said, "Good quiet," stroking the dog's head as he gobbled up the treat.

"What is that?" Mary asked. "He loves it."

"Dried liver," Ruth told her. "Great odor if you're a dog, and all protein with no additives. You could also try smelly cheeses like Limburger, Roquefort, or Muenster, hot dogs cut into tiny pieces, and peanut butter if he needs variety."

Bolt resumed barking as Elizabeth waved and headed for the house, so Ruth repeated the process.

"This is step one in the learning not to bark sequence," she told Mary. "I like to teach 'quiet' first and then add 'speak.' Every trainer does it a little differently." She went on to explain the whole shaping process, and then they watched another video together.

"I'm only going to have him for a week," Mary said. "The people who will be fostering him long term will be back from vacation on Sunday, I think. But I'm certainly going to pass on all this information and the internet links you gave me."

"They're welcome to contact me if they want to continue what he's learning. You can show them these first steps and get them moving in the right direction. He'll be a much more adoptable dog if some of that wild puppy behavior can be curbed. Also, remember to give him plenty of exercise. A tired dog is a more manageable dog, in most cases." She rose. "Now let's work on those basic obedience commands. You can practice them when you take him for walks."

"How many commands are there?" Mary asked.

"You can teach a dog to do lots of tricks," Ruth said, "but I consider the foundation of basic obedience to be 'sit,' 'down,' 'stay,' and 'leave it.' When Bolt learns those four things, and 'quiet,' of course, he'll fit into many households."

Mary felt encouraged by the woman's matter-of-fact assumption that Bolt was going to improve. He wasn't the least manageable dog in the world after all!

CHAPTER SEVEN

Martha and Elizabeth made the trip into Lancaster after a very quick supper to visit with Anya Presser and her husband at Lancaster General Hospital, where Anya was being treated for a ruptured appendix. Although the new responsibility would be a bit stressful, especially at the last minute like this, Martha was glad she was available and able to take on the oversight of the book sale so Anya could rest and not worry too much.

The fountain in the middle of the terraced landscaping out front had been turned on, another welcome sign that spring was truly here to stay. The sisters entered the spacious tiled foyer and headed for the elevators, taking one to the floor where surgical patients were housed.

"Hello, girls." Anya extended a hand from her bed as they arrived at the door of her hospital room. She was still on an intravenous drip, being loaded up with antibiotics to ward off peritonitis after her surgery, and the tall IV pole loomed in the corner. Anya's husband got up and excused himself while they visited.

"Hi there." Martha moved around the bed and took Anya's free hand, since the other sported the IV catheter in the back of her hand. Her friend looked pale and wan, with her usually elegantly styled French twist in a simple, messy bun. "I was looking forward to seeing you this week, but this wasn't quite how I'd envisioned it."

Anya sighed. "Me neither. I love the book sale. I can't believe I have to miss it." She released Martha's hand and gestured at a file folder on the corner of the rolling table where the aides set her food. "There's the folder with all the organizational information in it. Volunteers, schedules, hours, when to lower prices and start the books-by-the-bag sale—the works. Pretty much everything's been done already, and all the volunteers have been given their shifts. You only need to be available to oversee it and make sure everyone shows up ready and willing to work. And you can allocate that to someone else if that will be a problem for you, since I know you have to work at your shop. Do you know Pollie Muller?"

"Oh yes," Martha said. "She and I shared a checkout shift at last year's book sale."

"Wonderful. She would be a great person to ask to oversee the times you can't be there. She's very reliable, just a little hesitant about taking charge. But if she thinks you're in charge and she's just helping, she'll jump right in."

Martha laughed. "Thanks. I'll call her tonight, since I know there'll be times I won't be able to be there."

"Oh, and I think I wrote this down, but I'd better remind you," Anya went on. "Get change before the sale for all three days and divide it into a bag for each day. I have a list in there of the money I start with each day. And at the end of the day, the deposit bag goes into the library safe, where the treasurer will collect it."

"Sounds manageable," Martha told her. "Don't worry about a thing. I'll take care of it."

"I know you will." Anya chuckled. "I've had my eye on you for a leadership position since you moved back, and I saw what a worker bee you are."

Martha's eyebrows rose, making Elizabeth chuckle. "A worker bee?"

"I think that's an excellent description," Elizabeth told her sister. "You're hardworking and reliable. When I leave something in your hands, I know it's going to get done and done right."

"You're also a natural leader," Anya said. "You have a confidence that people can sense and rely on."

"Well...thank you both." Martha felt her cheeks begin to warm. "I hope I'm worthy of your faith in me. I'll do everything I can to make sure the book sale goes well."

After leaving the hospital, the two sisters headed back toward their home and picked up Mary. Instead of going into the house for a relaxing evening, they drove out the lane again and along Classen Road past the Fischer and Stoltzfus farms to the home of Rachel's sister Sally. Sally had invited all three sisters to the baby shower she was hosting for Rachel's daughter-in-law, Leah.

A host of buggies and a few cars were parked at Sally's home when they arrived. Sally welcomed them with a warm smile.

Rachel was there, as were her two elder sisters Marietta and Leora. "I'm glad you could join us," she said.

Elizabeth smiled. "How did you get out of making sure all the homework was done and everyone washed behind their ears?"

Rachel chuckled. "I left those jobs to Phoebe and Luke. It is very pleasant to have a night off from the evening tasks." The pair were her two eldest children still at home and although Phoebe had Down syndrome, she was quite capable within the routine of her familiar household. Elizabeth had long admired the way Rachel and her husband Silas treated Phoebe as they did all their other children. The only difference had been school. Elizabeth knew Phoebe had been a bit older when she'd started school, and Rachel had taught Phoebe at home after the first few years so she could ensure the girl learned simple reading, writing, and figuring well enough to function with the work of the Amish. Elizabeth doubted Phoebe would ever marry, but she seemed quite happy and well adjusted.

"I have a favor to ask," Martha said to Rachel. "Is there any way you could work for me at the shop Thursday? I have to fill in for a hospitalized volunteer at the library book sale."

"Even if you can't stay until five," Elizabeth said, "I'm sure Mary and I could manage that last hour or so."

"Phoebe and Hannah can ready the meal," Rachel said. "I will plan something not too hard for them. I will just stay after morning quilting circle ends until close."

"Oh, thank you," Martha said. "I really appreciate that."

"I hope your friend recovers," Rachel said. "If you would like to share her name, I will pray for her."

"Thank you." Martha smiled and reached for a notepad. "I know that would be greatly appreciated."

"Rachel," Elizabeth said, "I also have a question for you, but this one isn't about the store. Have you had any trouble with a fox lately?"

Rachel hesitated. "One of our barn kittens went missing yesterday, and the twins said they thought a fox got it. But they didn't see it, so I am not sure why they think that. I believe one of my sons saw one a few days ago, so they may assume a fox took the kitten because of that."

It sounded plausible to Elizabeth, after the theory she and Mary had about Barnie's disappearance. She related Mary's story about the missing hen and told Rachel about the hole they'd boarded up in the chicken coop. "And Mary saw a fox with her own two eyes," she added.

"That is not good. You had better get that coop fixed up." Rachel looked grave. "Silas will shoot it if he sees it. I did not tell him about the kitten." She paused, and a smile appeared. "I have some sympathy for Mr. Fox, although I am afraid at this time of year, it may be Mrs. Fox trying to feed her young ones."

"That's quite possible," Elizabeth said. "But I sure don't want him or her eating any more of our hens. Mary loves those birds." She paused. "I haven't told you about the strange thing that happened at church yesterday."

"A mystery?" Rachel looked intrigued.

"Maybe." Elizabeth recounted the story of the girl in the over large jacket she'd seen at church and then encountered earlier today at the library. "And Fanny at the library saw her taking apples off the table at story time last week," she reported.

"Isn't that just the oddest thing? No one has been able to speak with her at any length. I would have liked to, but she rushed off too quickly for me to even ask her name."

"You gave her money," Rachel repeated, smiling. "That was a kind act, Elizabeth. I will pray that she is using it for a wise purpose."

"I certainly am as well," Elizabeth said. "I'd hate to think I gave a child money for drugs."

They looked at each other, horrified by the thought. But then Rachel shook her head, smiling.

"You must trust your judgment, I think," she said. "If you believe she needed money to help someone in some way, you probably are right."

"I can't help thinking that she needs more help than just a little donation," Elizabeth confided. "On one hand, I feel the Christlike imperative to give and trust that it will be used well. But on the other, I have a similar feeling that perhaps I am His instrument of change, that maybe I am needed in that girl's life. That's why, I think, I feel so compelled to find her. It's not simple curiosity. I feel as if she needs assistance."

"Trust your judgment," Rachel said again. "Let it guide you."

"I think I have to," Elizabeth said before taking a seat with her sisters. "I told Rachel about our mystery girl," she told them.

"Your mystery girl," Martha said. "Mary and I haven't done more than hear you talk about the glimpses you've had of her."

Elizabeth shrugged that off. "Rachel told me to trust my judgment. You know, about trying to find out more about her."

"And what's your judgment telling you?" Martha inquired.

"I think I need to find her and see if she needs more help than one twenty-dollar bill can offer," Elizabeth said. "It's not simple curiosity anymore, and it's not just mild concern. Now I'm beginning to feel really worried."

At home, Mary gathered a few scraps from the pork loin Martha had cooked in the slow cooker and served for dinner. Elizabeth had related her conversation with Rachel about the fox, and now Mary felt even more conflicted than she had before.

She walked out to the edge of the pasture farthest from the edge of the house and scattered the leftovers near a copse of oak trees. "There, Mr. Fox," she said, "or Mrs., as the case may be. If I feed you, will you leave my hens alone? Oh, and stay away from the Fischer farm too, if you know what's good for you. I may not be happy with you, but the last thing I want is to see you catch a bullet."

Hiking back across the pasture, she detoured toward the henhouse. It was growing dark, and she was determined to make sure all her hens had found their way into the coop. After she'd unbolted the door, she stepped inside and flipped on the light in the tiny anteroom where the egg basket, supplies, and feed were kept. Then she opened the door into the main room where the chickens were roosting and began counting. Yippee! They were all accounted for.

Except for her poor little Barnie. Mary felt her spirits sink. She looked around the interior of the coop, wondering how long it had been since any improvements had been made. The little building really was in appalling shape. From in here, she could see rotting beams and loose boards, and she knew there was a soft spot in the floor in one of the far corners. Really, the entire thing needed to be replaced.

Once the thought occurred to her, it stuck like a burr in a wool stocking. "How hard could it be?" she asked aloud. One of the Wyandotte hens half-raised her wings and then resettled herself as if to indicate that she didn't appreciate being disturbed. "Sorry," Mary whispered. "But really, how hard could it be to build a henhouse?"

Elizabeth had suggested they ask Bill to check over the structure and repair it. But the suggestion didn't feel right to Mary. Bill had willingly helped them in so many ways since they'd reopened the shop, but she didn't want to become dependent on him for repairs, particularly since he rarely let them pay him. And then there was the whole "developing relationship" thing, which she really wasn't sure how to handle. So far, she'd mostly just avoided anything more than simple friendship...but one thing she did know—she didn't want to get into the habit of hollering for Bill every time she needed help. Friendship had its limits. She had learned to value her independence, and she wasn't about to start depending on a man again anytime soon.

Suddenly determined, she closed the inner door, shut off the lights, and secured the outer door carefully before hurrying back to the house. She had to take Bolt out for a little exercise and training session, and then she would sit down at the computer and do some research. You could find anything online. She was willing to bet there were collections of building plans for chicken coops for sale.

Elizabeth thought that Tuesday was a better day at Secondhand Blessings in regard to Bolt's behavior. Martha had been vocal about not allowing him to return to the store, but when Elizabeth had agreed with Mary that the beagle needed frequent training sessions and opportunities to properly greet people if he was to improve, Martha had capitulated. Not happily, Elizabeth thought, hiding a grin, but her middle sister liked the little dog too, and she suspected her protests had been mostly for form's sake.

Mary was quite firm with Bolt. She wore his leash around her waist. Each time the door opened, and she sensed that he might react to a customer, she immediately told him to heel and waved a treat beneath his nose, after which she began a series of obedience exercises and fed him treats, praising him lavishly for sitting, heeling, and staying.

As the day wore on, Bolt began to look at Mary every time the door opened, rather than scrambling to his feet and watching the door. Elizabeth and Martha even began telling customers to make sure they stopped to greet the little beagle in the back if they were dog lovers. They kept a supply of treats on the counter and gave them out so people could approach Bolt with a treat in hand as soon as his behavior was appropriate.

All in all, it was a significant change from the debacle that had been Monday.

The phone rang just before lunchtime.

"Oh no," Elizabeth heard Martha say. A moment later, Martha hung up.

"What's wrong?" Elizabeth asked.

Martha turned to her sisters, worry plain on her face. "One of the book sale volunteers just called. The two large posters that we display on easels at the front and back door of the library during the sale were stored in the attic of a volunteer's home, and they got water damage over the winter. The person didn't know it until she went to get them down last night." Martha sighed.

"Oh goodness." Mary laughed. "I thought it was something serious. I can make you a couple of posters, Martha."

"Really?" Martha's eyes widened with hope. "Are you sure?"

"Of course," Mary assured her. "Do you have images of the old ones? Or can you tell me what they need to say?"

"I don't, but I'm sure we can come up with some ideas," Martha said, relief plain in her tone. "Thank you so much, Mary. I'll get you details—and money for supplies—as soon as the library opens."

"We have plenty of that heavy-duty fiberboard in the back," Elizabeth reminded her. "Remember the lady who cleaned out her craft room and gave us all those supplies? Mary can use two of the large framed ones that are unfinished."

"Oh, that's perfect," Martha said.

"Why don't you write down what you want them to say?" Mary suggested.

Martha took a pen and notepad from a drawer. "Obviously, we need 'book sale' in large letters, and the days and times.

But I'd love to put a quote about reading on them. I saw some good ones the other day. I'll have to look them up."

Martha scrolled through her phone. "Oh, here we go. How about, 'The reading of all good books is like conversation with the finest minds of the past centuries.' That's a quote by Descartes."

"I've always liked, 'Fill your house with stacks of books, in all the crannies and all the nooks,'" Mary said. "Can you guess who said that?"

Martha chuckled. "Dr. Seuss. Oh yes, use that one too, please. A different one for each poster."

"Okay. Any preferences for theme, such as flowers or animals, or...?"

"Towering stacks of books?" Martha laughed. "I trust your judgment. Thank you again."

Mary took Bolt up to the house over lunch, and when she returned, Elizabeth took her lunch out to the picnic table they had placed behind the barn for taking breaks in good weather. But she had no sooner set out her sandwich and apple than Martha came rushing outside.

"You need to go inside," Martha said urgently. "The Pearce family just walked in."

Elizabeth understood immediately. Ellie Pearce was one of the girls who had been mentioned as the name of the mystery girl. After the things that Frannie had confided about the Pearce family, Elizabeth had thought that Ellie might have a very good reason for trying to supplement her family's food stores.

She walked back into the shop. Anticipation rose. It would be nice to know the name of the girl she'd given money to.

A woman and a slender teenage girl stood near a table filled with neatly folded stacks of towels, sheet sets, blankets, dishcloths, and other fabric items for the home. The woman had graying red-brown hair pulled back in a messy twist, while the girl beside her had dark red curls that fell past her shoulders. She was a young teen in jeans and a blue T-shirt, but even before the pair turned to face her, Elizabeth knew she wasn't the mystery girl.

Her young friend's hair had been longer, wilder, and much less tame. This girl, Ellie Pearce, had distinctly red tones in her deep copper curls, and those curls were neatly pulled away from her face with a headband.

"Good afternoon," Elizabeth said cheerfully. "Welcome to Secondhand Blessings. May I help you?"

"We're just browsing," the woman said hastily, lifting her hands from the bath towels she'd been examining.

Elizabeth continued to smile. "Well, browse to your heart's content. If you have any questions, one of my sisters or I will be near the counter." She picked up a set of high-quality towels she'd folded earlier that morning and shook them out. They looked as if they were brand-new. "Aren't these pretty? I was just about to mark them down to half-price, in case you're interested."

As she leisurely strolled to a nearby aisle, she saw Mrs. Pearce examine the towels before laying them in the shopping basket she carried over one arm. The girl, Ellie, wandered off a bit to a bookshelf where the sisters had displayed a collection of classics. She picked up *The Call of the Wild* and splayed a hand across the cover almost reverently and then returned it to the shelf.

Elizabeth strolled around to the book display. "Hi. I'm Elizabeth. Have you read any of these classics?"

Ellie nodded. "A few."

"I love to read. When I was about your age, my mother subscribed to a book club that sent us four classics condensed into one volume about every six weeks. I could hardly wait until those books arrived. My favorite was *Jane Eyre* by Charlotte Brontë."

"I've read that. And *Wuthering Heights,* which was written by her sister Emily."

Elizabeth smiled, nodding. "Isn't that funny to have two successful authors in one family?"

"There was another sister who was an author too," Ellie told her.

"You must read a lot. Do you go to the library often?"

Ellie smiled for the first time. "Every chance I get. I'm glad summer's coming, because I'll have a lot more time to read."

"I know just how you feel. I used to love summer. I would come home from the library with a stack of books *this* tall." She spread her palms vertically from her waist to her chin to demonstrate. "Say, I have a library question that perhaps you could help me with."

Ellie looked intrigued. "What is it?"

"I'm trying to find a girl that I know goes to the library. I spoke to her once, and I want to give her something. But I don't know her name. Maybe you've seen her while you were browsing in the stacks?"

"Maybe. What's she look like?"

"She's about your age, I guess, and about your height. But she has long curly hair that's very dark brown, and light-colored eyes you wouldn't forget if you'd met her. And I think she often wears a tan jacket that looks several sizes too large."

Ellie nodded immediately. "Oh, I think I know who you mean. There's a new girl at school, and I've seen her several times at the library. She fits your description pretty well. Could that be who you're looking for?"

The library! Elizabeth hoped her exhilaration didn't show. "I bet it is. Do you know her name?"

Ellie shook her head. "No. She's not in my section."

Elizabeth's hopes took a dive. But still…it was more than she'd had before. "Thank you so much." She picked up the Jack London novel the girl had been cradling so lovingly. "As a thank-you for your help, would you be willing to accept this book?" Seeing refusal on the girl's face, she added, "I know it's not much, and you probably can find a nicer copy at the library book sale that's opening on Thursday, but I'd really like to thank you in some small way."

"Well," said the girl weakly, accepting the novel, "I guess if you insist. But I'd better ask my mom." She rushed over to her mother with the volume clutched to her breast.

After a moment of animated conversation on Ellie's part, the mother's gaze met Elizabeth's. "Thank you," she said across the aisle, but her smile looked stiff and forced.

"I appreciate your daughter's assistance," Elizabeth said. "And her love of literature. I didn't know there was a teenager alive who knew all three of the Brontë sisters."

Mrs. Pearce's face relaxed. "She loves to read. If I can't find her to help with chores, I know she's off lost in a book somewhere."

Elizabeth laughed. "A girl after my own heart. I bet she's a good student."

The mother's face softened further. "Straight As. I'm so proud of her."

Elizabeth hurried to the register to ring them up herself so she could include the "half-price discount." As she completed the sale, she said, "Don't forget about the library book sale. It runs Thursday through Saturday, and if you wait until Saturday, they have a bag sale. You buy all the books you can fit in a bag for a dollar."

Ellie's eyes popped wide open. "Really?" She clutched her mother's sleeve. "Mom, can we go?"

"I think we can probably spare a dollar," her mother said with a smile. "We'll go by on Saturday."

"First thing," Ellie insisted. "Before they get too picked over."

Her mother was laughing as the pair left the store, and Elizabeth was smiling as she closed the cash register.

The shop closed early on Tuesday afternoons. Martha was just about to sling her handbag over her shoulder when the phone rang. Debating leaving it for a millisecond, she hesitated and then picked it up. "Secondhand Blessings. This is Martha. How may I help you?"

"Hello, Martha, I was hoping to reach you at the shop. This is Natalie Jones."

Natalie was one of the Friends of the Library volunteers. She and her teenage sons had signed up to help sort books tonight. "Hi, Natalie. What can I do for you?"

"Well," the woman said, "I tried to call Anya, and her husband told me what happened, and that you're in charge of the book sale now. Both boys woke up with the flu this morning, and I'm pretty sure I'm getting sick too. I'm so sorry, Martha, but we're not going to be able to make it for our shift."

Martha took a deep breath. She only had six volunteers on the schedule for that time period. Now half of them couldn't be there. "These things happen when you have a family. We'll miss you."

"I feel terrible for the short notice," Natalie said. "I apologize."

"Just take care of yourself and your family," Martha said. "That's what's most important."

Only Mary was standing outside, since Elizabeth had left a bit early to run some errands. She and Bolt waited while Martha put the deadbolt in place and locked the keyless entry. As they walked up the lane together, Martha said, "Would you want to come to the library with me and help sort books from five to seven tonight?"

"Oh, Martha, I don't know," Mary replied. "This is kind of short notice. I was planning to paint this afternoon and evening, and I want to make those posters for you."

"Forget I asked. I understand," Martha said glumly.

"Don't you have volunteers lined up?"

"Natalie Jones and her sons have the flu," Martha said. "They were half my volunteer team tonight. I wasn't planning on going in, either, but now I'll have to make the time."

"That changes things," Mary said with feeling. "Of course I'll come. I can paint any old day, and I'll still have time for the posters before Thursday. Maybe Elizabeth can come too, and then you'll have all the help you need to replace what you lost."

Relieved and grateful, Martha chuckled. "Probably more, since two of them were teen boys. Those two are a handful."

Arriving home, Martha decided to begin her prep work for the baking she would do later for tomorrow. She reviewed several recipes and checked her ingredients to be sure she had everything she needed. Tropical Muffins were on the list for the first time since last summer. She hadn't made them through the winter, but a customer had asked yesterday when she planned to offer them again. She also wanted to try a pretty rolled cookie called a Lemon Curd that she planned to cut into the shape of a daisy. They were actually two cookies pressed together with a "window" hole cut out of the middle of the top one. She would spread lemon curd on top of the bottom cookie and press a "window top" onto it so the curd would show in the center.

The third recipe she intended to take to the shop soon was Cream Wafers. It was an old recipe that her grandmother used to make, but Martha had never tried it. Now, she thought nostalgically of Grandma Lois's Cream Wafers. That was what she would call them, she decided. The concept was roughly the same as those of the macarons often served in the South, but the cookies were not quite as light. They actually looked a bit like Ritz crackers once they were carefully pricked with a fork before baking.

Since she'd frozen a bumper crop of rhubarb the previous year, and she still had a lot left, she also decided to make several "Spring and Fall Pies," as her mother had called the rhubarb, apple, and cranberry pies she'd made during both spring and autumn seasons. Martha had no idea why she'd never made them midsummer. Probably because there were simply so many other types of berry pies to be baked when everything was coming ripe and needed picking over the summer.

While Martha was immersed in her kitchen craft, Mary said, "I'd like to paint for a bit. Do you mind watching Bolt, or would you like me to kennel him?"

"Oh, that's all right," Martha said. "I can keep an eye on him while I make these muffins."

"Thanks," Mary said, to the tune of Bolt noisily lapping from the water bowl. "Just don't forget, he's a sneaky one."

Martha looked at the little dog as he finished his drink and then innocently gazed up at her. "Oh, don't worry," she said. "It's the kennel for him if he misbehaves."

CHAPTER EIGHT

Elizabeth drove to Mount Zion Mennonite Church as soon as she left the shop. The only car in the parking lot when she arrived was a battered silver Honda that belonged to the church secretary. Pastor Nagle must be doing house calls or something, because she knew from experience that his day off was usually Friday.

She parked next to the Honda and walked up the sidewalk to the side entrance to the church. The big double front doors were usually locked on weekdays, and the only entry was through the side door that passed the suite of offices and the library. She waved through the glass of the office door at Louella, the secretary, but didn't stop. Beneath a coatrack in the vestibule outside the sanctuary, there was a box marked Lost and Found. There was always a collection of miscellany in the box: single gloves and mittens, a woolen scarf, a Bible and other books, some child's forgotten pacifier. Occasionally there were other interesting things. Today there was even a cell phone in one corner. But another larger item claimed Elizabeth's attention. A pale petal-pink jacket in a size three was perfect for her purposes. A three was a junior size and would fit a petite teenager.

Draping the jacket over her arm, she walked back toward the office. She paused and opened the office door.

"Hi, Louella."

The secretary looked up. "Hi, Elizabeth. How are you?"

"Fine, thanks." Elizabeth held up the pink jacket. "Do you know how long this has been in the lost-and-found box?"

Louella shrugged. "I couldn't tell you weeks or months, but it's been there for a while. I figured someone forgot it last fall and didn't notice all winter because it was too cold for a light jacket. Do you know who it belongs to?"

Elizabeth shook her head. "No, but may I borrow it? If I don't find the owner, I'll bring it back."

Louella waved a hand. "Sure thing."

Back in the car, she headed for the McClaine address, which she had looked up in the church directory the night before. After parking in the driveway of the neat little white Cape Cod home accented by frilly tied-back curtains, Elizabeth ascended the three concrete steps to the little porch and rang the bell.

Within seconds, the door opened. The tall, slim woman who appeared in the doorway looked surprised, but she smiled and pushed open the storm door. "Hello, Elizabeth. How are you? Come on in."

"Just for a second," Elizabeth said. "I'm on an errand." Spotting movement in the kitchen through an adjacent door, she said, "I picked up a jacket at church that Brittany may have lost." Which, technically, could have been true, although it wasn't her primary motive for the visit.

Immediately, a girl peeked into the room. A long, sleek fall of straight dark hair fell around her face. As she stepped into the room, it was apparent that she was slender and easily as tall as her mother already. And most importantly, she was not the girl Elizabeth had met. She eyed the jacket Elizabeth was holding out and shook her head. "Sorry, not mine."

"Just thought I'd check," Elizabeth said cheerfully. "Any idea whose it could be?"

The girl and her mother both shook their heads. "It doesn't look familiar."

"Oh well, it was worth a try."

"You could put it in the lost-and-found box in the vestibule," Brittany said helpfully. "That's the first place everyone checks when they lose something."

Elizabeth's lips quirked. "That's a great idea. If I don't find the owner, I'll do that."

After thanking the pair and leaving, Elizabeth felt discouraged. Was she being ridiculous? Trying to find one teenage girl felt like seeking the proverbial needle in the haystack. And really, why was she pursuing it? It certainly wasn't going to affect her in any personal manner.

But she couldn't shake the feeling that the youngster needed help. The fervent way in which the girl had thanked Elizabeth for the money replayed in her memory. *"It will make all the difference in the world,"* she had said. The kid hadn't just been dumpster-diving for kicks. She had needed that cash.

When she'd used the church directory to find the McClains' home, Elizabeth had written down the address of Sheila Canner's family, and it wasn't far away. Since she was out and about, she decided to try her excuse one more time.

Driving along several roads through fields that would soon be starting to show the first seedlings of the crops they'd hold, she found the Canner home. It was a frame farmhouse with peeling white paint and faded blue shutters. A few chickens scratched in the dirt along the driveway, while daffodils, undaunted by the weeds that undoubtedly choked out summer flowers, poked up here and there along the side of the house.

Elizabeth stepped carefully on the cracked cement sidewalk. It would be easy to turn an ankle on the uneven surface.

Stepping up onto the front porch, she didn't see a doorbell, so she rapped on the frame and waited. No one answered. No dog barked, nor was there any sound from inside that indicated someone was home. And, she realized, there was no car in the driveway either. She tried to remember if anyone had mentioned whether the Canner parents worked, but nothing came to mind.

She rapped again and listened for any sound. Still nothing. Well, she should have expected this in the middle of a Tuesday afternoon, but she couldn't help being disappointed. Now that she was finally resolved to figure out who her mystery girl was, she was frustrated that she couldn't make things happen faster.

She turned to leave the porch and head back to her car. Just as she stepped off the porch, a big yellow school bus came roaring along the road. It screeched and squealed to a halt at the end of the driveway. The driver sent her a friendly wave, which Elizabeth returned, but her attention was focused on the girl alighting from the steep steps of the bus.

It had to be Sheila. She wore a black jacket, tight black jeans adorned with silver studs and chains, and clunky black boots. Beneath the jacket was a black T-shirt bearing a design of ribcage bones. Her hair was very short and black with blue streaks, and as she sauntered closer, Elizabeth noticed that she sported a line of stud earrings up each ear and a small hoop through one eyebrow.

"Hi. My mom's at work," the girl said.

"Actually, I think I'm looking for you. Are you Sheila?" Elizabeth asked. "I'm Elizabeth Classen. I go to your church."

"Good ol' Mount Zion," Sheila said scornfully. "Yeah, I'm Sheila. Whatcha want?"

"I found a jacket." Elizabeth held out the pink jacket, unable to suppress her amusement at the thought of this girl wearing the stylish pink coat. "But now that we've met, I doubt it's yours." She didn't even try to hide her grin.

Sheila eyed the jacket. As her gaze met Elizabeth's, she grinned too. "What was your first clue?" The smile made her look much more approachable and friendly.

"Call it a hunch," Elizabeth said. "But I do have another question for you. I'm looking for a girl about your size with long, dark hair. Very curly. She may wear an oversized khaki-colored jacket with big pockets, but she's really slender. I've seen her at the church during the social hour and at the library."

"You think the jacket is hers?"

Elizabeth shrugged. "I don't know." She didn't want to get into her reasons for finding the mystery girl, and she really *wasn't* lying about the pink jacket. She didn't know who it might belong to.

"The new girl in eighth grade. I saw her a couple of weeks ago hanging around church for a little while, but she didn't actually come to church that I know of." Sheila snapped her fingers. "Just moved here at the beginning of the school year, I think. I'm not sure of her name…Mara or Marla, maybe? A teacher might know."

"Thanks." Elizabeth smiled. "I appreciate the help. Nice to meet you, Sheila. I'll look for you at church."

"Nice to meet you too." Sheila smiled back at her and started toward the house.

Elizabeth chuckled the whole time she buckled her seat belt, started the ignition, and headed back toward Classen Road. That exchange had gone about as well as it possibly could have.

Martha watched all three dogs sprawl on the floor in the kitchen as Mary took her painting satchel, folding stool, and easel and headed back out the door.

Alone in the house, Martha hummed to herself as she pulled yet another recipe, this one for Strawberry Bread, toward herself. She'd been wanting to try something a little different and distinctive for a while. This recipe, with a few variations that she'd pulled from the reviews, might just do the trick. Just in case it didn't turn out as she expected, she didn't double the recipe as she often did, but followed the directions.

Carefully, she read through the recipe she had altered slightly from the original.

First, she took strawberries from the refrigerator. The recipe had called for fewer, but she'd read several reviews that had suggested doubling the amount because they reduced so much when baked. She sliced half of them, lightly sprinkled sugar over them, and set them aside. Next, she pureed the other half and set the resulting mixture aside as well.

Then she preheated the oven and buttered and floured two loaf pans before assembling the rest of the ingredients. She combined all her dry ingredients and mixed them thoroughly with a fork. In another large bowl, she stirred together all the wet ingredients with a large spatula, continuing to follow the directions until she had a distinctly pinky-red strawberry batter. It looked so delicious it made her mouth water. She hoped it was as good as it looked.

Finally, she stirred in pecans and divided the batter equally between her two loaf pans. Just as she finished scraping the last of the gooey mix out of the bowl, the timer dinged, signaling that it had finished preheating.

"Perfect timing," she muttered to herself. Carefully, she transferred the two loaf pans to the oven and set the timer for forty-five minutes.

While the bread baked, she washed up the mess she'd made with bowls and utensils and wiped down the counters. Then she got out a pen and one of the double-fold recipe cards that fit into the large recipe book in which she filed her "keepers." She started to transfer the recipe she had written on a sheet of paper, but her pen wouldn't write.

Martha scribbled for a minute, hoping it was just a block, but when the pen still wouldn't produce ink, she sighed and rose to her feet. After tossing the pen into the trash, she walked to the office. Elizabeth always had a tray inside the top drawer of the big desk filled with pens, pencils, and highlighters.

She selected a pen and took a cursory swipe across the edge of a much-scribbled-on sheet of wastepaper. It made a mark immediately, so she returned to the kitchen—and stopped suddenly in the doorway, aghast.

The little beagle stood squarely in the middle of the kitchen table, tongue lolling, white-tipped tail waving madly.

"Bolt! Get off there!" The pen skittered across the floor as she lost her grip on it, gesturing at the dog.

At her stern tone, his head cocked as if to ask, "Why?" But then, seeing her advance across the kitchen, he scrambled down by way of the chair she'd so helpfully left pulled out for him, and quickly planted his bottom on the floor. He looked up at her apprehensively, and Martha, about to punish him, melted. She recalled something Mary had told her about praising animals for behaviors you liked immediately after they performed them.

"Oh, buddy," she said, kneeling to pet him. "Good 'off,'" she told him, fondling the drooping silky ears. "I guess we never told you to stay off the table, did we? And then I left that chair in exactly the right position to tempt you. Totally my fault."

Rising, she retrieved the pen she'd dropped when she'd rushed forward and took a seat at the table to write her recipe and notes.

Bolt, appearing to think that all was now well with his world, headed for the water bowl and noisily slurped up a big drink before returning to settle on the floor with his head across one of her slipper-clad feet.

Martha had to laugh. "You sure don't hold a grudge, pal."

There was a jingle of tags from the living room as their border collie, Pal, rose from his spot and came out to see why she'd called his name. Right behind him came Tink, the sweet little dachshund, determined not to miss out on anything.

Martha chuckled again. "All right. Treats all around."

At the familiar word, all three dogs grew more animated, milling around her legs. It hadn't taken Bolt any time at all to learn that one, she reflected with a grin as she reached for the cookie jar in which she kept the peanut butter treats she baked for them.

The doorknob turned, and Elizabeth stepped inside. "Spoiling the dogs, Martha?" she asked with a grin.

"Maybe." Martha grinned right back. "Sit, and I'll spoil you too."

Three rumps hit the floor at the first word, even though it had been directed at her sister.

"Stay." Two dogs stayed, but Bolt surged to his feet as Pal delicately took his cookie from her.

"Bolt, sit," Martha reminded him, and he sat again. "Stay." She reinforced the command with a hand signal, and this time he waited while she gave Tink a treat before offering him one, although his whole little body quivered, and he followed her every move with soulful brown eyes.

"Progress," Elizabeth commented, setting her handbag and a light pink denim jacket on the kitchen table. "That was actually quite a bit of progress."

"He's improved a lot in a very short time," Martha said. "Although apparently none of us have thought to explain that the kitchen table is off limits."

Elizabeth's eyes grew round. "Oh no. What did he get into?"

"Nothing. He was just standing there looking at me," Martha told her.

Elizabeth laughed. "Well, thank goodness for small favors."

Martha chuckled. "That's for sure." Then she looked quizzically at the jacket. "New purchase?"

"Hardly." Elizabeth laughed. "Not really my style. Or size." She held up the jacket, which looked as if it might fit a very slender teenager. "I got it from the church lost-and-found box, and I'm slightly ashamed to admit I used it as a pretext to meet two of the girls on my list."

"Not a bad idea." Martha looked impressed rather than horrified. "So you asked them if they were the owner?"

Elizabeth bent to pat Bolt. "I didn't tell any lies," she said honestly. "I mean, it is a lost jacket."

"And you're using it to try to find the girl from church?"

Elizabeth nodded. "I eliminated Ellie Pearce earlier today. But Ellie thought she might have seen the girl around the library. I wanted to be sure it wasn't one of the other girls who's been suggested to me, so I borrowed this jacket from the church and stopped by Tammy McClain's home to ask her daughter Brittany if it could be hers and then by the Canners' to see Sheila. Turns out the jacket doesn't belong to either of them, but more importantly, neither one is the girl I met behind the library. Also, Sheila knew exactly who I meant. She says she's a new girl at school and that she saw her hanging around church."

"So who's left on the list of the names that were suggested to you?" Martha asked.

"Just Jean Ann Brean, the one everyone says doesn't go anywhere without her folks."

"And I can picture her. She's not small and skinny." Martha pointed at the jacket. "If the girl you're looking for would fit in that jacket, it's definitely not Jean Ann. So what next?"

Elizabeth sighed. "I guess I'll try to follow up on what Ellie Pearce told me. She thought she'd seen the girl at the library. And I did see her behind the library, remember? Also, Sheila Canner thought the girl was an eighth grader at her school. She suggested I ask a teacher."

"That's a pretty good idea."

"Oh, there are no flies on that one," Elizabeth said, laughing.

Martha's face softened. "I haven't heard that expression in a long time. That was another one Mama used to say."

"Usually about Mary," Elizabeth said, and they both chuckled fondly.

Martha patted the pink jacket. "Borrowing this lost jacket was a pretty good idea too."

All three sisters went together in Martha's car to the library shortly before five, when three other volunteers would be meeting them there to sort books that had been donated for the book sale.

The community room where the sale was being held had been a recent addition a few years ago. Large windows ensured it was filled with light, and room-darkening shades could be pulled to show movies if darkness was required.

Elizabeth surveyed the room with raised eyebrows when they walked in. "This sale starts Thursday, you say?" Thursday was only two days away, and the room was a wreck, with piles of books and box after box stacked anywhere there was room.

Martha nodded, and Elizabeth could see she looked worried. "I hope no other volunteers have to cancel. This is a big job to finish in two nights."

"Hi, girls!" The speaker was a small, birdlike older woman with tightly curled gray hair. "I didn't know you'd be here."

"Pollie!" Elizabeth exclaimed. "How nice to see you! Are you volunteering tonight?"

Pollie Muller had been a babysitter to Martha and Elizabeth when they were very young children many, many years ago, back before Pollie married and raised her own family. She was at least a dozen years older than they were, but her volunteer activities were legendary in the community. Elizabeth wasn't at all surprised to see that she had a hand in the Friends of the Library's work.

"I am," Pollie said. "And Joe and Tina Hamilton are coming in this time slot too, I believe. I heard about Natalie's boys getting sick, and I figured she'd have to cancel, so I also asked Donny and Gilda Flory to come in."

"Oh, you're the best. Thank you." Martha looked relieved. "The eight of us ought to be able to make a nice dent in this mess, and then there's another group coming from seven to nine. So hopefully tomorrow night will just be fine tuning."

"So how does this work?" Mary asked. She looked dubiously at all the boxes, obviously wondering where to start.

"It's easy." Pollie pointed to the signs on the walls above the tables of books and those hanging over the tables in the center.

The signs were labeled BOARD BOOKS, MYSTERY, FICTION, CHILDREN'S FICTION, SCI-FI, COOKING, and many other popular genres of books. "You just go through the books yet to be sorted, find the right table, and lay them on it. If it doesn't fit into any particular category or you can't figure out where it belongs, let me know. Later, we'll sort them and stack them better, but we don't have to alphabetize them or anything. We're just categorizing them so the historical fiction lovers and the romance readers and the moms looking for kids' stories can find the sections easily. That's all we need to do."

"That sounds easy enough," Mary said. "Let's get started." She picked up a grocery bag full of books from the pile yet to be sorted and started pulling titles out, and Martha and Elizabeth did likewise.

Elizabeth's first bag of books appeared to be mostly nonfiction World War II history. In the bottom were a few gardening books, also nonfiction. It didn't take her long to get into a rhythm as she began to memorize where the various categories of books were located. The other four volunteers arrived within minutes, and soon they all were busily zipping back and forth from pile to pile, adding more and more books to each one.

Martha was surprised, and a little relieved, to see how quickly the stacks of boxes were diminishing. Before long, there were more books on tables than there were in boxes, and Donny Flory stopped sorting and started breaking down the boxes so they could store them in the basement until they were needed.

"Don't break them all down," Martha reminded him. "We'll need some for the leftovers once the sale is over."

Shortly before seven, Minerva Helman stuck her head in the door. "Anyone need anything before I lock the front door and leave?"

Everyone shook their head.

"Martha, did Anya give you the key to this door?"

Martha nodded. "Yes. Pollie will be staying for the second shift, so I gave it to her."

Pollie held up a shiny brass key on a key ring that looked like a miniature book. "Do I need to set an alarm or anything?"

Minerva shook her head. "Just lock both the door and the deadbolt locks from the outside, and we'll be fine. Text me when everyone is done and out of the building, and I can set the alarm remotely."

"Ooh, that's fancy," Mary said.

"But very helpful," Minerva said, "especially when we rent out this room for evening events. I can just give out a key, set the alarm remotely after they lock the door for the evening, and the renter brings it back again the next day."

"I'll text you once we're all out and locked up for the night," Pollie promised.

"Thank you." Minerva looked around. "And thank you all for your hard work. The Friends are a great source of support to us, and this book sale allows us to purchase things that we simply can't do within our annual budget."

As the librarian turned and left, Elizabeth followed her into the adjacent hallway. "Minerva? I have another question for you related to the girl I saw."

"Sure thing." Minerva paused.

"I spoke with Sheila Canner and Brittany McClain today, and neither one of them is the girl I saw. Is there anyone else you can think of who might have been the girl I saw?"

"If I think of anyone else who fits the profile, I'll let you know. And if I see that girl in the tan jacket again, I'll try to engage her in conversation, try to get a name. I talk to everyone about books." Her eyes lit up. "Maybe I can help her get a library card."

"That would be a bonus, wouldn't it? Thanks," Elizabeth said. "I appreciate your help." Although Elizabeth had a funny feeling the girl wasn't coming to the library strictly for reading material.

"Ready to go, Elizabeth?" Mary was standing by the door. "The next shift of volunteers is here. Martha's talking to them about what happens after all the boxes are emptied, and then we're leaving."

CHAPTER NINE

At home again, Mary took the dogs for a short walk down the lane to the store and back again. Bolt was well behaved, trotting along beside her without dragging at the lead so much, and Mary felt encouraged that the training was yielding some results.

By the time she returned, Martha and Elizabeth had prepared a late supper of chicken salad sandwiches and a spinach salad dressed with mandarin oranges, candied almonds, and a tangy cider vinegar dressing. The dogs were banished to the living room or, in Bolt's case, his kennel, to await their turn for supper.

Martha offered a brief prayer and concluded it with a request for Anya Presser's continued healing, and Mary surprised Elizabeth by saying, "Lord, bless Elizabeth's efforts to find and help Your child in need."

"Amen," they all chorused in unison.

The mealtime conversation consisted largely of discussing several consignment requests that Secondhand Blessings had recently gotten. One was a collection of salt-and-pepper shakers, which all three sisters agreed they should consign. They also agreed to make an offer on six boxes of household goods from the home of a church member's recently deceased mother, practical items like utensils, cookbooks, tea towels, and trivets that surely would sell, and another of baby toys and items like a high chair and swing that a young mother moving out of the toddler years was ready to part with.

Another consignment request was more problematic. A widow had brought in a variety of items she and her husband had purchased when he was active-duty military, and they were stationed abroad. The pieces ranged from an ornate Italian spelter clock to a set of Chinese porcelain plates to several World War II Polish army medals to Japanese netsukes. The consignor did not want to consign the items individually but was insisting that the sisters take it all.

"The problem," Martha said, "is that while I think we have a market for those plates, the rest of the items are not typically things that are of interest to the patrons who come through our shop."

"The clock, maybe," Elizabeth said.

"We do get a lot of tourists though," Mary said. "You just never know who's going to be a collector of what."

"People, in general, seem to be collecting less these days," Elizabeth cautioned. "It's not like it was when we were growing up and every household had china and silver and collections of various items. Young people today are living much differently, and they don't want all our old stuff, no matter what sentimental value we attach to it."

"You can see it in our sales statistics," Martha added. "Household goods sell better and much faster than sheerly collectible items. I vote no if this consignor insists that we take it all."

"I vote yes," Mary said stubbornly. "I think there are still people out there who are seeking pieces that are aesthetically pleasing, like those little netsukes. I admit, the Polish medals may be a tough sell, but who knows when an army general who collects World War II memorabilia might wander by with his wife on a tour bus to Longwood Gardens?"

Both sisters looked expectantly at Elizabeth, each set of blue eyes compelling her to cast her vote for a certain point of view.

Elizabeth sighed. "I agree with you both. Household goods are easier to move than collectibles in today's market. But there are still folks seeking that special something whose eye may be caught by a ridiculously elaborate gilt-and-marble Italian clock. What if we told her we'd take them for six months, and at the end of that time, she would take back anything that didn't sell?"

"Hmm." Martha nodded consideringly. "Not a bad idea. Would we ask a fee for displaying the items for that time?"

"Maybe a small one," Elizabeth said, "and we'd consider it a deposit that would come out of any sale. If nothing sells, the deposit would be forfeit."

"She's not going to want to do that," Mary objected.

"Then our problem would be solved," Elizabeth said. "We wouldn't have to turn her down flat, but we wouldn't have to take her items either."

"I don't know what to hope for," Martha said. "I vote yes to Elizabeth's idea."

"Me too." Mary smiled. "Always the peacemaker, that's our Elizabeth."

As they were cleaning up the kitchen after dinner, Mary turned to Martha. "I smelled that strawberry bread you made earlier. Any chance we might get to taste test it?"

Martha chuckled. "Absolutely. Someone's got to do the dirty work, right?"

"I've got to run outside first. I'll make it quick," Mary said.

As she gathered scraps from lunch and dinner that she'd saved and headed for the door, Elizabeth said, "Where are you going with those? Slops are for hogs."

Mary probably looked as sheepish as she felt. "I thought if I left some easy-to-forage scraps out for the fox, she might stop trying to get into the chicken coop until we get a sturdier one in place."

Elizabeth raised her eyebrows. She looked aghast. "Mary, if you start feeding that fox, he'll be coming around every single night for handouts!"

"I've, uh, already been feeding him," Mary confessed. "Rachel mentioned that 'he' might be a 'she' trying to feed her family, and I'm just not hard-hearted enough to make her life even tougher."

Elizabeth rolled her eyes...but didn't offer any more protests as Mary slipped out the door with the scraps of food.

When she returned, Martha had cut three slices of strawberry bread and garnished each with a dollop of whipped cream and a sliced strawberry. She handed a plate to each of her sisters. "Be honest," she warned as they all settled down in the living room. "I'd like to perfect this and add it to our items for sale."

Mary took her first bite. "Umm-yum," she said. "The texture's great, the flavor explodes in my mouth. Oh, Martha, this is a winner. You don't have to change anything."

"I agree," Elizabeth said. "This is terrific." She forked up another bite and looked down at the hopeful beagle wagging his tail at her feet. "Not a chance, you little mooch."

"Bolt, come lie down." Mary patted the sofa cushion, and the young dog hopped up beside her, circled once, and lay down. Mary took another bite of her dessert. "Fabulous."

After she finished off the last bite of the delicious strawberry loaf, Mary brought her laptop into the living room and began a search for chicken coop building plans.

Within minutes, she was overwhelmed by the plethora of ideas she found. There were plans for large coops and small coops, coops that looked like cute little cottages, and others that looked like nothing more than exactly what they were. They could be painted one color or liberally decked out with contrasting trim. One even looked like a miniature Swiss chalet, while another looked exactly like a Lilliputian farmhouse. It was not hard to imagine that a builder with some skill could design a coop that would look exactly like one's home in miniature. She had to suppress a chuckle at the thought of a Victorian-themed chicken coop with its bricks painted in warm cream with green and lavender trim to match their stately old home.

Some had runs or covered yards to protect them from predators. She especially liked the ones that were raised on stilts so that when the sun was beating down there would be some shade underneath the coop, although those were generally for a fairly small number of birds. She imagined a raised coop would be ideal for Southern climates. But she thought it made more sense here, where it could get bitterly cold occasionally, for the coop itself to meet the ground so there would be less need for additional insulation beneath. What they could do instead was affix a tarp to the roof of the run so there would be some shade outdoors during the day if the chickens were not given free range for any reason.

One reason being a rascally fox, she thought crossly.

Some of the coops she looked at had feeding and nest boxes that could be accessed from the exterior for easy feeding and cleaning. Those caught her eye. How would it be not to actually enter the coop in order to feed her hens and gather eggs?

Weird, she decided. She was used to a henhouse with a small antechamber for supplies and cleaning materials. She wasn't aiming to change her methods that much. She pulled up another website and was confronted with ever more fancy structures. One made her laugh aloud when she saw it had a laser cutout of a rooster on the door with window boxes for flowers.

"What's so funny?" Elizabeth asked.

Silently, Mary turned the laptop around so both Martha and Elizabeth could see the fussy, funny little chicken coop.

"Oh my," Martha said. She began to chuckle.

"Those are some well-loved chickens," Elizabeth said with a grin. "I wonder if they water their own window boxes."

Mary laughed again as she went back to her search for the perfect chicken coop.

It took several more websites of chicken coop construction designs before she found one that wasn't as elaborate. Finally, her eye was caught by a coop that looked a bit like the one they had now. The floor plan showed a small room into which a person could step and shut the door behind them before opening the main door into the henhouse. That way, there would be no escapees unless the doors to the ramps were opened. One ramp led into the enclosed run, while another could be opened when one wanted to allow the birds free range.

"Look at this," she said to her sisters. "Here's a nice little shed-type chicken coop similar to ours with an attached run. I think this might work. The plans say ideally it holds sixteen chickens. We only have twelve now—"

"Eleven," Elizabeth interrupted. "Right?"

"Right." Mary's excitement dimmed as she thought of poor little Barnie. "Anyway, this would be a good size, and it looks like a no-frills project. It says it's easy to build."

Elizabeth rose and came over to perch on the arm of the easy chair in which Mary sat. "That does look like a good plan," she said. "Bill should have no trouble knocking that out in a day or two."

Mary cleared her throat. "Um, I was thinking that we probably don't need to ask Bill. This looks pretty simple. I bet we could do it ourselves."

Martha looked up sharply from the recipe book she was perusing. "Build it ourselves?" She snorted. "I measure in cups and ounces, not feet and inches. No way."

"I mostly meant I'd build it," Mary said, stung by her sister's immediate refusal. "All I'd need from you guys is the occasional assistance holding a board or some wire in place, that kind of thing."

"Have you ever built anything before?" Elizabeth asked.

"Well, not on this scale," Mary admitted. "My project exper-tise has mostly been a few scaffolds for the kids' musical theater shows when they were in high school. But this plan looks very straightforward, and I know how to measure and hammer. If I buy all the wood precut, how hard could it be?"

Elizabeth smiled. "Probably a bit harder than you'd like to think. Bill would be happy to help us with it."

"I'd like to try to do it without having to ask him," Mary said. "Wouldn't it be great to be able to build something on our own without having to ask for help?"

"You don't want to be beholden to Bill," Martha said. "Right?"

Mary was silent. "I don't know if that's exactly it...but some-times I feel that we're awfully quick to ask him to do our out-side work for us."

"And even some of the inside stuff," Martha said. "There's a reason. It's because he's good at it."

"Is it that he rarely lets us pay him?" Elizabeth asked. "If that's the problem, we can tell him either we pay him, or we hire someone else who *will* accept payment."

"I think this might be more about Mary and Bill's relation-ship than it is about accepting help from a friend," Martha observed.

Irked, Mary said, "I am not 'in a relationship,' thank you very much. Why is it a problem that I want to build a chicken coop instead of asking someone else to do it?"

Elizabeth resumed her quilting, letting silence stretch for a moment, while Martha only smiled, which infuriated Mary even more. Finally, Elizabeth said, "Now that you ask, I can think of a couple of reasons that we are not out of line for questioning you. First, you don't have any demonstrable carpentry skills that I've ever seen. Second, you just admitted that you've never built any kind of serious structure before."

Mary opened her mouth, but Elizabeth held up a finger. "Swing sets don't really count, because they come ready to assemble." Her eldest sister paused, obviously choosing her next words with care. "I don't want to be a wet blanket, but the materials for this will not be cheap, and we can't afford to foul it up and have to pay someone to fix it. It has to be sound, it has to be well-roofed so our birds don't get wet and get pneumonia and die, and it has to be secure against intruders like our friend the fox. Are you certain you can do all those things?"

Mary swallowed. "No," she said honestly. "But I'd like the opportunity to try it, at least."

Martha and Elizabeth looked at each other.

"That's fine with me," Elizabeth said, "as long as you promise to be realistic and ask for help if you run into problems beyond your capabilities."

Martha nodded. "And with me. I'll even help you when I can, although I make no promises about my skill level." It was, for Martha, an apology, and Mary was ready to accept it.

"Thank you," Mary said. "I'll give it a try. I really think I can do this."

Just then, her ears caught an odd sound from the direction of the kitchen. "Uh-oh," she groaned. "I think Bolt's into something." She indicated the empty sofa cushion where the pup had been lying.

"I didn't even notice him get down!" Elizabeth said as they all leaped to their feet and rushed toward the kitchen.

The trash can, normally kept beside the sink, lay on its side, emptied of its contents, and trash was strewn all across the floor.

"Mercy me," Elizabeth said as she stepped into the kitchen behind Mary. "This is like having a toddler. We can't leave him for a minute."

Martha grimaced. "Having two well-behaved dogs makes it tough to remember there's one we've got to watch. I saw him get up, and I guess I assumed he was just going for a drink. I didn't give him a second thought."

Mary sighed, surveying the paper, coffee grounds, egg-shells, and more that would need to be picked up before the floor could be cleaned. "Oh, buddy, you give new meaning to the phrase, 'in the doghouse.'"

Martha tugged Bolt across the kitchen to his kennel and placed him inside. "And that's where he's going to have to stay any time we can't be with him from now on." As Bolt settled down on the thick blanket in the crate, she latched the door. "That trash can will live in the pantry until this dog is gone."

"I should have already put it there." Mary was gathering up the refuse strewn around by the exuberant pup. "That's what Ruth told me. It'll be less convenient, but we can't have this. And you know there will be moments when we forget to watch him closely."

"I didn't forget," Martha said a bit testily. "I expected that he would get a drink and come back to his spot like our dogs do."

"And you weren't wrong," Mary said, hoping to soothe her irate sister. "He's just ruled by his nose."

"And he has no manners whatsoever," Martha grumbled.

Mary rolled her eyes and gave up, letting her sister have the last word.

The sisters opened the store as usual at ten on Wednesday morning. Elizabeth took the bills and coins from the bank bag and placed them neatly in the cash drawer in front of the stamps they used for checks and the special marking pen they used to check for counterfeit bills when someone gave them anything larger than a twenty. Martha unlocked the door. And as she had the day before, Mary took Bolt to the back of the store.

Elizabeth looked up with a smile on her face, prepared to offer a polite welcome as the first customer entered, but her expression warmed with genuine pleasure as Bill walked in. She wondered fleetingly if his ears had been burning last night when they'd been talking about him, and her smile grew wider.

"Morning, Elizabeth," he said. "How's business?"

"It's a little early to tell yet," she said, grinning. "How about you?"

"Busy." Bill gave her a thumbs up. "I'm finishing a bathroom remodel today, and tomorrow I'm starting a deck addition for a different client."

"Unless it rains," she said with a laugh.

"Don't worry," he said. "If it rains, I have a list of small odd jobs different people want me to fix for them."

"That's good to hear," she said, noting with amusement the way his gaze moved around the store. He was looking for Mary, unless she missed her guess. "Mary's in the back," she offered.

A tide of red crept up his neck and bronzed his cheeks. "Thanks," he muttered. "I wanted to check out the tools and see if anything's been brought in that I'd like to have." But she noticed he wasted no time making a beeline for the back of the shop. Mary, she noted, was just coming out of the stockroom with several bolts of fabric someone had consigned stacked in her arms. Bolt was tethered to her belt loop so he couldn't sneak off.

"Hi, Mary," Bill said.

Seeing a new friend to greet, Bolt forgot all his manners training. He immediately began to bark and lunged, pulling Mary forward. She juggled the stack of fabrics and just barely managed to keep from dropping them everywhere. Once she'd set them on a stack of books nearby, she grabbed the tethered leash and hauled the dog back to her side.

"Hi, Bill." She didn't sound thrilled to see him. "Bolt, that's enough. Sit!"

"Who's your little buddy?" Bill knelt, but Mary ignored him. She pulled a treat from her pocket and waved it in front of the pup's nose, getting his attention. "Sit," she commanded again. And wonder of wonders, Elizabeth thought, he did. "Stay," she told him, putting her foot on the lead to prevent him from ignoring her.

"This is Bolt," she told Bill. "He's a foster dog."

"I didn't know you were thinking about fostering dogs," Bill said.

"He's from Safe Harbor Beagle Rescue. We only have him until Saturday." Mary took a few moments to explain the little beagle's history. "We're trying to modify some of his more interesting behaviors," she said with a grimace. "You can greet him but step back if he doesn't stay seated."

Bill took a step forward, and the dog immediately leaped to his feet.

Bill stepped back.

Mary gave the "sit" command again and waited until Bolt complied.

Bill stepped forward, and Bolt jumped up.

Three more times they went through the routine, while Elizabeth held her breath, wondering if the pup would ever get it. Finally, Bolt appeared to realize that if he stayed seated, he got to meet the guest *and* get a treat. Elizabeth had to admire Mary's perseverance.

"Hey, buddy," Bill said. He stroked the satiny ears, and when Bolt promptly rolled over, he vigorously rubbed the dog's belly. "Aren't you a good boy?"

"That's definitely up for debate," Mary said, laughing.

"But we're working on it," Elizabeth insisted, from where she'd moved to gather up the fabrics.

Just then, Martha walked toward them from where she'd been assisting a customer. "Hi, Bill," she said. "Want a dog?"

"I don't think my work schedule would be great for him," Bill said, sounding regretful. "But someone's going to fall for him."

"I hope so," Martha said. "Hey, has Mary told you about her chicken coop project?"

Elizabeth winced. There were times when she wished Martha could be just a tiny bit more tactful. It was inconceivable to Elizabeth that Martha did not realize that a comment like that was bound to put Mary on the spot.

"Chicken coop project?" Bill asked. "I noticed the old one's sort of falling apart. It's on my list to get to, but if you're ready to start, I can make it a priority."

"You don't need to bother with it." Mary's smile had faded. "I found plans online that look simple enough. I'm taking the cut list to the hardware store later to pick up the things I need."

"Oh. Okay." Bill hesitated, concentrating on petting Bolt. "Well, if you need help, I'm just a phone call away."

After a pause that stretched long enough to be awkward, Mary said, "Thank you. I think I can manage it, with a little help from Elizabeth and Martha."

There was another pause. An overly long one. Bill looked as if he was sorry he'd even come into the store. Before Elizabeth could find words to throw into the silence, Bill stood. Stepping back a pace from Mary, he said, "I've got to get going. Good luck with your project."

And before any of them could say another word, he turned and made his way out of the store, raising a hand without turning when Elizabeth called, "Goodbye."

"Now look what you've done," Martha said to Mary. "You hurt Bill's feelings."

"Me? Why did you have to bring up the chicken coop? It's none of his business," Mary responded heatedly. "Did we ask him to build us a new coop? No, we did not."

"He's a builder, and he's a family friend," Martha retorted. "Why on earth wouldn't we tell him about it? Besides, it's not like he won't see it the next time he comes over."

This was going nowhere, and it was about to get uglier, judging from the expression on Mary's face. Bolt's tail was down between his legs, and he was looking up at Mary anxiously.

"Mary," Elizabeth said, "I think Bolt may need to go out." She wasn't sure it was true, but it had the instant effect of diverting her younger sister. She rose and led the dog out through the stockroom without another word.

Elizabeth rounded on Martha, exasperation getting the better of her. "Why did you bring that up? You knew Mary felt strongly about trying to do the coop herself. And you know Bill well enough to know that he would want to do that for us if he knew we were worrying about it. Argh!" She threw her hands in the air and walked away, stalking up front, where she straightened a crooked stack of dishes with hands that trembled. She hated conflict, and she hated it even more when her temper got the better of her. She owed Martha an apology…and she would offer it, just as soon as she could speak without her voice trembling.

She was at the cash register again when she sensed a presence behind her.

"You're right," said Martha in her ear. "I'm sorry. It was insensitive of me to bring up that stupid chicken coop. I was amused by seeing the two of them dancing around whatever this is going on between them, and I wasn't thinking. I'll apologize to Mary."

"There may be *nothing* going on between them," Elizabeth pointed out. "Mary certainly doesn't seem inclined to be leaping into another relationship."

"For which I commend her," Martha said. "I just get a little…
matchmaker-y feeling sometimes, when I see them together.
Don't you?"

Elizabeth had to smile, and her annoyance dissolved. "Yes.
But we have to give her time to find her own way. Neither you
nor I have ever experienced the kind of rejection that her heart
has. It must be devastating, and I'm sure it takes a long time to
heal and be able to trust again. I think we need to respect the
fact that she may never choose to enter another relationship."

As she turned back to the register, the door of the shop
opened, and a gaggle of ladies came in, exclaiming over the variety of items displayed. Clearly tourists, with big bags, sneakers,
and umbrellas stowed inside pockets in case of rain, several
made a beeline for Martha's goodies while the rest scattered to
scan the shop for special finds.

"Oops," Martha said. "I've got to get over there. I promise
I'll talk to Mary though."

Pleased that she'd made her point without angering her
sister, Elizabeth went to greet their customers.

Thirty minutes later, the group departed.

Martha said, "Whew!" as the door closed. "I guess I'm
going to have to make more of the strawberry loaf next time.
It's almost gone already! That group went through it like
locusts in a field."

Elizabeth laughed. "They were rather like locusts, weren't
they? They discovered those hand-crocheted throws that we
just consigned last week, and every single one of them sold."

"And the hand-blown glass ornaments took a big hit as
well," Martha observed. "We're going to have some delighted

suppliers when they receive checks and requests for more of the same very soon."

"Did you happen to notice the Italian clock went out the door?" Elizabeth asked with a grin, shaking her head. "Mary just put it on the shelf this morning. I can't believe it. Ugliest thing I've ever seen."

Martha laughed. "Oh my. So we made a hundred dollars' profit on something I'd never even have brought in. Guess that tells you what my judgment's worth."

"Well, Mary is the one with the artistic eye," Elizabeth reminded her.

"I'll let her know about the clock." Martha turned toward the back of the store. "I'm going to talk to her now. Back in a minute."

Elizabeth busied herself with one or two customers who were browsing and then straightened up the linen section, which the group of ladies had riffled through looking for finds. Just as she finished, both of her sisters came toward the front of the store. They were smiling and chatting, Elizabeth was relieved to see. Apparently, Martha's apology had been sincere and accepted.

Mary still had Bolt attached to her belt loop. The arrangement seemed to be working well. She had been able to catch and forestall his wildest impulses several times, with the exception of his behavior with Bill earlier, and he was beginning to learn that good behaviors got him treats.

Behind her, Elizabeth heard someone say, "Oh!" in a tremulous tone.

CHAPTER TEN

Elizabeth turned to see a woman walking toward Mary and Bolt, one hand pressed to her bosom. "Is that…is his name Bolt?" the woman asked Mary, obviously on the verge of tears.

"Yes. Do you know him?" Mary sounded as confused as Elizabeth felt.

"He belonged to Dolores Knepper, a friend of mine who passed recently," the woman said. "I'm Eleni Caragianis." She paused, gulped, and then went on. "Dolores's daughter wouldn't tell me anything about him except that she gave him away. I was so worried that he might not have landed in a good place."

"He was surrendered to a shelter," Mary told the woman. "And then a beagle rescue stepped in. I'm fostering him short term until the people who are going to foster him long term return from their vacation."

"Oh, I'm so glad he's safe." The woman knelt and embraced the little dog, and Elizabeth was fairly certain she was crying. "Hi, Bolt. Hi, baby boy. Oh, I'm so glad to see you." Enthusiastic as Bolt was to meet everyone in his path, he seemed especially joyful to see this woman. She set down her handbag and plopped right down on the floor in the aisle, and Bolt burrowed into her lap, licking her chin. When the woman finally looked up, her eyes were wet. She surely was mourning her friend as well as being relieved to see the little dog. "Dolores sat on the floor with him every evening doing puppy massage and rubbing his belly," she said. "He would get so relaxed he would just moan."

"Oh, that's precious." Mary's eyes looked a little moist as well, Elizabeth thought, fighting tears of her own.

"What rescue group are you with?" the woman asked.

"Safe Harbor Beagle Rescue," Mary answered. "They can answer any questions you have about his care. I can tell you that he's done very well with us so far this week."

"I can't tell you how relieved I am to know he's in a safe, loving home. Perhaps I could make a donation," the woman said. "Do they have a website?"

Mary nodded. "There's donation information right on the home page. I'm sure they'd be grateful, and you could make the donation in your friend's memory."

"Oh, thank you. And bless you for fostering him," Eleni added as she gathered her things and gave Bolt a final caress.

Martha's strawberry loaf had all been sold. "I can't believe it," Martha said to Elizabeth, who had to agree that the new dessert had flown off the shelf. It seemed that every customer who entered Secondhand Blessings noticed it and felt compelled to leave with at least one slice.

Martha had just sold the last slice not long after lunch when Mary came up from the back, where she'd been working on the requested posters in between customers.

"I've got one finished," Mary said, holding one of the pieces of fiberboard with the illustrated side facing in. "Would you like to see it?"

Elizabeth, dusting some dishes nearby, chuckled. "What a silly question. We both would." She came over and stood attentively beside Martha.

With a flourish, Mary turned the board around.

"Ohhh!" Elizabeth drew in a sharp breath.

Martha clasped her hands to her mouth, seemingly as amazed at what she saw. "Mary, that's stunning. It's not just a sign, it's a work of art."

It truly was. The information about the book sale stretched across the very top, and then there was a bit of white space before the illustration began. A charming garden of whimsical, oversized flowers occupied the main space beneath it. Amid the flowers was a staircase made of books. A little girl in an Alice-in-Wonderland style dress was mounting the steps, preoccupied with a book she was reading, while at the top an open doorway glowed brightly. The rays that were softly radiating from within were actually children's book titles. Elizabeth could make out *James and the Giant Peach*, *Goodnight Moon*, *The Wind in the Willows*, *Charlie and the Chocolate Factory*, *Where the Wild Things Are*, and more. The longer she studied it, the more she saw. Across the bottom was the Dr. Seuss quote.

"How on earth did you do this in just one morning?" Martha asked. "I hate to inflate your ego, but Mary, this is truly genius."

Mary grinned. "Working with light layers of acrylics and a fan helped a lot. It still needs to set. I wouldn't suggest taking it in until tomorrow morning."

"Are you doing a second one like it?"

Mary shook her head. "I have a different idea for that one. You mentioned 'towering stacks of books,' remember?"

Martha laughed. "Oh, perfect."

"Hey, I have an idea," Elizabeth said. "Why don't you raffle them off during the sale? People could put their ticket in a box for the sign they like, and a winner could be drawn at the end of the sale."

"Oh, that's a great idea," Martha said. "Yet another way to make money for the library. Mary, would that be okay with you? After all, they're your pieces."

"I'd be delighted to donate them," Mary said. "As you say, more money for the library."

Martha, generally not given to exuberant displays, clapped her hands. "Excellent! People are going to love this."

The afternoon was slow. Elizabeth found herself thinking about her mystery girl when there was little else to occupy her. Now that she had met and dismissed Ellie, Brittany, and Sheila, the only girl who remained from her original list was Jean Ann. She felt certain the girl was unlikely to be Jean Ann, who by all accounts was rarely unaccompanied. The mystery girl she'd seen at church and met behind the library had to be the new girl Sheila had seen "hanging around" church, as she'd put it.

"The new girl," she murmured to herself. Angie Rempel had been the first to mention her, though she didn't know her name, and Sheila had thought of her as soon as Elizabeth had mentioned that distinctive jacket. Sheila had thought her name might be Marla. And at least two of them had thought she was in eighth grade. Who could Elizabeth talk to about that girl?

Rhythmically tapping her fingers on the counter, she reviewed her friends and acquaintances who had connections to the middle school. Angie was out—she'd already said she didn't know the child's name. Most of her closer friends' children were significantly older than thirteen, except for Rachel's, and the Fischer children attended Amish schools and had little acquaintance with students from the public schools. Acquaintances... She thought through the other members of various community organizations she'd been involved with, but no one came to mind. Next she thought about her fellow Mount Zion members.

There were several teachers and others who worked in schools who attended Mount Zion. She brought them all to mind and tried to remember what grades or ages they taught. One was a music teacher at an elementary school. If indeed the girl was new and had transferred from outside the district, or even from another school, she wouldn't have known her.

Another deacon at Mount Zion was a physical education teacher at the high school who also coached cross-country running. She judged that the chances that he would know the girl were slim. A third was the director of meal services for the school district, but Elizabeth didn't think she had a lot of contact with individual students.

She brightened a moment later. One of the men who sang in the choir was an English teacher at the middle school. Did he teach eighth grade?

"Martha," she called, "do you know what grade Ian Pulaskey teaches?"

"Eighth, I think," Martha said. "Why?"

"I want to ask him about the girl I saw."

"Oh, right. Good idea." Martha joined her at the counter and reached beneath it for the church directory that each member or family received. They had gotten two for some reason, so they'd brought one to the shop. "Here you go. Ask him."

"Now?"

Martha smiled at her. "Why not?"

But Elizabeth hesitated. "He probably can't tell me much, if anything. And on the phone, he's likely to be even less forthcoming."

Martha frowned. "Oh, I see your point." She narrowed her eyes in thought. "Wait, I'm pretty sure there's choir practice this evening after the potluck. Don't you have something you need to do at the church?"

Elizabeth snapped her fingers, brightening. "Yes! I need to return that jacket, since no one I know owned it. Perhaps Ian might have seen a student wearing it at school."

The sisters attended a potluck supper at church that evening.

Elizabeth followed her sisters through the buffet line, trying to take small portions of the many delicious-looking dishes various families had brought. In a twist from the usual, everyone had been asked to fill out a little place card made of a folded index card that identified their food. Elizabeth thought the cilantro-lime bean salad and the creamy pecan crunch grape salad both were delicious, but really, everything she tried was, from the pulled pork deviled eggs to Martha's Cajun mac 'n' cheese made with andouille sausage and shrimp. And the desserts!

She couldn't resist the devil's food cake Maida Nagle made with chocolate fudge frosting, but the butterscotch blondie gooey bars were terrific as well. Mary traded her a bite of her August pie, filled with apples, cherries, and blueberries, for the devil's food cake, which was so rich it was probably a sin to eat a whole piece anyway.

Martha eyed the pie as Mary sliced it in two. "August pie," she said thoughtfully. "You really could make that with any fruits you wanted that were in season or canned. I could make a peach pie with—"

"Don't change your peach pie recipe!" Mary said hastily. "It's perfection. Why mess with perfection?"

Martha looked amused. "It's not like I have to choose one or the other," she said. "I can experiment and still go back to the old standby if it's better."

"It's better." Mary nodded decisively. "Take it from a peach pie connoisseur. Yours is incomparable."

"Thank you," Martha said modestly. Then her attention was arrested by something behind Elizabeth, and she reached across the table and tapped Elizabeth on the forearm, lowering her voice. "Don't turn around and look, but I believe Jean Ann Brean and her parents just took a seat at the table behind you."

Elizabeth's gaze flew to Martha's. Her heart rate picked up. She had been reasonably sure her mystery girl was not Jean Ann—but she could be wrong. "All right," she said in an equally quiet tone. "I'm just going to oh-so-casually get a refill on my drink." She raised her voice to a normal pitch. "Would either of you like a refill?"

"I'm good," Mary said cheerfully. She was sitting beside Elizabeth, so she couldn't sneak a peek either.

"I'm fine," Martha said. "You go ahead."

Elizabeth rose and pushed in her chair to make room in the aisle. Turning, she smiled at the table behind her.

The girl she saw was not the girl she'd seen on Sunday. That was clear at a glance. Jean Ann had straight brown hair and was quite a bit bigger than the mystery girl.

After the supper ended, Elizabeth made her way toward the room where the choir practiced. Mary and Martha helped clean up the fellowship hall while they waited for her.

A tall, thin man was walking down the hall just ahead of Elizabeth, and she recognized Ian Pulaskey, the middle school teacher she'd been hoping to see.

Elizabeth called, "Ian?" When the man paused and turned with an inquiring smile, she said, "Hello. How are you?"

"I'm fine, thanks. How are you, Elizabeth? Joining the choir?"

She grinned. "No. Just taking something to the Lost and Found." She held up the pink jacket. "Recognize it? You teach students about the age I'd imagine this fits."

Ian gave the jacket a thorough once-over, taking it from her and holding it up as they stood in the hallway. "Doesn't look familiar. But I may not be the one to ask about clothing. As long as it's clean and fits reasonably well, it's fine by me."

Elizabeth smiled, thinking that was probably true. Ian wore khaki trousers and a light blue shirt, and she realized she nearly always saw him in a similar outfit. She took back the jacket and folded it over her arm. "I showed it to a couple of girls from the congregation, but none of them claimed it." Her eyes danced. "Of course, one of them was Sheila Canner, who probably wouldn't claim it if she did own it, considering the amount of stark black enhanced with skeleton motifs that I saw on her."

Ian chuckled. "Sheila's a character. But she's a terrific student with a wonderfully creative turn of mind. I've told her I expect to see her writings in print someday."

"That's wonderful," Elizabeth said. "I liked her a great deal." She patted the coat. "By the way, she mentioned that this might belong to a new girl in school. She couldn't recall her name, though. Marla, maybe? Dark hair, wears a big, oversize tan jacket?"

Ian's questioning look faded almost immediately. "Oh, it's not Marla. It's Marlee. She's new this year." He smiled. "I kind of doubt that's her jacket. I've never seen her wear anything other than that giant coat. She even wears it in class. Does she go to church here?"

"I'm pretty sure I saw her at the fellowship time last Sunday."

"Hmm. That's odd. I usually see new attendees from my perch in the choir, but I haven't noticed her. I'll have to look next week." He grinned and shrugged. "Hope you find the owner of that jacket."

"Oh well." Elizabeth turned toward the hallway where the lost-and-found box was located. "I'll just put it back in the box, and hopefully the owner will come along."

"If you want to ask Marlee about the jacket in person, you could always come by the school at dismissal and try to catch her then." Ian waved before he headed off to the choir room, leaving Elizabeth feeling a little guilty for misleading him.

Driving home with her sisters, Elizabeth was relieved not to be carrying around the jacket anymore. She hoped the owner hadn't come looking for it while it had been temporarily removed from Lost and Found.

"So her name must be Marlee," Martha said, when she told them about her conversation with Ian.

"I think so. Between Sheila and him both immediately recognizing the description, I feel almost sure it must be."

"Now all you have to do is find her again," Mary said with a chuckle. "Easier said than done, maybe."

Tomorrow was Thursday, the last day of school before the Easter break. If Elizabeth wanted to follow Ian's suggestion and try to catch up with Marlee as she got out of school, she either had to do it tomorrow or wait until Tuesday, since the kids were also off school on Monday.

Right then and there, she decided she was going to be at school at dismissal time tomorrow.

On Thursday morning, Mary's alarm was set to go off at six, but she had awakened a few minutes earlier and turned it off, sitting up so she wouldn't fall back to sleep, and enjoying the peace and quiet of the still house in the early-morning hours.

Moments after slipping into her work clothes, she was out the door with the three dogs, drawing deep draughts of the chilly early April morning air. It was a beautiful day, and the next few leading up to Easter were also predicted to be mild and lovely, although Easter morning itself was probably going to be too chilly for children to hunt eggs outside without jackets.

She started off across the field with the dogs for a bit of a walk before she fed the goats or got the eggs, as she normally did. Bolt was on a longe line she'd found in the barn, and the minute he caught sight of the pygmy goats, he began to chuff and race back and forth. Before his behavior could escalate to the inevitable baying that would disturb the quiet of the morning, Mary reeled him in and started a series of obedience exercises, feeding him treats from the stash in her pocket to keep him focused on her and not the goats.

To her amusement, Pal circled back and began to perfectly obey every command. She fed him treats just as she did Bolt, and the little scheme seemed to enhance Bolt's concentration on the exercises. After a few minutes, they were able to walk past the goats without incident. Still, she knew returning would require the same attention, and she'd need to put him back in the house before she dealt with feeding the outdoor animals and gathering eggs.

Just then, she heard a distant yip from Tink, who had ranged ahead of them. Pal surged forward, and she struggled to control Bolt, who wanted to follow. She glanced up to see what had Tink all atwitter—and was just in time to catch a glimpse of a plumed red tail tipped in white disappearing into some brush. Tink immediately followed, being long and low and built for exactly that type of hunting. Pal had to stop and run around the brush, since he had the sense to know that his long, thick coat would catch in the dense vegetation.

The quiet morning was forgotten as Bolt began to bay, and Tink, out ahead of them, began to bark with the loud bark of her breed, always surprising given how small she was. A moment later, Pal joined in, not because of the love of the hunt, but because he was always happy to have an excuse to expend energy, and barking and racing across the field was just the ticket for that.

"Hey," she yelled at the fleeing fox. "You stay away from my coop, you chicken thief! Go on, Tink. Get him!" She'd completely forgotten her concern for the potential of kits, but as she came to her senses, she remembered. "Oh no!" She immediately began to call the dogs back to her. The last thing she wanted was for Tink to kill a baby fox. Tink might appear to be a sweet little house pet, but dachshunds were bred to scent, chase, and flush out game such as badgers, or in the case of the miniature versions, rabbits. Tink was perfectly capable of any and all of those behaviors.

Pal, on the other hand, would probably try to herd the animal if he was lucky enough to catch up with it.

"Come on, Tink, good girl." Mary praised her lavishly as the panting dachshund reluctantly abandoned the chase and returned for a treat.

Pal followed more slowly. The fox had vanished, and he wasn't sure what had happened to all the fun they'd been having.

Allowing Bolt a bit more freedom on the long lead as she walked back toward the house, Mary was more determined than ever to get the new chicken coop built as soon as possible. She wasn't about to lose one more chicken to that black-stockinged marauder, even if it was a mother hunting food for her kits. Maybe she could talk her sisters into helping with the construction project tomorrow.

Martha rose shortly after she heard Mary go out with the dogs. Since the strawberry loaf had been such a hit, she decided to make another batch for today. She tripled the recipe before realizing she only had four loaf pans. Muttering beneath her breath, she rushed to the pantry and pulled her two Bundt pans from the shelf before filling them with the last two loaves' worth of batter.

The whole time the loaves were baking, she was on pins and needles. The pans were not the same size or shape as her loaf pans, which baked perfect strawberry loaves at three hundred and fifty degrees. In her experience, cakes in Bundt pans often baked a bit slower than in loaf pans, but this might be a different consistency than the heaviness of, say, a pound cake. But she didn't dare keep opening the oven door to check, because every time she let out all the heat and the oven had to get back to three-fifty again, she was changing the moisture content of the bread.

In the end, she sat by the oven and peered through the window every minute or so, trying to gauge if the loaves and the Bundts looked the same. It was almost impossible to tell until the timer went off at precisely minute forty-five, and she opened the oven to check.

To her everlasting relief, the Bundt strawberry loaves were baked just as perfectly as the others. The bread in the unique design of the Bundt pan looked so gorgeous she thought she might enter it in the fair or some other baking contest this summer, given how delicious every customer who tasted it declared it was.

Martha had just finished removing the cakes ever so carefully from the pans when she heard shrieking outside.

After pushing the cooling loaves well back on the counter to keep them safe from prying canine noses, she ran outside. "What's wrong?"

Mary was coming toward the house with Bolt. She'd taken him out for a romp, and apparently she'd decided to give him some space. The longe line was usually used for horse training, but Martha could see how it would also work well for a little dog who wanted to run much farther and faster than his handler did.

What had happened?

"I—have—*had it*!" Mary hollered. She gestured wildly at the dog. "I try to be nice. I try to give him a little modified freedom, and what does he do? He rolls in something dead. He smells like roadkill after it's been out all day on the hottest day of the year." She made an exaggerated gagging sound.

Martha raised her eyebrows. Mary's reaction seemed a little extreme—and then her sister and the dog drew nearer and she caught a whiff of the indescribable odor accompanying the pair. Maybe not such an extreme reaction after all, she decided, backing off a bit.

"He bayed at the Fischers' cows and startled them all into running. They galloped over half the field! That can't be good for dairy cows, can it? Silas is going to hate us." Her shoulders slumped, and she went on before Martha could speak. "He's going to need another bath, after we just gave him one on Sunday. Fostering a dog was the worst idea I have ever had. *Ever!*"

"It seemed like a good idea at the time." Martha surveyed the filthy dog and her irate sister.

"I know, but I feel like he's made an enormous amount of extra work for all of us."

"You, mostly, since you've taken on the lion's share of socializing him." And that was probably another reason for Mary's ire. She'd all but lived with the dog for the past four days. "Do you want to return him to the rescue for the rest of the week?" Martha hadn't seen Mary sound this discouraged in a long time. Perhaps, even, since her marriage had ended.

"I don't know." Mary gathered up the long length of rope with her free hand as she tugged the little dog toward the hose.

"I'll help you." Martha got the dog shampoo and two towels from the kitchen and rejoined her sister in the yard. Whew, the dog stank. "What on earth did he roll in?" she asked.

"It may have been a groundhog." Mary was smart—she was breathing through her mouth, Martha noticed, copying her. "I suspect one of the neighbors shot it over the winter, and now that it's warming up, it's rotting. But boy, was it ever ripe." She vigorously hosed water over Bolt, who stood panting in his default happy attitude.

Martha poured a line of shampoo down his back and began to massage it into his fur. "This will help."

"Every time I think we've gotten past the worst of the things he can get into, he finds something new," Mary said mournfully.

"He's a hound dog," Martha said practically. "It's in his job description."

That drew a small smile from Mary, as she'd intended. "I guess we should keep him," she said. "We—I—made the commitment until Saturday, and that's only two more days."

Martha put a hand on her sister's arm. "You're doing a really good thing," she said. "When I saw that poor woman earlier, his owner's friend, so happy and relieved that he was safe and well...I'm glad you suggested this. Well," she added, pointing down at the smelly pup, "not *this* specifically."

Mary's smile was the reward she'd been hoping to see.

Mary realized that her work clothes smelled distinctly of whatever Bolt had rolled in. She changed into clean things and tossed the befouled ones straight into the washer. Then she headed for the barn and her chores.

As soon as the animals were cared for, she made a beeline for the garage. The evening before, she had laid out all the materials she'd purchased in the garage. She wasn't sure how long the chicken coop project might take, and she didn't want her things to get rained on. After it was built, it was sure to get wet, but those boards couldn't get warped before she'd even had a chance to use them. She'd purchased plywood for the inner walls, insulation and additional wood for the exterior, and she planned to paint the exterior with weatherproof paint. She had mesh for the ventilation hatches, and she had figured out the best way to angle the coop so the front was facing the sun.

She had a moment of panic when she reworked her figures. Had she purchased too small a design? She wanted to be sure her chickens had more than the minimum recommended amount of space. After all, in winter there were periods when they couldn't go outside much for days, and she didn't want them to feel cramped. Then she realized she'd made a mistake in her figures. Putting one little decimal point in the right place made a world of difference. Her birds would have plenty of space, even if they had to be contained in their outdoor run every day, which they generally would not.

The first step, she read, would be the four vertical posts that needed to be set in concrete. She didn't have time to start that this morning, but she selected the four posts she needed. Two of them were eight feet long and two were six feet, so that when they were cemented in an upright position, they would form the supports that would allow the roof to be angled for rain runoff.

Slowly, she read through the rest of the directions. Although they were supposedly written for someone with no experience, there were a lot of directions that appeared to have the assumption that basic carpentry skills were a given. How did she make the supports stand straight up? How would she know if they were leaning? She supposed she'd need to find the level that she knew was somewhere in the basement among the tools. But the only thing she'd ever used a level for in her life was hanging pictures. She was certain there was more to it than she was being led to believe with these instructions.

Crystal clear in her mind's eye, she could see the sales assistant who'd helped her select the lumber she'd needed. He'd tried to talk her into pressure-treated wood and been slightly supercilious when she'd declined. He had explained that the newer technique did not use arsenic in the copper treatment method and was therefore nontoxic to both chickens and humans. Even so, she'd declined and asked for cedar.

"Have you ever built anything this big before?" he'd asked her.

Mary had hesitated. But honesty won out. "No," she'd said.

"I really think you should consider the new wood. It's infused with pesticides to prevent burrowing insects from destroying it." He had all but rolled his eyes.

But she'd read all about that online yesterday, and she still believed that rot-resistant hemlock or cedar would be a choice with which she was more comfortable.

His silence had underscored his disapproval when she'd told him. Victoriously, he'd said, "You know it's much more expensive, right?"

She hadn't.

Maybe she should ask Bill for help. This probably was child's play for him. But a stubborn streak rose and refused to allow her to pull her phone from her pocket. She did not need a man to help her with this. She had been getting along just fine without one for several years now, and she could continue to do it.

CHAPTER ELEVEN

Shortly before it was time to leave for the shop, Mary brought the second of the posters Martha had asked her to make downstairs. She had a few tiny elements to complete with a shade of acrylic paint she hadn't owned and had stopped to buy today. It would dry quickly and be taken to the library for the opening of the sale this afternoon.

Martha and Elizabeth were discussing plants as they finished breakfast. Martha had seen a TV show about landscaping with native plants, and she and Elizabeth were debating about whether butterfly bushes would qualify in central Pennsylvania. Martha loved the showy shrubbery for its looks as well as its ability to attract and nourish the fragile insects from which it took its common name.

Mary set her painting down and pulled out her phone. In minutes, she had an answer. "It's not a native plant," she said. "Buddleia were brought to this country as an ornamental shrub back in the early 1900s from China. It can be invasive if not managed, and it's recommended to keep it from getting established in the cracks of buildings and masonry as the root systems can do a lot of damage."

"They're still gorgeous," Martha said. "And talking of gorgeous things, is that the second poster? Is it finished?"

"Almost," Mary said. "I still need to add titles to the spines of some of the books." She picked up the frame and turned it to face her sisters. "Voilà."

"Oh, wow," Elizabeth breathed, as she and Martha studied the painted poster.

Martha appeared speechless for a moment. Finally, she cleared her throat and asked, "Where did my baby sister acquire such formidable skill? Mary, your artistic sensibilities are simply stunning."

Elizabeth nodded. "You're amazing. This one is wonderful too," she said. "I'm going to buy raffle tickets and put some in the box for both of them."

"But I'm part of the organization raffling them off, and you're my family," Martha said. "Is that allowed?"

Elizabeth laughed. "I helped too, remember? We're all volunteers. I can't imagine why not. It isn't as though I'm profiting in any way from this sale."

"I guess that's true," Martha admitted. She rose and came closer. "Oh, Mary, you have such talent. How do you even think of a scene like this, much less execute it?"

Mary shrugged, embarrassed by her sisters' praises. "Once I can see it in my head, I just paint it."

Mary's vision for this poster was that of a library of some sort. The Descartes quote ran across the top, and the book sale information across the bottom. The main body of the poster was taken up by bookshelves in the background crammed with books of every shape and style. Some were meant to represent fiction, and others were given the uniform look of something like reference tomes. In the foreground, a teenage boy lay on his stomach on a rug engrossed in an open book, one page of which had a minute illustration that was clearly a dragon.

Mary's favorite element, though, was a transparent dragon, designed to be imaginary, with an equally transparent boy like the reading teen on its back, soaring above the stacks. The implication, Mary hoped, was that the reader was experiencing the story as he read it.

Around the oblivious boy on the floor, books were stacked haphazardly on a reading table, on two comfortable-looking overstuffed chairs, on the floor in front of the shelves, and scattered around him. Those in the foreground bore titles that could be discerned, while others farther away from the viewer's perspective were indistinguishable.

"I still need to add titles to this stack." Mary pointed to a group of books leaning perilously near the boy's foot. "Any ideas?"

"*The Crystal Cave* by Mary Stewart," Elizabeth said immediately.

"Already done." Mary pointed to a book close to the boy's head that bore the title.

"*Little Women*," Martha said. "I've always loved that book."

"Any of Jan Karon's Mitford titles," Elizabeth suggested, trying again. "It's one of my favorite series."

"They don't all have to be fiction," Martha said. "What about a cookbook or one on plants or animals?"

Mary carefully laid the painting on the table in the corner and pulled the chain on the hanging light with the stained-glass lampshade with the dragonfly design above it. She squeezed a couple of drops of the paint into a plastic tray and loaded the brush she'd brought down with her. It had the finest of fine points, mere whispers of fiber. Holding her breath, she wrote LITTLE WOMEN on the spine of the topmost volume. On the second, she wrote BIRDS OF AMERICA.

Elizabeth, leaning over her, said, "Oh, nice choice."

Silently, Mary used the end of the paintbrush to point to the nearby bookshelf where *Birds of America* by John James Audubon was clearly visible.

Elizabeth chuckled in delight as Mary went back to work. Martha came to see what was so funny and stayed to watch as the rest of the books took on titles. The next book in the stack soon became *At Home in Mitford* and the next *The Joy of Cooking*. The fifth and final she titled *Puppy Training for Dummies*, which made both her sisters laugh aloud. Mary propped up the poster to dry and took her paint tray and brushes to the kitchen to clean.

Martha was going to the library this morning so she could make sure all was in place for the opening of the book sale at noon that day. Rachel would be there working with the quilting circle, but if her sisters needed help, Rachel would be able to step away and assist them.

Pollie Muller had called the evening before, and although Martha felt sure the capable volunteer had thought of everything, she was extremely anxious to have Martha approve of all that she'd done. Leadership was an extremely funny thing sometimes, Martha decided.

Before heading to the library, she stopped by the bank. She had three bank bags, each with a list requesting a set amount of change in exchange for one hundred dollars, as Anya's directions instructed. Once she had the necessary change in coins and small bills, she turned her car toward the Bird-in-Hand Free Library, where the sale would soon begin.

Arriving at the library, she slung a large bag with the change and other supplies over her shoulder, placed a deep market basket's handles on one arm, and picked up the two lovely framed posters Mary had painted.

"Hi, Martha. Let me help you." Fanny, the assistant librarian, rushed over to hold wide the door for Martha. She took one of the posters from Martha's grasp. "I guess all this is for the book sale—oh!" She had turned the poster over and was looking at the one with the Dr. Seuss quote. "This is magical. Who did this?"

"My sister Mary," Martha said proudly. "She's enormously gifted. We're going to raffle off both the signs at the end of the book sale."

"You're selling tickets?" Fanny asked. When Martha nodded, the librarian said, "I'm buying some. I'd love to own that!"

She helped Martha carry everything back to the community room, where Pollie was already busy with last-minute book sorting.

"Morning, Martha," Pollie said as Fanny hurried back to the front desk. "We've got a great selection of different genres of books this year. I think it's going to be a good sale. And here are the two rolls of raffle tickets you asked me to pick up."

"Thanks." Martha took the red and blue ticket rolls absently as she surveyed the stacks and stacks of volumes for sale. She certainly hoped the sale would be a hit. Whatever hadn't sold would be boxed up after Minerva looked through the leftovers in case there was anything she wanted for the library. Then the remainder would be sent to auction. The sisters had briefly discussed selling the books through their shop, but books took up a lot of space for very little profit, and many of those left over were things that sold poorly, so they'd decided against it.

"So where are the posters you're going to raffle off?" Pollie asked. "We've never done anything like that before."

"They're over here." Martha could tell from Pollie's tone that she wasn't sure about the wisdom of a raffle. "This is what Mary made for us." With perhaps a bit more flare than was strictly necessary, Martha turned over the two posters that were propped against the wall.

"Oh my stars." Pollie gaped. She put a hand to her chest and patted, as if she needed air. "What an amazing talent."

Martha nodded proudly.

"And she's just *giving* them to us to raffle off?" Pollie looked like she couldn't believe it.

Martha understood the feeling. The two posters were incredibly compelling. She nodded again. "She is. I'm so grateful to her for stepping in after the other posters were ruined."

Pollie snorted. "I would have ruined them myself if I'd known Mary would replace them with these!"

She and Martha shared a laugh as together they set up the checkout station, stashed dozens of recycled plastic bags beneath the counter for those customers who hadn't brought their own, and reviewed the laminated instructions placed at checkout for the volunteers who would be completing the sales. Pollie hid the stack of paper bags for Saturday's bag sale in a closet for the moment so they didn't inadvertently get used by the cashiers on the preceding days. The market basket for the raffle was placed between the two cashiers' seats so people who purchased raffle tickets for the posters could deposit them before leaving. Two rolls of raffle tickets, red for one sign and blue for the other, awaited behind the basket. Index cards describing each poster were affixed to the basket so hopeful ticketholders could buy the right color ticket for the poster they wanted.

The last thing Martha did was set up the easels and place Mary's lovely posters on them. One, the fellow reading amid the stacks of books with the dragon overhead, greeted customers as they arrived. The Alice-in-Wonderland-style sign was placed at the far end of the room near the tables full of children's books. Raising the easel as high as it could go ensured that the inspiring poster could be seen from practically anywhere in the room.

When they had finished, Martha looked around. It was 11:25, and the other sale volunteers were beginning to arrive so they could look through the books and be able to help people find what they wanted. The sale would run from noon until the library closed at seven today, from nine to five tomorrow, and from nine to five Saturday. The bag sale, when people could buy however many books they could fit into a paper grocery bag for a dollar, would run on Saturday right before the end of the sale. Pollie was the supervising volunteer tomorrow, and Martha would take on the final day.

Martha felt inordinately pleased that everything was going so well, even though she really hadn't done much of the planning. The sale practically ran itself.

Elizabeth, Mary, and Rachel were swamped when Martha returned to the store shortly before noon. The quilting circle was just beginning to disband.

"Do you have everything organized?" Elizabeth asked, observing that Martha was smiling and looking as if she was pleased.

"Absolutely. They are ready for customers to walk through the door," Martha reported. "And Mary's signs are a huge hit. Fanny, that junior librarian, already bought ten dollars' worth of raffle tickets for one of them!"

Mary clapped her hands. "Oh, that's nice to hear."

"I may have purchased a few myself," Martha said.

"Oh, you." Mary laughed, evidently not realizing her sister was serious, before hurrying off to greet some new arrivals.

"Has it been this busy since you opened?" Martha asked.

Elizabeth nodded. "Oh yes. I'm really thankful Rachel was here. She's a godsend. The quilting circle practically runs itself, so she was able to give us a great deal of help." She gestured to the baked goods over which she'd been presiding. "If you'd like to take over here, I'll check on those ladies who've been looking at the Royal Doulton figurines we got in last week."

When Martha nodded her assent, Elizabeth crossed to the pair. It turned out they were sisters trying to decide if their mother, who collected such figurines, already had the "Bonnie Lassie" made between 1934 and 1953.

"Would you like to see it?" Elizabeth asked. It was one of a handful of rare, more expensive collectibles they kept in a locked case. When the ladies said they would, she returned to the cash register and retrieved the key so she could let them see the very good condition of the piece.

"I could hold it for you for twenty-four hours," she offered. "You could come in or call by, say, noon tomorrow and let me know if you want it."

"That would be fantastic," the shorter of the sisters said. "I'm headed over to Mom's this afternoon, so I'll check her collection when she nods off for her afternoon nap. Then I'll call you and let you know yes or no. You don't even need to hold it past five today."

"That's perfect." Elizabeth got the woman's name and number and placed a discreet RESERVED tag beneath the seated porcelain lady with her basket of flowers before her. She waved as the women left and then turned to see where else she was needed.

Mary was back in the housewares section with a customer, and Martha was checking out someone else Rachel had been helping.

Elizabeth put her hands at the back of her waist and stretched out her back.

Rachel smiled. "It was a busy morning."

"And I'm very grateful for your help," Elizabeth said.

"I am still praying for the girl you gifted money to," Rachel said. "Have you learned anything more about her?"

"I have, just last evening," Elizabeth said. "Everyone who's ever seen her says she wears that big jacket all the time. I'm pretty sure she is in eighth grade at the public middle school, and her name is Marlee. That's such an unusual name, I think I have a chance of finding her."

Rachel's eyes widened. "Marlee? I think I might know her," she said.

"What?" Elizabeth almost dropped the key she had used to relock the curio cabinet. "Where might you have met her? I think she's new to the area. Someone called her 'the new girl' at school. "

Rachel nodded. "But as you say, the name is unusual, and the girl I met said that was her name."

"Where did you meet her?" Elizabeth asked.

"Before Christmas, a friend referred her to me for a purchase she wanted to make. She was looking for a goat." Rachel had a small dairy herd. People paid well for goat's milk over at the farmer's market, and Rachel was one of their regular suppliers.

"Looking for a *goat*?" That sounded distinctly odd. "What would a teenage girl want with a goat? Was it a gift?"

Rachel lifted her shoulders. "She said she needed goat's milk. I told her how to care for it, but I told her goats are herd animals and won't be happy alone. She said in the spring she would buy another if she could afford it."

Elizabeth felt a pang of sadness for that poor goat. She refrained from pointing out that Rachel could have refused to sell off a single goat and focused on what she needed to know. "So your customer's name was Marlee?"

Rachel nodded, wrinkling her brow. "But I can't remember her surname. It was not Amish, that I know."

Elizabeth pretty much could have discerned that, but she didn't say so. "Did you deliver the goat? Where does she live?"

But Rachel shook her head. "No delivery. She walked to my farm, and she walked away leading her goat."

Walked? So the girl had to live relatively close by. Exhilaration rose. Even though Rachel hadn't really provided any helpful specifics, it should be easy to track down the girl named Marlee now. Oh, Elizabeth hoped things would settle down in the shop in the afternoon. She only had today to get over to the middle school for dismissal, and since Martha was already going to be leaving to return to the book sale, she wouldn't be able to get away if they were so busy. It wouldn't be fair to leave Mary and Rachel alone.

Fortunately, business slowed over the lunch hour. Martha left at one forty-five, and at two o'clock, Elizabeth felt it would be safe to leave for an hour. She'd learned from a mother who'd come into Secondhand Blessings that the middle school let out at 2:35. Leaving at two should give her plenty of time to arrive, park in a convenient location, and watch the students as they emerged from school at the end of the day.

The more rural public schools were not enormous like some in other locations, since quite a number of Lancaster

County's rural student scholars attended Amish schools. Rachel hoped she'd be able to locate Marlee.

There were two middle schools close to Bird-in-Hand, but given that Rachel had seen the girl walk away with the goat, indicating that she probably lived close, Elizabeth chose the one nearest, on the north side of Route 30. The name had been changed two years ago from Conestoga Valley Middle to the name of a recently retired school superintendent, but many people still called it CVM.

Elizabeth drove along Mount Sidney Road and back again, seeking a spot with the best visibility. Buses were already beginning to pull into the loop where the students boarded, and she was afraid she might fail to see the girl if she wasn't eagle-eyed enough.

As dismissal time drew nearer, she realized that there was a good chance she could miss the girl altogether from her limited viewpoint. A few students were beginning to emerge from the school. She had to make a plan immediately.

After another moment's debate, she got out of the car and walked up the sidewalk toward the school. She felt conspicuous. There wasn't another adult anywhere in sight except for a school security guard chatting with one of the bus drivers.

She was just about to check the time when the bell went off. Instantly, the entire tenor of the scene changed. The school doors opened, disgorging hordes of students exuberant at being sprung from their day of education. They walked, they sprinted, they dawdled. They whooped and hollered and shrieked. Many dug out cell phones from pockets or backpacks, while others searched for friends, greeting them as if they'd been separated for years rather than hours.

They wore a kaleidoscope of colors. Denim and khaki still appeared to be the shorts or trousers of choice for many boys, but the girls' outfits were far less homogeneous. Dresses, jeans, skirts, capri pants, jackets, sweatshirts, sweaters…Elizabeth saw them all.

She felt like a salmon trying to swim upstream. Kids poured down the sidewalk toward her, parting at what felt like the last instant to pivot around her. A few, absorbed in their phones, walked straight into her before they mumbled an apology and moved off to one side or the other.

And then she saw her.

She moved steadily, but she gave the impression of stillness. She didn't interact with anyone around her, simply walked toward the buses with her head down, her long dark hair a wild cloud that covered much of her face. The jacket, large and enveloping, and the jeans and sneakers were the exact same uniform she'd worn on Palm Sunday. They were different enough from the contemporary clothing many of the other girls wore to make her stand out from the crowd.

Elizabeth took a deep breath. She started forward again, fighting her way through the surging mass of students intent on escaping the building. The girl was heading for one of the buses near the back of the line, and Elizabeth feared she might miss her.

She stopped and cupped her hands around her mouth just as the girl reached the open stairway of the bus. "Marlee!" she called.

The girl froze. She paused before she boarded the bus, and looked in both directions. If she'd looked behind her, she'd have seen Elizabeth, but she didn't. A second later, she darted quickly up the bus steps and out of sight.

Elizabeth turned away as well. Moving out of the lemming-like stream, she hurried back to her car. There was no question in her mind now. The girl she'd seen at church was named Marlee. She'd clearly responded when Elizabeth had called the name.

Marlee had boarded bus number twenty-seven. Elizabeth intended to follow it and see where her young friend got off. Quickly, she hurried back to her car, half walking, half running.

The first of the buses was pulling out with a roar and the scent of exhaust. Elizabeth slipped into her driver's seat and quickly fastened her seat belt. Some of the buses headed north, up toward Horseshoe Road and Hartman Station Road. Others turned south on Mount Sidney and headed straight down to the intersection with Route 30. Number Twenty-Seven and the ones behind it quickly turned off Mount Sidney onto Stumptown Road. When they came to the intersection with Beechdale, the bus on which Marlee was riding turned again. The direction made sense, given what Rachel had said about the teen walking away with the goat she'd purchased.

Elizabeth followed at a cautious distance, letting two other cars go ahead of her. The bus was not going to be hard to keep track of, and she didn't want Marlee to spot her from a back window. The bus stopped several times, letting kids off before turning onto Church Road and allowing more kids to exit the bus. Then it turned onto North Ronks Road.

Elizabeth leaned forward, feeling herself tense. If Marlee lived near the Fischers, she'd be getting off somewhere along this road, probably before it met Classen Road where it intersected and where Elizabeth's own business and home were located.

Twice it stopped, but no Marlee.

Could she be wrong?

But the bus roared on, and then its flashing lights warned motorists once again that students would be getting off. It slowed and stopped, and Marlee emerged. She checked the mailbox of a tiny brown-shuttered two-story home before walking up two stone steps and over a cracked sidewalk to the concrete porch.

The house sat alone amid a patchwork of Amish farmers' fields. A stone fence enclosed what must be a small backyard, although the stone hid everything except the top half of one tree. A single-car driveway angled up to a small porch beneath an overhang at one side. It was currently empty, and there was no garage or other outbuilding on the property, making the little house look very alone and isolated. The one thing that saved the house from total drabness was a glorious flowering cherry tree to one side of the front porch that was currently in bloom, its soft pink blossoms drawing the eye as one passed the house.

The bus drove away, and the single motorist still in front of Elizabeth followed it. Elizabeth had no choice but to drive on unless she wanted to park and try to talk with the girl. But she didn't feel ready for that. She needed to ponder her next move, she decided as the teen pulled open the battered screen door and vanished. Elizabeth drove on, passing the dilapidated little house with its leaning chimney and aged rocking recliner sitting on the front porch. She felt positively elated. She'd figured out the girl's name and where she lived.

Now she just needed to find out what the girl really needed food and money for. Maybe there was some way to help her. Marlee's words from when they'd met behind the library echoed in her head again: *It will make all the difference in the world....*

Elizabeth knew teenagers were notorious for their drama, but somehow, she believed that twenty dollars she'd given Marlee really would make quite a difference in her life.

Exactly what that difference was, she was determined to learn.

CHAPTER TWELVE

Elizabeth returned to the store and related her fact-finding mission to Mary and Rachel.

"I'm impressed," Mary said, grinning. "You sleuth, you. We're going to have to start calling you Nancy Drew."

"So what will you do next?" Rachel asked.

"I'm not sure," Elizabeth said honestly. "I don't know whether to march up to her front door, knock, and ask why they need money, keep sleuthing, find a way to run into her and offer her more money, or what. Suggestions are welcome."

"Let's think about it a bit," Mary suggested, "and discuss it after dinner with Martha. She may have some helpful thoughts."

There wasn't much afternoon left, and a few customers came and went as the three women cleaned up the store. At five o'clock, Rachel began the short walk home, while Elizabeth and Mary headed up the little rise to their house.

Martha had run up to the house at midday and put a spaghetti sauce with meatballs in the slow cooker. It was nearly ready, and the entire house was fragrant with the aroma of dinner. Elizabeth immediately began to boil the water for pasta and preheated the oven to warm some Italian bread.

"Yum, that smells delicious," Mary said as she stepped into her barn boots to go out and take care of the goats and chickens.

"I'll second that," Elizabeth said. "Let me feed the dogs. The faster we finish with the animals, the sooner we can eat." She suited words to action.

Martha arrived just as Mary walked out the door.

"How was the opening of the book sale?" Elizabeth asked.

"Busy," Martha said. "It's a major event around here."

The evening chores did not take long, and Mary returned soon. Martha already had the table set and was pouring ice water at each place.

"Hey," Mary said as she washed her hands at the kitchen sink, "if you two helped for a little while after dinner, I bet we could get a pretty good start on the chicken coop."

Martha looked dubious. "We have to be at church at seven. I'm willing to lend my support, but I can't guarantee I'll be much help, and we'll only have about forty-five minutes."

"I can read directions," Elizabeth said cheerfully. She was still feeling exhilarated after finding out where Marlee lived. "Let's give it a shot."

And so they did. After spaghetti and meatballs served with warm Italian bread and a classic garden salad garnished with cherry tomatoes, onion, and purple cabbage curls, they headed out to the barn.

"So…we mix the concrete and put the posts in first?" Elizabeth asked. "I guess that makes sense, but how do we make them stand up? What if the posts lean sideways overnight?"

Mary looked nonplussed. "I never thought of that."

Martha had had the foresight to bring her iPad outside with her. Busily, she typed and swiped for a moment, before she said, "Here's a Youtube video on how to set posts in concrete. Maybe we should watch it. It looks like we have to dig the hole first, then set the post in the hole and make sure it's level. They recommend bracing it with a sideways board nailed to it, see?"

All three sisters clustered around the little screen, watching intently.

"That looks easy enough," Mary said.

Elizabeth coughed meaningfully. "Let's try it before we pronounce ourselves master carpenters."

They all trooped out to the site of the new chicken coop, which they'd decided to build close to the old one. Then when the new one was complete, they'd knock down the old one and use that area for a spacious outside run.

First, Mary directed as they measured the dimensions of the coop and marked it with string. The chief difference, other than the increase in size, was the orientation of the coop. Everything she'd read said that it should face the direction from which the sun came most of the year.

After they'd laid out the dimensions, Mary picked up a sturdy shovel and started digging the first hole. "Yikes! This ground is hard as rock."

"I'm not surprised," Martha said. "Our swath of Lancaster County is mostly limestone, isn't it?"

Elizabeth nodded. "I believe so. The farmers sure spend enough time getting the stones out of their fields. People around here joke that they grow new rocks every year."

"Someone else's turn," Mary said, holding out the shovel.

Elizabeth took it gingerly. The hole Mary had started look awfully small compared to the hole in the video. And they had to dig how many of these? She decided she didn't want to know the answer. Propping the shovel vertically against the ground, she then hopped up and pushed down hard, digging it into the soil. She barely buried the tip.

"Ugh," she said, jumping up on the shovel and trying to jam it into the ground again. "How come this looks so easy when I see someone else do it?"

"Because that someone else is usually a man," Martha said succinctly. "Bigger, heavier, and he's probably done it dozens of times, to your one."

"Oh, well that explains it." Elizabeth rolled her eyes. She hopped on the shovel again with more force, jamming it deep into the soil. "Ha. I used to work in the garden. I can do this." She picked up the shovel containing a heftier clot of soil than Mary had managed, dumped it, and went back for another.

By the time each of them had taken two turns with the shovel, they had a respectable hole that resembled the one in the video.

Mary hefted the bag of concrete and dumped it into the bucket sitting in the wheelbarrow in which they'd carried everything out of the barn. "Now we set the post," Mary said, "and then we mix the concrete and pour it into the hole."

"I don't think we should start that tonight." Martha glanced at the time on her phone. "We have to leave soon, and if something goes wrong, we'll have wasted the concrete."

Mary frowned. "The longer it takes us to get started, the longer it's going to take to complete."

"I fear," Elizabeth said gently, "that given our busy schedules and our general lack of experience, it's going to take quite a while to complete this." She was careful not to imply that any of them were incompetent.

"Oh dear," Mary said. "I really hope we can move faster than that. I'm afraid we could lose more chickens if that fox is determined enough to try alternate ways to get into the coop. It's so rickety."

Martha and Elizabeth were both silent.

"What?" Mary asked.

"It's just that we weren't planning on turning this into a family project," Elizabeth said gently. "We both have other things to occupy our evenings. You would have no leisure time to paint, which I think you need."

"You know," Martha said, "I've actually thought that per-haps we don't need to keep chickens at all. We could easily get eggs from the Fischers, and then we wouldn't have to worry about predators and chicken feed and cleaning out that dis-gusting coop."

"Not keep our chickens?" Mary sounded completely flum-moxed. "But I love our chickens."

"Mama always kept chickens," Elizabeth said quietly. She couldn't pretend the suggestion didn't shock her a bit. "I can't imagine this place without them."

"It's just an idea," Martha said quickly. "Something to think about. Are we putting our energies in the right place?"

Cleanup was very quiet after that. Mary replaced the tools in the barn. They all headed back indoors to don clean clothes and drive to Mount Zion for the Maundy Thursday commu-nion service.

Sitting in church after communion, Elizabeth took one more look around. She'd been hoping to spot Marlee during the service, but it didn't appear that the girl was among the worshippers. As she waited in line to have her feet washed by Pastor Nagle, she forced her mind away from the puzzle of the young teen and strove to focus on the Easter story. Tonight the minister would literally minister to her by washing her feet. It was, on the surface, an act of service and humility, certainly two virtues to be practiced. But, as the pastor had shared in his message, Christ had intended the act to symbolize a deeper, more spiritual meaning. Those who did not have their sins washed away, who would not repent and forgive others, could not enter the kingdom of heaven.

Once more, Elizabeth's thoughts strayed to Marlee. The teenager apparently needed food. Elizabeth could provide that. But did Marlee have a church family to help her understand the message of the Crucifixion? What about food for the soul? Perhaps Elizabeth could be more than an instrument of assistance to the girl on a physical level. Her spiritual welfare was equally important.

The sisters gathered in their living room for a short while before bedtime.

Martha watched as Mary settled on the rug before the couch and called to Bolt. The little beagle was peacefully snoozing beside Pal, but at the sound of his name, the inevitable tail wagging began, and Bolt joyously came over to rub all around her and snuggle. His unabashed pleasure was too cute for words. Mary waited him out until finally, the little dog calmed and settled in her lap. Soon he was stretched out full length on her legs. She rubbed his tummy and stroked the silky ears, and he groaned with contentment.

"He loves having his belly rubbed," she said. "Remember the woman who recognized him in the store mentioned that his owner always used to give him massages and rub his belly in the evening? I bet he's been missing that."

"He looks pretty blissful," Martha observed. "Then again, if someone offered me a massage every evening, I'd feel pretty blissful too."

Mary laughed. "I'll second that."

"I imagine he's been grieving too, just like human family members," Elizabeth said. "It must have been so bewildering to be in a loving home one day and then *boom*, the next you've been shuffled off to who knows where with perfect strangers who have no idea of your routine and don't know the commands you're expecting to hear."

"And he's going to feel that way again, probably more than once," Mary said regretfully. "I wish we could continue to foster him until a permanent family is found, but he just isn't working very well with our schedules."

"Fortunately, most dogs seem to adapt well to changes," Elizabeth said, "and he's young. Look how quickly he's settled in here. He'll do it again."

"We can write up a summary sheet of his daily routine for the next family who cares for him," Martha suggested. "And make sure they know the evening puppy massage is something he was accustomed to with his original owner as well."

"And write down the commands we've taught him, and what obedience training we've worked on and our methods,"

Mary added. "Oh, that would make me feel a lot better when it's time for him to leave us."

"I can start a list right now," Martha said, rummaging in the side table for a notepad and pen. She could not get the mingled grief and relief on the face of Bolt's owner's friend out of her mind. They might not be able keep the little beagle, but they could ensure that he went to his next home with every advantage, including having his new family treat him with the same familiar routines he currently knew.

Elizabeth rose earlier than usual on Good Friday for an extended time of personal prayer and reflection. The promise of the resurrection and eternal life offered through Christ's death on the cross was vital to their Mennonite faith. The Son of God had chosen to die in order that they could be offered salvation. It was sobering and humbling.

Afterward, she helped Mary with the barn chores. The work was almost done when Mary appeared from the chicken coop, where she'd gone to gather eggs while Elizabeth took care of the goats.

"I just scared the fox away from the henhouse," Mary blurted.

Elizabeth sucked in a gasp of breath. "He's growing bolder. You just saw him yesterday." Mary had told her sisters about the dogs chasing the fox when she'd returned. "Did he approach you?" First and foremost, Elizabeth was concerned that the animal could be rabid.

"No." Mary shook her head. "One look at me, and he took off like his tail was on fire."

"Oh, that's good." Elizabeth was quite relieved. An animal with rabies could put their dogs and goats—and even her sisters and her—at risk.

"We've got to get this coop built," Mary said soberly. "We can't let him pick off our hens one by one."

Martha had breakfast ready when they came in, a simple meal of scrambled eggs and toast. Before the meal, Elizabeth read a Scripture and led her sisters in prayer. After Mary told Martha about the latest fox sighting, the meal was a quiet one. Elizabeth didn't want to mention the loaded subject of the chicken coop again. Mary seemed so intent on building it without asking for anyone else's help that Elizabeth feared opening the topic would be likely to start their day on a disagreeable note.

Shortly before the sisters left the house to head down to open Secondhand Blessings, the telephone rang.

Elizabeth picked it up. "Hello?"

"Hello, this is Pollie Muller, a book sale volunteer. May I speak to Martha, please?" The woman's voice sounded anxious and strained.

"One moment, please." Elizabeth held out the phone to Martha. "Pollie Muller about the book sale."

A short conversation ensued. "What?" Martha exclaimed after greeting the caller. "How did that happen? I thought we had those hidden."

Elizabeth could hear the excited chatter from the other end of the phone, and Martha shook her head. "I see. Well, there's nothing we can do now but round up some more."

When Martha hung up, Elizabeth raised her eyebrows in inquiry.

"The paper bags for tomorrow's bag sale are gone," Martha said. "Some library volunteer cleaned out the closet where we stored them and sent them for recycling."

Elizabeth's eyes widened. "Oh no!"

Mary, standing nearby, took out her phone and began urgently swiping and tapping. "Well, that's ridiculous," she snapped a moment later. "Paper bags are expensive! You'd spend too much of the book sale proceeds to buy more, even if you were able to get them here before tomorrow, which I doubt. Could we use something else?"

"Plastic grocery bags may not all be the same size. We need something that's uniform," Martha said.

"We can get paper bags from several local stores, I think, as long as we don't take too many from any one place. What if we asked every volunteer coming in to stop at a different store and ask for paper bags?" Elizabeth started ticking off stores on her fingers.

"That's a workable idea." Martha nodded. She took a deep breath. "I guess I need to call Pollie back and get her to start calling our volunteers to make 'bag calls.'"

"Send her a script," Elizabeth suggested. "Write down a concise, simple request. She can e-mail it to everyone who's calling so they don't waste so much time on the phone. Have people drop the bags off at the library today or tomorrow morning."

"Great idea." Martha reached for a pencil and paper. "I'll work out the wording now and e-mail it to her."

Good Friday was celebrated by the Classens' Amish neighbors with a morning of fasting and prayer. There was no school or work, and at noon, extended families often gathered together for a meal. After lunch, the Fischer family had established a custom of caroling over the years.

Fischers and Easter caroling were paired in Mary's very earliest childhood memories, so she knew exactly what was going on when she heard the sound of voices raised in hymns of praise outside Secondhand Blessings.

Everyone inside, customers and Classens alike, flocked out to the parking lot, craning their necks to see the source of the sweet voices raised in song as the wagonload of Fischer family members slowly trundled into the parking lot. The carolers launched into another, "Now the Green Blade Riseth," by British priest John MacLeod Campbell Crum:

Now the green blade riseth from the buried grain,
Wheat that in dark earth many days has lain;
Love lives again, that with the dead has been:
Love is come again like wheat that springeth green.

There was not a hymnbook in sight. Everyone had the songs memorized. The musical moment was one of Mary's favorite traditions surrounding the Easter holiday.

When the last notes died away, the spectators, which included a number of tourists, burst into spontaneous applause.

The Fischers didn't react except with broad smiles. They had not sung *for* praise, but *to* praise.

"Come in, everyone, and have some dessert," Martha invited.

"Just a wee bit. We have other stops to make," Silas advised the exuberant teens and children, as everyone headed inside to sample the slices of strawberry bread, butterscotch brownies, and coconut macarons Martha had made. She had mentioned they would probably be serenaded by carolers today and prepared accordingly.

"This is wonderful, Martha," Rachel said. She held up a slice of the strawberry bread. "I must get this recipe from you."

"I'll write it down for you next time I make it," Martha promised.

Mary was carrying an armload of quilted table runners they'd consigned over to a display rack where she intended to hang them. The sound of a man's voice calling her name from the direction of the counter stopped her in her tracks.

"Hi, Lyle," Mary said, smiling as she set the table runners on a nearby display and detoured to greet the speaker. Lyle Barriman owned a local nursery. Mary had met him the previous summer, when he'd worked on a project to protect monarch butterflies with her. "Are you looking for something in particular?"

Lyle grinned. "I heard through the grapevine that Martha was making a new and fantastic recipe for strawberry bread. My mother's arriving tomorrow for Easter, so I thought I'd pick some up. And I also saw those stone garden gnomes out front when I drove in. Where'd they come from?"

"A local woman had them all tucked into her landscaping," Mary told him. "When the house was sold, the new owners didn't want them. Are you interested?"

"Not just interested," Lyle said. "Determined. Your price is very reasonable. I'll take them all if they're for sale."

"They are indeed," Mary said, grinning. She was especially pleased with the sale, since she'd had to talk Martha and Elizabeth into buying them from the owner, who didn't want to be bothered with consigning.

"By the way, I was at the book sale yesterday afternoon, and I saw two gorgeous posters on display. I heard you were the artist."

"Guilty." Mary indicated the bread. "How much of this do you want?"

"I'll take that whole loaf there." Lyle indicated the Bundt-formed bread Martha had baked again. "Looks delicious."

"It is," Mary said. "There are nine of those gnomes. Do you really want them all?"

"Absolutely." Lyle reached for his wallet. "I bought some raffle chances on those posters. Mary, you really have a gift. Those posters are collectible quality."

"Thank you." Her response was genuine. It still was mildly surprising to her that people were so enthusiastic about her artwork. "I'll wish you luck."

"I saw them also." Rachel, who was still there with one of her youngest children, joined the conversation. "You have an eye for charming drawing and painting."

"Thank you," Mary said, sincerely touched. Most Amish were not given to artistic self-expression. A very few painted or drew, and most women expressed themselves only through their fine stitching or cooking, while men distinguished themselves with superior quality woodwork. All of those, of course, were artistic endeavors in Mary's eyes, but she knew most of her Amish friends abhorred prideful behavior and would be horrified if they knew she considered some of what they did artistic.

She finished ringing up Lyle's purchases and walked outside with him to help him load the gnomes into the back of his pickup. Returning to the shop, she felt a warm glow remain at his compliments on her artwork. It was wonderful to feel that she was good at something.

Wryly, she thought of the chicken coop she was trying to build. If she was honest with herself, the thought of attempting to build it without more expert hands to assist, at the very least, was intimidating.

Maybe, she thought, it was time to admit defeat. Or maybe not defeat, so much as realism. She'd just gotten a wonderful compliment on her painting. That was something she truly excelled at...unlike building anything other than a rough easel.

As Elizabeth approached with a basket of items to hold behind the counter for a customer who was still shopping, Mary asked, "Do you think it would be a good idea to get Bill to help us build the chicken coop? Or maybe just build it for us?"

Elizabeth was clearly trying to hide a hint of amusement. "Second thoughts about your carpentry prowess?"

"Third and fourth thoughts," Mary said dryly, unoffended. "It's not fair to expect you and Martha to help with something I'm clearly unsuited for."

"I would agree that calling Bill would be the most efficient way to get the job done," her eldest sister said diplomatically.

Rachel, still within earshot, turned. "My family could help tomorrow. We could have a 'coop-raising.'" She chuckled, delighted with her own joke.

"Really? That would be terrific." Mary reached for the phone. "Let me call Bill and see if tomorrow would work for him."

"I could work here in the store, and then you could help," Rachel said, obviously thinking ahead to the logistics of keeping the store open.

"We close at two tomorrow because of Easter," Elizabeth reminded her. "If the men came by and set the posts early, would we be able to do it at two?"

"I think Silas could do that," Rachel said. "I will ask him when I go home."

"We would be very grateful," Elizabeth said. She and Mary both understood their Amish friends would be offended if they offered to pay them for their kind offer.

"I'll go call Bill now." Mary headed for her cell phone, stored in her bag in the back of the shop.

Elizabeth left the shop at four thirty after Martha, tied up with customers, asked her to run by a nearby store and pick up some large plastic Easter eggs. The sisters had purchased children's socks to put in them for the church's Easter egg hunt, in which the Mount Zion children found the eggs and opened them before sorting them into groups of items to donate to a local family ministry for victims of fires. Martha had bought regular size eggs and then realized the socks were too bulky to fit into them.

Elizabeth left the store and followed the parking lot around the side of it to the exit. She was just about to turn onto the highway when she caught sight of a girl peering into the dumpster behind the next-door convenience store. Long dark hair. Oversize khaki coat. It all registered in seconds.

Without stopping to think, Elizabeth rolled down her window and called, "Marlee!"

The girl's head jerked up, dark hair flying around her. Her eyes were wide and shocked, and before Elizabeth could react in any other way, the girl took off running past the dumpster and around the far side of the building.

Elizabeth was stuck in a one-way exit lane behind another car trying to turn left. When it finally did, she immediately turned right and cruised along the street slowly until someone behind her honked impatiently. Reluctantly, she increased her speed and continued down the highway. There were shops with houses behind them all along this stretch, small streets leading back into a warren of residential homes that petered out into country roads. Marlee could be hiding anywhere.

Recognizing the futility of trying to search for the girl, Elizabeth reluctantly turned northward off the highway and headed for Ronks Road and the Classen farm.

CHAPTER THIRTEEN

The Tenebrae service that evening was lovely. As scriptures were read throughout the progression of the service, candles were extinguished one by one. The slow death of light symbolized the flight and despair of the disciples and the isolation of Jesus the night before His crucifixion. By the conclusion of the service, only one candle remained lit, a large pillar on the altar at the foot of the simple cross hung from the wall. It threw somber shadows over the scene, powerfully highlighting the death of the Savior. Finally, that one also was extinguished, and the congregation sat reflecting in silence, broken at last by a loud noise that represented the earthquake that occurred at the time of the resurrection. Afterward, the single pillar at the foot of the cross was lit again, and everyone silently made their way out of the church.

The Classen sisters did not speak on the way home. Mary was still absorbed in thoughts of what Jesus must have gone through during His final days, knowing as He did that He would be denied by His disciples, betrayed by one of them, and subjected to a cruel and horrifying death. He was human, and surely that prospect must have made Him fearful. And yet His death and subsequent resurrection had been so powerful that two thousand years later, people still remembered it and worshipped Him.

The sisters were still silent as they entered the house. Mary let Bolt out of his kennel and put him on his lead for a short excursion outside with the other dogs. Bolt was his joyous self, and Mary thought sadly that she was going to miss her little friend when he left tomorrow, despite the extra work he made for her.

When she got back inside, she removed Bolt's leash and turned to the sink to wash her hands.

When she turned back around, she realized that when she'd gone outside, she'd pulled out a chair from the kitchen table and set her handbag on it. Now Bolt had his front paws up on the chair and looked as if he was just about to make a foray up onto the table.

"Bolt!" She laughed. "You are such an opportunist."

The moment he heard her voice, the beagle scrambled down.

She went to the chair and removed her purse before pushing it in. They'd all gotten better about taking preventative measures to control the dog's behavior. But one slip, and you could see what happened.

"Come on, Bolt," she said affectionately. "Let's go join the others."

Pal and Tink had already gone into the living room where Martha and Elizabeth were seated. Mary walked in to join them, and Bolt hopped up on the couch beside her, turned in a circle, and lay down.

Just then, her cell phone rang. She pulled it out and answered it. "Hello?"

"Hi, Mary, it's Deb O'Hare from Safe Harbor Beagle Rescue. I assume since I haven't heard from you, everything has gone well with our little friend Bolt this week."

Mary laughed. "More or less. We had a pretty steep learning curve trying to stay one step ahead of him, but we've come to terms."

"Good, good." Deb chuckled. "I hope he hasn't been too challenging."

"Well," Mary said honestly, "we've learned a lot. We're keeping notes for his next foster on the techniques and commands and reinforcement we've used to shape some of his, um, less desirable behaviors, shall we say?"

"That's terrific," Deb said. "I'd like to pick him up later tomorrow and take him to his new fosters if that works for you. I can take your notes with me."

Mary swallowed, realizing anew that she would miss her constant companion, despite his antics. "That would be fine. Just text me a time. I should be here."

"Great," Deb said. "Thanks again, Mary. You were a lifesaver this week. Are you interested in fostering again?"

"Anytime," Mary said. "I don't know that we're ready to become long-term fosters, but we certainly could help out when fosters go on vacation and times like that."

"Great! Got it," Deb said. "If you're serious, I'll add you to our sub roster. Thanks so much. I guess I'll see you tomorrow."

"See you tomorrow," Mary echoed.

When she ended the call and set her phone down, both of her sisters were looking at her.

"What?" Mary asked.

Martha smiled. "I think we both expected you to say you wanted to keep him. He's a pretty endearing little fellow."

"He is," Mary agreed. "And part of me would love nothing better than to give him a forever home. But…"

"But perhaps we're not the best fit for him?" Elizabeth asked.

"That's really the thing," Mary said, glad that her perceptive eldest sister had framed it so well. "We all work, so he either has to be kenneled or he has to go with me, which puts a lot of pressure on him to behave in the store. We don't have a fenced yard, which I think we all know he has to have, otherwise he can never be off-lead, and that wouldn't be any fun for him."

"And with Martha baking as much as she does," Elizabeth said, "it makes it very difficult for us to allow him to be loose in the house. His instinct is to follow his nose to all those wonderful odors."

"So the short answer is, of course I'd like to adopt him," Mary said. "I'd like to adopt every dog in need I see, wouldn't you? And he's a sweet, happy little dog. But we're not the right home for Bolt, so he'll be leaving us tomorrow evening."

The Mount Zion Easter egg hunt was going to be held at eleven on Saturday morning.

At eight, as Martha reviewed her plans for the day ahead, she felt a little overwhelmed. First she needed to run a large selection of paper bags she'd received from several people to the library. Then she was helping with the church egg hunt, and after that she needed to hustle back over to the library to help with the bag sale and the conclusion of the book sale, while Rachel, Elizabeth, and Mary watched the store. Martha was relieved their plans to close early today would give them more flexibility.

At two, the Fischers and Bill would be coming to the house to raise the chicken coop, so she'd need to have refreshments to offer them. Then after dinner, Bolt was leaving, and she needed to do some of her Easter baking, including making the Paska bread that was one of their family traditions.

She set out at ten fifteen, stopping first at the library. The sale had slacked off a bit later yesterday, according to the volunteers, but this morning, the room was positively packed with shoppers filling their grocery bags for the bag sale.

"Oh, thank goodness," Pollie Muller said as Martha appeared with several dozen more bags. "We're down to our last few bags. I've never seen it this busy!"

"With luck," Martha said, "we'll sell all the books, and there won't be any left to dispose of." At the conclusion of the sale, all the leftover books had to be boxed up for resale, but the alternative was to send the books to an auction.

Leaving the library, Martha drove on to the church with the plastic Easter eggs stuffed with socks that she'd put together last night. Several dozen other volunteers clustered about tables in the large social hall, mixing eggs of all sizes into bags that they were about to carry outside and hide for the children who would be arriving shortly.

The egg hunt was the brainchild of their former pastor's wife, Ruth Zook. The idea was a sort of in-gathering of items local families in need might want for their children. Anything that would fit in an egg worked, and many larger items were donated as well. Those were generally placed right on the sorting tables, but smaller things, like underwear and T-shirts, infant pacifiers, thermometers, utensils, packs of crayons, socks, and mittens, were placed in different sizes of plastic Easter eggs. The church's children hunted and then opened and sorted everything. It was a lovely concept tailored to the Mennonite focus on service to others, and the children seemed to enjoy the tradition. It also was occasionally amusing, as it had been last year when one member had found plastic eggs the size of basketballs to stuff. Those had been a coveted find among the children, hidden as they'd been deep in the shrubbery surrounding the building.

Soon the church grounds were filled with the lively sounds of children giggling, shrieking, and calls of, "I found one!" The older children had to work harder to hunt theirs, while the smallest children picked up eggs lying in plain sight in a special toddler area.

Martha smiled as she observed the commotion. It brought back sweet memories of her own children's Easters. Her husband, Chuck, had loved holidays of all kinds and had thrown himself into preparations, whether it was traipsing all over a tree farm to find the perfect Christmas tree, hiding Easter eggs in such unconventional spots as a bird's nest in a low bush, or organizing autumn hayrides and bonfires for the youth of their church.

Next she thought of her five grandchildren. Her eldest, Kevin, was probably old enough that he thought hunting Easter eggs was silly and childish. But the others, Dylan, Elliott, Celeste, and sweet little Mick, would still be all about finding eggs. Maybe next year, she thought, she'd spend Easter in Kansas. Even though life here, working at Secondhand Blessings and living with her sisters, was supremely fulfilling, she missed those special holidays with her babies.

It didn't take long for the children to find the eggs, and with adult assistance and supervision, they soon had all the donated supplies sorted and packed up to take to the organization they were helping. Shortly after noon, Martha was on her way to Secondhand Blessings for a quick pop-in, and then she'd head to the library.

She almost groaned aloud as she approached the old barn at the foot of their lane. The shop was packed with vehicles, everything from an Amish buggy to SUVs to a tour bus. There was no way she'd be able to walk out and leave her sisters and Rachel to deal with this. Fortunately, they were closing at two, so she'd just have to wait and go to the library then.

After she'd parked behind the barn, she went in and headed for the register, surveying the mob as she went. Mary, Elizabeth, and Rachel were all busy with customers. Martha slipped a shop apron over her head and tied it as she hurried to the register, where she figured she could do the most good.

"Oh, I'm glad you stopped," Elizabeth muttered. She smiled brightly at the woman following her with overflowing arms. "Here you go. Martha can get you checked out." And off she darted to help someone else.

Ten minutes later, a woman approached the register. "Is Mary working today?"

Martha recognized her face. "You're the lady who was Bolt's owner's friend? I'm sorry, I can't recall your name. Mary's tied up right now, but I could give her a message. Or you could wait and speak to her when she's not busy." Mary was outside, helping two clients who were trying to decide between several sets of patio furniture they'd consigned. It would be a big sale, and Martha was loath to interrupt her at the moment. Martha gestured around her. "Although I honestly am not sure that will happen until we close at two."

"Eleni Caragianis," the woman said. She smiled wryly at Martha's words, looking at the bustle around them. "I wanted to speak with her about Bolt," she said. "I'm thinking of applying to adopt him."

Martha did a double take. "Really?" She remembered how happy the little dog had been to see someone familiar, and she'd watched how gently the woman had cuddled him in her lap on the floor of the store. She grabbed a pencil and notepad and pushed them toward Eleni. "If you write down your name and number and your e-mail, I'll have Mary get in touch with you as soon as possible."

"That would be wonderful. Thank you. I really can't stick around until after two."

"You, er, know he's a handful, right?" Martha didn't want the woman to feel obligated to adopt Bolt in her friend's memory if she wasn't really prepared for his level of energy and inquisitiveness.

Eleni laughed. "Oh yes. And he's a beagle to boot. But I adore him, and I'm wise to his ways. I had coonhounds for years, so I understand hounds. I have a fenced yard, because you know you can never let a hound out off lead."

"Oh, we know," Martha said dryly. "We learned that the hard way."

Eleni laughed. "I bet."

"Oh, this is perfect," Martha said fervently. "I'll be sure to have Mary contact you. Thank you so much, Eleni." She pocketed the paper containing the woman's contact information. "If you do adopt him, you have to promise to bring him by for some Classen sister snuggles from time to time."

Eleni chuckled, her eyes twinkling. "Oh, I'm pretty sure I can make that promise. After all, I'd never have found my little buddy again if it wasn't for you."

Slowly, the line dwindled at the register. The tour bus pulled away in a cloud of disagreeable-smelling exhaust. It was nearly two by then, and the three sisters were wilting. But Rachel grinned as she tidied up a helter-skelter assortment of napkins and dish towels that looked like a whirlwind had hit them. "That was fun!"

"You're crazy," Elizabeth said with a chuckle.

Mary blew out a relieved breath. "Can we turn over the CLOSED sign yet?"

"Two minutes," Elizabeth said. "And then we get to go build a chicken coop. Yay." There was a distinct lack of enthusiasm in her tone.

"The men will take care of most of that," Rachel assured them. "And we will let them, *ja*?"

"Ja," Mary replied with a heartfelt chuckle. "I told them we'd give them cookies and drinks. I'm thrilled, quite frankly, not to be the one wielding the hammer and nails. Worst idea I ever had."

"Was it like this all morning?" Martha asked.

"It was," Elizabeth said. "Honestly, it was manageable until the tour bus arrived. And that only happened a few minutes before you arrived, so I'm glad you came back. How was your morning?"

Martha gave her two thumbs up in answer. "The egg hunt was a success. Now I'm anxious to get to the library to help with the end of the book sale and see how we did."

"I'll come by after I run an errand," Elizabeth said. "I'll be happy to help pack up the leftovers."

"I was there this morning before I came here," Rachel said. "I do not think there will be too many books to pack. They were selling a lot."

"Good!" Martha felt a stir of optimism. She really wanted the book sale to do well under her guidance, late as she'd come into it.

Elizabeth drove away from Secondhand Blessings feeling pleasantly tired but accomplished after keeping all the balls in the air during their frantic morning. She wasn't really needed for the chicken coop raising planned for this afternoon—*thank heaven*—but she had another errand she was anxious to attempt.

Anxious. Yes, she decided, that was the right word for how she was feeling. Was this the right thing to do? She had prayed about it for some time last evening, and she felt that she had to make this effort.

Carefully, she drove the short distance to the run-down little house along the north side of Ronks Road.

As she pulled into the driveway and parked behind an ancient little Honda Civic with rust spots along the bottom, she noted that all the blinds appeared to be closed in the house. Maybe the presence of one car didn't mean someone was home.

Elizabeth didn't know what to hope for. Was she sticking her nose into private business? Probably. But when a child was so hungry she was hanging around free food and dumpster-diving in the community, that child and her family clearly needed help.

After getting out of her car, Elizabeth softly closed the door and avoided the uneven chunks of concrete in the sidewalk as she made for the front door. There was no doorbell, and up close, the light beige paint was cracked and faded, showing bare wood around the doorframe in places.

Elizabeth took a deep breath and knocked.

The sound of footsteps approached from the interior, and a moment later, the door of the small house was pulled open, and a small, heart-shaped face surrounded by long locks of dark hair peered out.

"What do you want?" The girl was clearly shocked to see Elizabeth standing on her doorstep. She stepped out, pulling the door closed behind her, and Elizabeth could almost see the child mustering her courage.

"I want to talk to you," Elizabeth said. "Your name is Marlee, right?"

The girl jerked her chin up and down in a single, defiant nod. "I don't have your money anymore, but I'll pay you back. I knew people didn't really just go around giving away twenty bucks." The last words contained a weary bitterness that tore at Elizabeth's heart.

"I don't want the money back." Elizabeth paused, trying to frame the words in a way that wouldn't get the door slammed in her face. "I just…I want to understand."

"Mar-wee? Mar-wee!" The sound of a young child's voice came through the door, and Elizabeth could hear a little one tugging at the doorknob, turning it but unable to open it. "Mar-wee." The last call was a wail, and Elizabeth saw the defiance drain out of the girl. She turned back and opened the door, then hefted a small child into her arms. Immediately, the little boy threw his arms around her neck and put his head on her shoulder, burying his face against her.

"Marlee? Who's at the door?" A woman's voice came from inside.

"Just a salesperson, Mom. Don't get up." The girl's gaze never left Elizabeth's. "So," she said, "how can I help you?"

Elizabeth eyed the little boy. He was probably around three, she thought, just a little older than Martha's youngest grandchild. "My name is Elizabeth Classen, and I live not far from here. I don't know what's wrong," she said quietly, "but I'd like to help. May I come in?"

For the first time, the girl looked uncertain. "I guess so," she said. "But my mom's not real good, so don't upset her."

Elizabeth nodded, and Marlee turned back toward the door, opening it and indicating that Elizabeth should follow her.

The house was small and dark, with stairs to the second floor immediately ahead. There was a living room on one side of the entry, what was probably supposed to be a dining room on the other but looked like someone's bedroom, and a kitchen that she could see through an open doorway at the rear as Marlee led her into the living room space. In the room, a woman sat in a recliner, while it looked like Marlee and her brother had been on the couch. The floors were bare wood with a ratty oval rug in the center, and equally dingy-looking curtains hung crookedly at the windows. The woman picked up a remote device and turned off the Disney movie that had been playing on the television.

"Mom?" Marlee was walking ahead of her, the little boy on her hip. "A…friend of mine stopped to say hello. This is Elizabeth."

"Hello." Elizabeth stepped forward and smiled, extending her hand. "Elizabeth Classen. We're actually almost neighbors. I live at the intersection of Ronks and Classen Roads."

"I don't know the area real well," the woman said. She didn't rise, but extended her hand as well, so Elizabeth came closer and took it gently. "I'm Donna Belser. This here's Timmy, and I guess you know Marlee. You a teacher?"

Elizabeth shook her head, understanding the unspoken question. "Marlee and I met at the library." She glanced at the girl, who looked down immediately.

Marlee's mother had deep circles beneath her eyes. She was thin, frail, and exhausted looking, and Elizabeth wondered if she was just tired or if she had an illness. Still, she gamely smiled. "That girl loves to read."

"Umm, Elizabeth, want to come out back and meet my goat?" Marlee looked determined to get Elizabeth away from her mother as fast as possible.

"Me come!" shouted her little brother.

"Sure, Timmy." Marlee put up her free hand and offered him a fist bump. "Where I go, you go, buddy."

"No school," Timmy said sadly.

Marlee chuckled, shaking her head. "Right. You can't come to school with me. But you can come out with me now." She swung around and made for the door. "Mom, we'll be out back."

"Okay. It was nice to meet you, Elizabeth."

"You too," Elizabeth said, meaning it. Her curiosity was now thoroughly aroused as she followed Marlee and Timmy past the small side entry and around the house to the stone fence that surrounded the little backyard. They kept a goat in here?

Marlee unlatched the four-foot wooden gate behind the house. "You'll have to come in quick," she said. "We can't let Blossom get out."

When she opened the gate, Elizabeth stepped through as Marlee followed with the child on her hip, latching the gate deftly behind her.

Right away Elizabeth heard the distinctive "ma-aa-aa" of a goat bleating. She located the source almost immediately. The animal looked as if she was barely a year old, and she was extremely eager to see them.

Marlee walked over and set Timmy in a sandbox in the section closest to the house while the goat attempted to greet her, butting and rubbing and yelling in a bid for attention.

Elizabeth looked around. The yard was little more than hard-packed earth with a tiny ramshackle stable at the far end.

The building was the typical small outbuilding with maybe two stalls that dotted much of the countryside around rural homesteads, but it looked as if it had been patched and mended several times recently, with tar paper and boards tacked up to cover what presumably were holes in the walls. Even though the recent winter had been relatively mild, there had been a deep freeze for much of January that couldn't have been comfortable for one small animal all alone in the shed. Herds generated warmth that this poor baby wouldn't have had access to. One goat alone wasn't going to be able to do much to keep herself warm.

There were shrubs and small trees around bare flower beds, but there were no spring buds on them as there were on those at the Classens' home. The poor little goat was thin, and her coat was dull and patchy. She appeared to be a LaMancha cross and looked very much as if she was one of Rachel's, as her friend had said. And she must have eaten every shrub, every flower, every blade of grass within reach that she could find. Elizabeth was honestly surprised that the goat wasn't in worse shape.

Elizabeth had been helping to care for her family's goats of one breed or another since she was a child. They'd had dairy goats for many years until her parents had stopped doing much farming. They'd gotten rid of their goats for a while, but then her mother had taken in the three pygmy goats from a petting zoo, and they'd had goats in residence again.

Although her family had mostly raised Oberhaslis because her mother loved their sweet temperaments, she knew quite a bit about the various breeds and crosses, and about goat husbandry in general. As the goat nuzzled and nibbled and generally made quite a nuisance of herself, it was quite clear to Elizabeth that this was an underfed, hungry animal.

There wasn't even any grass in the yard, which really concerned her. Goats were browsers, she knew. They usually would not eat grass until they were really hungry. They preferred weeds, bushes, leaves, even the bark of trees, before they would crop grass. This goat had been hungry enough to eat all the grass she could find. And she was currently doing her best to nibble at the corner of Elizabeth's spring jacket.

"Her name's Blossom. She's hungry." Marlee sounded both defiant and ashamed, her hands gently caressing the little animal's floppy ears. "I don't have enough feed."

"She's pretty." Elizabeth could sense that the next few minutes might define her relationship with Marlee going forward, whether the girl would accept her help or reject her interference. "And she's very sweet. I can tell you spend a lot of time with her. Have you had her long?" Long enough for the pitiful little animal to denude the entire yard in search of food, for sure.

"I got her right before Christmas, not too long after we moved here," Marlee said. "From an Amish farm over on your road. I googled how to take care of her, and I used all my money from babysitting jobs to buy food and supplies for her." She looked down. "But I've kind of run out, and since we moved here, I don't know anybody to babysit for."

So it had been about four months, Elizabeth thought, calculating, since she'd gotten the goat. And presumably, she'd been able to buy feed for at least the worst part of the winter. It wouldn't have taken long for the goat to strip the yard like this once the feed ran out.

She thought of the apples she'd first seen Marlee taking from the church social hour. "So you've been doing your best to find things to feed her."

The girl nodded, her hair hiding much of her face as she kept her head down. Elizabeth understood pride, and she felt certain the child was fighting tears. Changing tactics, she said, "Does your mother work?"

Marlee shook her head. "She can't work. She gets a little support, though."

"Is she ill?" Elizabeth asked quietly, needing to understand if she was to help.

"She's got ankylosing spondylitis." Marlee shook her head. "Nobody knows what that is. Like arthritis. It makes her joints really painful."

"Where's your dad?"

"He died," Marlee said, so flatly that Elizabeth didn't ask any more questions. "They only counted his last year of SSI for us, so she's barely getting anything."

"I guess you were lucky to find this house." It wasn't much, Elizabeth thought, but it was better than nothing.

"Mom's aunt died and left it to her. We moved here when she found out."

"I bet that was a nice discovery."

"Better than nice," Marlee said quietly. "We were about to get kicked out of our apartment in Philly. And my brother—" She stopped, flushed. "Sorry. I don't mean to complain. We're lucky everything worked out."

"What about your brother?" Elizabeth asked. "He's adorable."

"He is." Marlee sounded defensive again. "He has some weird allergy, and he can't have cow's milk. But the doctor said goat's milk would be okay. Something about the protein, I think."

"Except that it's a lot more expensive," Elizabeth summed up when the girl stopped abruptly.

"Yeah." Marlee exhaled. "We can't afford it, so I thought if I bought a goat…" She trailed off.

"That was a pretty good idea," Elizabeth said.

"But it's turning out to be almost as expensive as buying the milk," Marlee said, sighing. "At least in the winter when there's nothing for her to eat, it is. And like I said, no babysitting. Plus, I don't really like to leave Tim with Mom if I don't have to, because he's like, too much for her sometimes, you know?"

"What does she do when you're in school?" Elizabeth asked.

"He watched a lot of TV this winter," Marlee said morosely. "Sometimes when I'm off school, I take him to the library for story time. He loves that."

And there, thought Elizabeth, was the reason Marlee had been in the library.

Unaware of Elizabeth's thoughts, in a burst of confidence, Marlee said, "I used the money you gave me to buy a mineral block and alfalfa. I know there's some other stuff Blossom needs too, though. I did a bunch of research at school on goats and milk production to make sure she's getting what she needs to produce milk."

"You milk her yourself?"

Marlee nodded.

Elizabeth was truly impressed with everything the youngster had done, even though there were some obvious flaws in her plan. She could see that Marlee was worried the goat would stop producing. Marlee was carrying much too big a burden, worrying about her family's finances and both her mother's and brother's health.

"Marlee," she said, "if I could find ways to help you with the goat, and maybe with some other things, do you think your mom would be too proud to let me help?"

The naked relief on the girl's face nearly brought Elizabeth to tears. "I could probably talk her into it," the teen said awkwardly. "But if you can't, I'll figure out something."

CHAPTER FOURTEEN

Martha was over the moon. The book sale had just ended, and the last customer had left. The Friends of the Library's treasurer's face told the story. She had been happy after the first day, extremely enthused after the second. But today, as the sale concluded, and she added the total of the bag sale and the raffle tickets, she was practically incandescent with excitement.

"We made eight hundred dollars more than last year, and last year was the best we'd ever done!" she announced.

"Anya's going to be so excited," Hilda Brunner, the president, said. "I can't wait to tell her."

Everyone in the room clapped, and someone added an ear-splitting zinger of a whistle.

"Well, we had all the books from the Hofstra estate sale," Pollie said. "That probably helped. And we all sold ticket after ticket after *ticket* for the raffle for Mary's paintings." She turned to Martha. "You'll tell her, won't you? And ask her to consider doing something for us again next year if she has the time?"

Martha chuckled, thinking of how astounded she and Elizabeth had been at the signs Mary had produced with little more than a day's notice. "Oh, I suspect she'll be able to fit it in," she said. "But I'll tell her that her artwork put us over the top."

They were just beginning the task of boxing up the few remaining books on the tables when Elizabeth came through the door. "I'm here to help," she announced, smiling, but Martha thought her sister's smile looked a bit forced.

"You okay?" she asked as she handed a box to her sister.

Elizabeth nodded. "I'm okay, but I've found someone who really isn't."

"Your mystery girl from church?"

Elizabeth nodded. "She's real, and she lives with her mother and baby brother on Ronks Road not far from us. They're poor as church mice, Martha, and the mother is disabled for all intents and purposes, and the little one has some health challenges too." Tears shone in Elizabeth's eyes. "And here's this poor dear child trying desperately to hold everything together." She stopped, holding up a hand. "I can't talk about it or I'll cry. Let's wait until we're home."

Martha nodded, rubbing her sister's shoulder briefly. "Until we're home."

The chicken coop was taking shape.

Oh, Mary had helped some, but her contribution had mostly been organizing supplies and fetching and carrying items for the men. And she was pretty certain the Amish men would have been happier if she'd simply left them to the task. But it was her henhouse, and she'd felt compelled to at least be on site for the process.

She knew she should be more annoyed that she hadn't been able to build it on her own. But as she carried a tray full of Martha's brownies and lemonade out to Bill, Silas, his brother Eben, and Silas and Rachel's three oldest sons, Adam, Luke, and Ephraim, all she could feel was gratitude.

It was a gorgeous, mild spring day. Their friends were giving of their time to help her and her sisters. Tomorrow they would celebrate the resurrection of the risen Christ. Why not be happy and thankful?

After she had offered drinks and brownies to her Amish neighbors, Bill ambled over. "This is going up fast," he said. "You chose a good design."

"Thank you." She smiled. "In my mind's eye, I could see myself building it, but when reality hit, I knew I was out of my depth. I appreciate you sacrificing your Saturday at such short notice to help."

Bill shrugged. "I wasn't doing anything important. And we can't have a fox snacking on your chickens again." He hesitated, his brown eyes on her face. "Going to church tomorrow?"

"Oh yes. It's Easter Sunday."

"Would you mind if I sat with you?"

Mary struggled not to feel flustered. She couldn't deny a warm flutter when Bill looked at her like...like he was looking at her now. "Of course not. You're welcome to sit with us any time."

"I'm not asking your sisters," Bill said. "I'm asking if I could sit with *you*, Mary."

"Oh." It was a tiny sound. Mary blew out a breath and met his eyes. "I'd like that."

Bill chuckled. "Great." He touched one finger to her cheek before turning back to the chicken coop construction. "I'll meet you there."

As Mary carried the empty cups, pitcher, and platter back to the house, she caught sight of her sisters' cars coming up the lane, one right behind the other. She wished she'd been able to help more at the book sale, but someone had needed to be here this afternoon.

Martha parked and was out of her car first. "Hey, guess what?"

"What? And oh, hi," Mary teased.

"I just saw you two hours ago." Martha brushed off her lack of greeting. "The lady who was friends with Bolt's owner came back into the store. She wants to adopt him!" She pulled the piece of paper with Eleni's contact information from her pocket and handed it to Mary. "I told her you'd get in touch with her."

"Wow!" Mary said. "That's great news." She slipped the paper into the pocket of her jeans. "Do you think she understands what she'd be getting into? I mean, I know she knew him before, but I wonder how much she saw of her friend with him."

Martha recounted Eleni's qualifications, mentioning her experience and her fenced yard, and Mary brightened at once. "Oh, so this really is a terrific placement! I wonder if she'd let me visit."

"I'm sure she would," Martha reassured her. "I already asked her to promise to bring him by the store."

Mary laughed. "You couldn't resist him either, could you?"

"Not for a New York minute," Martha said. "He's precious. But hey, guess what else?"

"More news? What?"

"The book sale raised the most money they ever had, and it was because of your painted signs! They begged me to ask you to do some next year if you have time." She rolled her eyes and laughed. "I wasn't about to explain to them that it took you less than two days to do both of them, or they might have asked for a dozen."

"I'd be happy to do a few more for next year," Mary said. "I've already had ideas. Once I turn on the brainstorming, it's hard to turn off."

"Terrific. You'll make some Friends of the Library volunteers very, very happy when they hear that." Martha lowered her voice. "Elizabeth found the girl. She's got stuff to tell us, and she doesn't seem very happy."

"Oh dear." Mary glanced back toward the men swarming over what was now the roof and walls of the chicken coop. "Do you think it can wait until supper?"

"I'm sure it can." Martha smiled as Elizabeth climbed out of her car and came toward them. "We're letting Mary and her crew finish up before dinner," she said, linking arms with their eldest sister and drawing her toward the house.

Over dinner, Elizabeth told her sisters the whole story of her visit to the Belser home and her introduction to Marlee and her family.

Martha's and Mary's reactions were as sympathetic as Elizabeth's. "That poor child," said Martha. "Who would expect her to know anything about keeping a goat?"

"A young girl who was raised in Philadelphia probably wouldn't know the first thing about it," Mary agreed. "And her mother is depressed, exhausted, and in pain, and not able to do much. And then add a little brother."

"What's that goat been eating?" Martha asked.

"There's a fair amount of stuff in that yard that's evergreen, like rhododendrons, mountain laurel, pachysandra, and some other ground covers," Elizabeth said. "She probably looked it at before snow fell and thought there was plenty there for a goat to eat."

"The whole situation makes me sad," Mary said. "The mom, the children. One poor little goat, all by itself. You said Rachel told her goats need pals."

"I'm pretty sure she couldn't afford more than one," Elizabeth said quietly. "Kids are not very financially savvy. I guess it probably seemed like a pretty good idea, a way to help get milk for her little brother, and I imagine she assumed her yard could support one goat. She had ideas about babysitting to earn feed money."

Mary shrugged. "And really, much of the time they aren't that expensive if you have a lot of browse and don't have to buy alfalfa."

"No, they're just escape artists, like Patsy Blue," said Martha, and they all laughed, thinking of one particular doe their mother had bought who had been able to jump over the top of a small car and who had often been found standing atop their father's tractor.

"I think this family really needs our help," Elizabeth said. She took a deep breath. "I'm just not sure where to start."

"Sounds like one thing we need to do is to get that goat taken care of," Martha said.

"I already ran by the feed store and bought a bit of alfalfa and some Bermuda pellets today," Elizabeth said.

"Maybe tomorrow afternoon Mary could sweet-talk Bill into going over there with her and trailering it up here. We could house and feed it for next to nothing, it would have buddies, and we live close enough that Marlee could hike over here and milk it morning and evening until it starts to taper off. I'm willing to bet she doesn't know that it won't just keep producing milk forever," Martha said.

"Hey!" Mary said. "You can sweet-talk him yourself." Then she smiled sheepishly. "Just kidding. I can ask him at church. He asked if he could sit with me, and I said yes."

Elizabeth looked at her with approval. "How nice," she said. "I'm happy for you, Mary."

"But back to Marlee," Martha said. "When can you talk to her about the goat, Elizabeth?"

"I was considering calling and inviting them to church tomorrow," Elizabeth said. "I know Marlee's familiar with the building, since we saw her there."

"Why don't you invite them to join us for Easter dinner? That might give you a chance to talk to her," Martha said. "And if they decline, we could always stop after church with a basket of food, since it's Easter."

"The longer-term problem is how to help the family with money," Mary said. "I think the mother is going to have to be approached to see if she's willing to accept help, and if Marlee wants to work, whether it's babysitting or something else, we can help her with that."

"Is she even old enough to work?" Martha asked.

"She's in eighth grade, so I assume she's thirteen going on fourteen. She may even be fourteen already, which means she's old enough to legally work."

"We could use her in the store," Mary said. "Rachel can't always help when we need someone."

"And she's interested in babysitting," Elizabeth said, "if she can get to know some families who need sitters."

"I wouldn't hit them with all these ideas at once," Mary suggested. "Perhaps tomorrow we mention the goat and see how that goes. If they think we're trying to take over their lives, they may refuse altogether."

"That's my fear," Elizabeth said. "You're absolutely right. It'll require a delicate approach."

"I can't think of anyone better suited to that than you," Martha said. "Heaven forbid being tactful fell to me."

That provoked another round of laughter before they began to clean up the remains of supper.

An hour after supper, Deb O'Hare from Safe Harbor Beagle Rescue came to pick up Bolt.

Mary had taken him for one last ramble after they'd eaten, and the sisters were sitting together in the living room when Pal's keen ears pricked at the sound of a car. A moment later, tires crunched on the gravel of the lane.

"Oh, Bolt," Martha said. "You've been quite the adventure." She rose and went over to pet the little dog's ears as Mary went to the door. "Part of me will miss you."

"But not the part that turns around to find him standing on the table," Elizabeth confirmed.

"Not that part." Martha smiled as Bolt rolled over so she could rub his belly.

Elizabeth joined her for some last beagle snuggles.

Mary ushered Deb into the room. "Martha, Elizabeth, you remember Deb. She's here for our boy."

Deb's ears pricked. "Sounds like someone's getting attached. Any chance you'd like to make this permanent?"

Mary laughed. "Is that how you get the dogs adopted? Make the fosters fall in love with them?"

Deb grinned without a trace of shame. "Whatever it takes."

"Well, it isn't going to 'take' this time," Mary said. "We are just a little too busy and distracted for such a young, active dog. However, I do have some good news. I have the contact information for a friend of his former owner. She's very interested in adopting him. I directed her to the website to fill out an application. She's got experience with hounds, she's got a fenced yard, and she knows his energy level."

"Wow! That sounds like a real possibility." Deb clapped her hands. "I'll look for her application. Thanks so much!"

"His food and everything else is in the kitchen," Mary told the foster care coordinator. She led the way from the room. "I have a notebook full of information here for the next person who takes him. We've been working on obedience all week, and he's really beginning to tune in. I'd be happy to get together with his next foster and show them what we've been doing so we can keep some continuity—and better behavior—going."

Deb grinned. "Was he pretty wild?"

"Not wild, exactly," Mary said. "He's just ruled by his nose, and he's young and very inquisitive." Ruefully, she admitted, "We had to bathe him twice in seven days."

"Oh my." Deb covered her mouth with her hand to stifle a guffaw. Bolt looked up at her and cocked his head inquiringly, and she laughed harder. "You brat!" she said affectionately. She extended a hand to Mary and then pulled her into a hug. "Thank you so much. I'll check in with you if we can use you to foster again. We really need great people like your sisters and you in our rescue family."

"We'll wait to hear from you," Mary promised.

She helped Deb out to the car with the supplies and the pup, kneeling to gather his warm, wriggly body against her one last time. "You be a good egg," she told him. "I have a feeling a wonderful home is waiting for you very soon." She kissed him atop his satiny head, handed his lead to Deb, and stepped back, determined not to cry. "Thanks for giving us the opportunity to foster."

"Thank *you*," the woman said with deep feeling. "I'll let you know when he's adopted."

When Elizabeth made the call to the Belser residence, Marlee answered the phone. After checking with her mother, the girl declined Elizabeth's invitation to attend Easter Sunday services and have dinner with them. To her surprise, Marlee sounded as if she really would have liked to attend.

"Oh, I wish we could," the girl said. "But my mom's not feeling well, and I don't think she'd be up to sitting on a church pew for such a long time tomorrow."

"What about if we picked up you and Timmy?" Elizabeth asked on a burst of inspiration. "Your mom could rest quietly at home while you two attend church with us, and we could bring you home after that. You could even take Timmy to toddler's church if you wanted. He might enjoy playing with the toys and other children. I thought it might be a good way for you to connect with families who might have some potential babysitting jobs."

Marlee hesitated. "I—I don't know...let me ask Mom if it's okay if we go without her," she said in a rush.

Elizabeth silently crossed her fingers and held them up to show Mary, who was standing in the kitchen dishing out some ice cream for an evening treat.

Marlee came clattering back to the phone. "Mom says she guesses that's all right, as long as we put Timmy's car seat in your car. And she says me and Timmy can stay for dinner. You know, if you want." She sounded uncertain.

"We'd love to have you," Elizabeth said.

"I know how to install the car seat the safe way," Marlee said, "so I can do that."

"Good," Elizabeth said, "because I have no clue." She laughed. "I'm delighted you can come. I'll pick you up tomorrow morning." They settled on a time before she ended the call, and then she turned to Mary, eyes shining. "The kids are coming to church and dinner!"

"That's wonderful," Martha said. "Why isn't the mother coming?"

Elizabeth related what Marlee had said about her mother's health. "I've been trying to think of ways to help them," she said.

"Gaining their trust is the first thing," Mary said without hesitation. "You can't march in there and start telling them what you want to do for them. It's going to require finesse."

"She said her mom gets a little bit of Social Security assistance from her father's death benefits," Elizabeth said, "but I wonder if there are other programs that may help. It didn't look or sound to me as if Mrs. Belser is well enough to work, and I'm worried the children aren't getting enough to eat and other things to meet their basic needs. Their home is extremely...well, they don't have a lot."

"How old is the little boy?" Mary asked. "There are preschool programs he might be eligible for. Sitting around the house watching TV with a disabled mother can't be good for his intellectual or physical development. He needs play opportunities." Mary and Martha were both devoted grandmothers.

"Oh, good idea," Elizabeth said. "I'll have to ask. I'm not a good judge, but he looks like maybe three-ish?"

"How disabled is the mom?" Mary wanted to know.

"I'm not sure," Elizabeth admitted.

"There may be ways to get her some medical assistance, maybe physical therapy, to help her as well."

"And the little one's allergic to dairy products from cows, you said," Martha added. "But he can have goat's milk, so we have to help them find a way to keep up with that."

Elizabeth sighed. "I applaud Marlee's ingenuity, but I'm not sure keeping a goat is the best way to go about supplying her brother's needs in that area. If you'd seen that poor little goat, it would have made your heart hurt."

"I still think we should offer to house it here as soon as possible," Martha said.

"It can't hurt to try," Elizabeth said. "If she seems open to discussing it at all today, I'll see if I can talk her into letting us board and feed it here."

"Do you think the pygmies will accept a bigger goat?" Mary asked.

"I think so," Elizabeth said. "The only way to know would be to try it."

"The cost wouldn't be significant for us," Martha said. "It's more a matter of the goats accepting it."

"Remember how Mama used to introduce new does when she was raising them back when we had a little dairy herd?" Mary reminded them. "We'd need to put Marlee's goat in a pen in a new pasture they don't use for a couple of days and let her explore it all. Then, after she's pretty familiar with it, introduce one of ours—probably Blynken, since he seems to adapt to change most easily—and once we're sure they're going to get along, turn out the other two. It'll help that she's larger than they are."

Elizabeth nodded. "Good plan." They'd all heard stories of goat introductions that hadn't been carefully managed.

Terrible injuries and even deaths could occur, usually to the new animal, because the existing herd banded together. "Now all I have to do is find a plan to get her to agree."

Martha and Mary both looked sympathetic.

"Better you than me," Martha said. "Teenagers can be so contrary."

"Not helpful," Elizabeth sing-songed, making both her sisters laugh. "Okay, so step one is gain her trust. Step two is help them with the goat, preferably bringing it here, and help Marlee do a better job with its care. Step three will be to investigate programs to benefit the family and find ways to help them without seeming pushy."

"Three small steps," Martha said. "No big deal."

Mary rolled her eyes. "Only because you're not the one trying to accomplish them. Elizabeth, I'll pray for your success."

Elizabeth had jitters in her tummy on Easter morning as she and her sisters got into her SUV. They were taking the big vehicle to have plenty of room for everyone, since they were able to convert the third row to seats.

It was a cool but beautiful April morning, with the sun casting the rolling landscape of the fields into sharp relief. Elizabeth was more dressed up than usual in honor of the special day, in a pretty new mint-green A-line dress with flowers on it, but she'd had to scramble at the last minute for a sweater to wear over it, since it was too chilly for short sleeves this early in the day.

By Elizabeth's reckoning, it was still a week too early for even the early tulips to make an appearance, but many of the homes they passed sported the bright, cheery yellows of daffodils as well as some in white and orange, along with white, yellow, and purple crocus, and hyacinths that would fill the air around them with a delightful scent.

When she pulled into the Belsers' driveway, Martha said, "Good gracious. I've passed this place a million times. I didn't even know anyone lived here anymore. Wasn't this the old Whistler place when we were growing up? And isn't that a gorgeous tree!" She was referring to the blossoming cherry tree Elizabeth had noticed.

"The place changed hands several times after the Whistlers passed away." Elizabeth explained about the aunt who had left the old place to Marlee's mother. "I never met the last owner."

"Well," Mary said, "it could use some work, but what a relief it must have been to have a place to live."

Elizabeth wasn't even out of the car when the curtain was whisked away from the front window, and a little round face appeared. It was Timmy, grinning and waving madly.

Marlee pulled open the door before Elizabeth could knock. "We're ready," she said. "Just let me get Timmy's coat."

Mrs. Belser—Donna—appeared in the hallway behind Marlee. She shuffled as if it hurt to walk. "Thank you for taking them to church," she said.

"Happy Easter." Elizabeth indicated a covered basket she carried over one arm. "We brought you a few goodies, and when we return your children, I'll bring some of our Easter dinner leftovers, so you won't need to cook today."

"Oh goodness." Donna looked flustered as well as wonderfully surprised. "Thank you so much. What a thoughtful thing to do. Marlee!" She raised her voice. "Can you take this to the kitchen, please?"

Timmy came running full-tilt at Elizabeth, and she automatically extended her arms to keep him from running off the porch. The little boy raced right into her arms as if he'd known her all his life, throwing his chubby arms around her neck. "Hi, Is'bef! I go wif you?"

She laughed, kneeling fully to hug him. "Hi, Timmy. Yes, I'm going to take you and Marlee to church with me today. Are you ready?"

"You need your jacket," Marlee said, returning. She extended a small garment and stuffed his arms into it, then spun him around and zipped it before snatching him up and kissing him. "There. We're ready to go."

Marlee herself appeared to have made some effort today. Her hair was brushed, and the front section was pulled back from her face with a ribbon. She wore the big jacket, but it was open, and beneath it was a blouse rather than a T-shirt. She still wore the ever-present jeans, of course.

Elizabeth didn't care, and God didn't either. She was just happy that Marlee had accepted her invitation.

"I'll get Timmy's car seat and put it in your car," Marlee said. She jumped off the porch and headed for her mother's car, leaving Elizabeth to lift Timmy into her arms. "Give your mother a kiss," she told him. "We'll see her again in a little while."

"Bye, Mama." Timmy waved merrily. "Me's going bye-bye wif Mar-wee and Is'bef!"

CHAPTER FIFTEEN

Taking Marlee and Timmy to church was amazingly easy, to Elizabeth's surprise. Marlee had the car seat in and Timmy buckled into it in no time. Elizabeth introduced Marlee to her sisters, and off they went to Easter services.

The small slope leading up to Mount Zion was carpeted in early spring with a cool blue blanket of glory-of-the-snow, courtesy of some dedicated landscapers in the congregation who had planted the tiny bulbs everywhere many years ago. They had multiplied madly beneath and around two Korean rhododendron, which were blooming a bright candy pink. As the SUV pulled into the lot, Marlee said, "Wow, that's really pretty."

More bulbs and blossoms greeted them as they disembarked and headed up the path toward the door. There were daffodils, narcissus, and crocus here too, as well as Siberian squill and the upside-down mauve and burgundy blossoms of several of the early-blooming hellebore, known as the Lenten rose. At one corner of the building, a star magnolia spread branches adorned in large blossoms of palest blush. It was a lovely display, and Elizabeth was thankful for the beautiful weather. She could recall Easters a foot deep in snow, and one memorable year when a terrible ice storm had coated everything in sparkling but destructive splendor. There had been no magnolia blossoms at all that year.

When they stepped into the house of worship, one of the first people they saw was Geraldine Goertz, who Marlee had spoken to at church on Palm Sunday.

"Well, hello and welcome back." Geraldine looked from the Classen sisters to Marlee and her little brother. "Do you still need that item you asked me about?" It was a kind and tactful reference to the money Marlee had asked for.

Marlee blushed. "I, er, I don't think so, but if you know anyone who needs a babysitter, I'd appreciate it if you'd recommend me." She looked down at Timmy and smiled, her small face lighting up in a way Elizabeth hadn't seen before, and then reached into a pocket and produced a business-size card. "This is my little brother Timmy, and I'm Marlee. I'm really good with little kids and babies. I have references from people I used to work for before we moved here if anyone asks."

Geraldine beamed, taking the card. "I'd be happy to let people know. You may call me Mrs. Goertz." She glanced at the card. "Happy Easter, Marlee."

"May I have one of those?" Elizabeth held out her hand.

Marlee blushed again as she withdrew another card and handed it to Elizabeth. It was simple, listing her qualifications as "Experienced babysitter, light housework, pet sitting," with her name, cell number, and an e-mail address.

"I check my e-mail at school or the library," Marlee said. "At least, I used to when I was getting regular jobs."

"I suspect you'll soon be getting some jobs again," Elizabeth said. "But you can't drive. How do you get there?"

"At home—in the city, I mean—I could take a bus. Out here, I'll have to walk or maybe ride a bike," Marlee said.

"There's an old one in the shed that needs the tires patched."

Or replaced, Elizabeth thought to herself, adding "decent bike" to the mental list she'd been making of ways to help the Belser family. "You're quite an enterprising girl," she said.

Marlee shrugged, although the compliment clearly pleased her. "Needs must."

Elizabeth did a double take. "My grandmother used to say that! I haven't heard that phrase in years."

"My grandmother used to say it too," Marlee said.

"Used to?" Elizabeth was curious about extended family. Maybe there was someone who could help these three that they simply hadn't considered.

"She died a couple of years ago, before Timmy was born. My grandpa died when I was little, but I remember him."

"Do you have no other family?" Elizabeth couldn't see a reason to keep prying around the edges. Better just to ask.

Marlee shook her head. "Dad's family doesn't want anything to do with us. It's just us three."

How sad, Elizabeth thought, that her relatives would never know how capable and smart and special this young girl was.

They took Timmy to toddler's church. Many of the children his age clung to their parents, but the little boy dove right into the toys on the shelves. When they left, Marlee looked back at him, sitting on the lap of a childcare worker who was reading him a book about trucks. "He sure doesn't seem to miss me, does he?" Her tone was a bit wistful. She'd intended to stay at first, Elizabeth knew, but when the church worker had given Marlee a little pager so they could contact her if they needed her, Marlee had decided to try going to church.

"You've given him a marvelous sense of security," Elizabeth said. "He knows you're coming back, so he'll enjoy himself in the meantime."

As they made their way into the sanctuary, Elizabeth went to great lengths to introduce Marlee to people and mentioned her babysitting skills as much as she could. Marlee handed out a few cards. Martha and Mary both asked if they could have a few to give to friends. "Also," Mary said, "you could put some on the counter at Secondhand Blessings, our shop. If people ask, we can assure them that we know you and you do indeed have great skills with children."

Marlee beamed. "That would be awesome. Thank you."

Bill was waiting in the vestibule for them. They all greeted him, and when they entered their pew, he took a seat on the far end beside Mary.

Elizabeth leaned over and whispered to Martha, "Ask Mary if she wants to invite him for Easter dinner."

But Martha shook her head. "I think we should let Mary manage this friendship, or whatever it becomes, at her own pace in her own way. He probably has other plans by now, anyway."

She was right, Elizabeth decided. Part of her would love to see Bill and Mary together as more than just friends, but Mary was still healing after the trauma of a marriage ending badly, and it wasn't fair to push her into anything. Far better to take it slow. As she was with John?

Elizabeth thought of how soon she'd see the handsome East Lampeter Township police officer who never failed to make her pulse speed up. Although she understood his reasons for not attending Easter services with her family, she was happy that he'd accepted her offer to have Easter dinner with them.

The service was beautiful and uplifting. The wooden cross, usually stark over the altar at the front of the church, was softened by a length of sheer white cloth draped over the front and hanging from each arm. Brilliant sunlight streamed through the clear glass of the windows on the east side of the church, while the sunlight was equally visible through the west windows, brightening the cemetery that spread out on that side. The whitewashed walls rang with a cappella harmonies that sent shivers down Elizabeth's spine.

When the entire congregation participated in the "Hallelujah Chorus" from Handel's *Messiah,* Elizabeth sneaked a glance at Marlee. Her young friend's eyes were wide and shining, and she actually smiled when her gaze met Elizabeth's. Perhaps she had never heard hymns of praise sung in such a way.

Perhaps, Elizabeth thought, Marlee had never been to church before. The expression on her face was wide-eyed, and she appeared to be taking everything in. And Elizabeth doubted she'd ever left her little brother in children's church— or anywhere else, for that matter.

As the service came to its glorious and uplifting conclusion, and the congregation began to disperse, the Classens and their friends made their way out of the sanctuary. Elizabeth was heading off with Marlee to gather Timmy when she heard Mary say to Bill, "Would you like to join us for Easter dinner? We're not eating until two, but you're welcome to come back to the house with us now."

"I'd like that. Thank you." Bill's words were quiet, but Elizabeth caught his grin of satisfaction. She didn't dare look at Martha.

Timmy was happy to see them and chattered nonstop about his new "fwens" and the many toys that he and his new friends had played with.

Before they left, Elizabeth asked Marlee if she minded taking Timmy for a brief walk around the church grounds while she and her sisters visited their parents for a bit.

"No problem," Marlee said. "Timmy's kind of a pest. He might be too much for old people anyway."

Elizabeth was startled into a chuckle. "Oh, Marlee, my parents aren't living. Believe me, they would have adored meeting you and Timmy." She pointed to the decorative metal fence surrounding rows and rows of gray and weathered headstones. "They're buried right over there."

"Oh." Marlee looked taken aback. "Sorry. Uh, sorry for your loss. That's what people said to us."

"It's a kind thing to say," Elizabeth assured her. Then she turned and caught up with her sisters, who were walking through the open gate at the driveway. It was a bit of a walk to the narrow path that forked back from the main road toward the slope her parents had chosen for their burial site. There were new leaves budding on the trees around them, and sunshine streamed through the spring day.

As she and her sisters passed the final resting places of church and community members they once had known, fond memories of yesterday floated into Elizabeth's memory and out again. Her piano teacher was buried just here, and over there, the first Sunday school teacher she could remember.

Her parents' headstone was at the top of a slope that looked out over a patchwork of Amish fields in the distance, fields that soon would be colored in shades ranging from celery to chartreuse to gold with new crop growth. The stone was simple, as befitted their faith and their lives, with an etched cross dividing their names and above that, the italicized inscription: *BELOVED FATHER AND MOTHER*.

Mary set down a pot of pink and lavender hyacinths that she'd carried from the church, where they'd been used as part of the Easter décor and supplied by the sisters in memory of their parents.

"Daddy and Mama," Martha said, "I miss you." She stopped abruptly, choking up, and Mary put a comforting hand on her sister's back.

"We all miss you. I wish you could see the chicken coop Bill and Silas helped us build," Mary said. "Well, to be honest, they built it. But I chose it. It looks nice, and it'll keep that rotten fox from getting any more of our hens."

They stood in silence a moment longer.

Elizabeth cleared her throat. "Mama, it's still hard some days. I'm just not used to being without you yet. A dozen times a day, I think of something I need to tell you. But I know you were ready to be with Daddy again, and I hope you're both enjoying watching the three of us making a life together." She held out her hands for her sisters, and the three of them linked hands in a rough circle at the foot of the graves. "Happy Easter. We believe in the promise of our risen Lord, and we look forward to the day we see you again. In the meantime, we'll keep doing our best to live the values you taught us and be good stewards of everything you left us."

Bill was waiting at the house when Elizabeth and her sisters piled out of the SUV with the Belser siblings.

"Who would like to color some Easter eggs?" Martha asked as Marlee unbuckled Timmy and lifted him down from his car seat.

"Wif cwayons?" the little boy asked.

Martha laughed. "No, with egg dyes I made. I hardboiled a dozen eggs last night."

"Who died?"

"Nobody died," Marlee told him. "This is a different word. To dye eggs means to dip them in pretty colors. Like in your book about Easter." To the sisters, she said, "We've never done that before."

The simple sentence made Elizabeth sad. Her memories of Easter as a child involved coloring a few eggs with dye her mother had made from various plants. One year they had blown out the yolks and made egg ornaments to sell in the shop. "There's a first time for everything," she said, summoning her brightest smile for the children.

They trooped inside with Bill, Mary, and Martha, and seated themselves at the old wooden table, where Martha served apple juice, vegetable sticks, and crackers with cheese to tide everyone over until mealtime. When they had finished nibbling, Martha tossed a large vinyl tablecloth over the table in case of spills.

Next, she set out a dozen large coffee cups filled with colored egg dye. "I've already made the dyes," she repeated. "These are homemade, so they take more work to get the brighter, deeper colors. You'll have to choose your color, dip and let them dry, dip and let them dry a bunch of times."

"How did you make the dye?" Marlee asked.

"I boiled water and added whatever I wanted to use to get the right colors," Martha told her. "Purple cabbage gives you sky blue on white eggs, green on brown eggs. Yellow onion skins make orange. Let's see…the spice called turmeric gives you a spectacular yellow, and red onion skins make lavender-pink. To get deeper purple, I use shredded beets. Grape juice makes a deeper blue. Red's a hard color to come up with. I had to use combinations of some of the other things. But I've practiced on my children and their children over the years, so I've got it down now."

She handed around spoons, and everyone took an egg. Elizabeth had set Timmy on her lap when they came in, so he'd be high enough to see. Marlee perched beside them, looking far more excited than Elizabeth had expected her to. Briefly, she thought of Sheila Canner, who surely would have sneered at coloring eggs.

Marlee chose the red onion skins and carefully set an egg down on a spoon and submerged it. Elizabeth helped Timmy, but they both got their fingers stained when he dropped his egg into the yellow with a big splash that made everyone laugh.

Bill chose purple cabbage to make light blue, and tried a brown egg in the same dye, hoping for green. Martha herself worked on making an orange egg from the yellow onion skins. After a few rounds of dyeing and drying peppered with light-hearted conversation and good-natured teasing, everyone's eggs were beginning to take on lovely colors. Some of them switched out for another egg in a different hue, and some, like Bill, diligently worked to deepen the shade of their colors of choice.

In less than an hour, the dozen eggs that had started as white and a few light brown boasted gorgeous hues. When they were all dry, Martha produced old cloth napkins and added a little bit of cooking oil to each one. "Now rub the oil on your eggs," she instructed. "You can dab at first, but then I want you to rub-a-dub-dub all over until your whole egg is shiny."

Timmy rubbed with such vigor that Elizabeth had to calm him a bit, fearing he would crack his egg. Everyone else did as Martha instructed, and soon the eggs took on a beautiful shiny finish. She produced an antique woven Easter basket filled with pink paper Easter grass, and as each egg was completed, it was laid in the basket.

"This will be the perfect centerpiece for our Easter dinner table," she proclaimed.

"I wish we had more eggs to dye," Marlee said wistfully.

Martha smiled. "I wish that every year. But that's what makes it special, right?" Looking around, she addressed the whole group. "We have about an hour yet until dinner for those who might like to go out and play for a while."

"Meeee!" Timmy hollered, scrambling down off Elizabeth's lap.

"Wait," Marlee said before he could slam out the kitchen door. "Miss Elizabeth and I are coming too."

Elizabeth felt warmed by the girl's automatic assumption that they were a team. Granted, it probably took two of them to keep up with the little boy's energy, but she liked it just the same.

Bill and Mary stayed inside the house with Martha to get the meal preparations completed, while Elizabeth and Marlee followed Timmy outside to play, letting Pal and Tink out in the process. Tink ambled around the yard for a moment and then found a patch of sunshine. Pal spied one of his tennis balls, dashed over to it, and came back to spit it out at Elizabeth's feet. Then he did an elaborate play bow, begging her to throw it for him.

Laughing at the dog's antics, Elizabeth picked up the ball and threw it far down the yard. Pal tore after it, snatched it in midbounce and came racing back.

"He's bringing you the ball!" Marlee said, as Timmy clapped his hands.

"He'll do that as long as anyone is willing to throw it," Elizabeth assured her.

"I twy? I twy?" Timmy demanded.

"Sure." Elizabeth smiled at him. "Just pick up the ball and throw it."

Timmy was thrilled when he realized that Pal would retrieve a ball and deposit it at his feet. Even though the little boy's throws were wild and erratic and occasionally went only a few feet, Pal obligingly played fetch.

"How's Blossom this morning?" Elizabeth asked Marlee. She had not forgotten that, although she had solved the mystery of who the apple-snitcher was, the girl and her family were in need of help. She was still trying to come up with a way to do so without offending Marlee's pride or making her feel less than capable.

Marlee shrugged. "She's okay. She really liked the feed you brought. It'll be better in a few months when there's more for her to eat." She brightened. "Plus, if some of the contacts you helped me make this morning come through, I'll be babysitting and making some money to buy her feed again." Then her face fell. "But I figure she only has maybe six more months of production before I'll have to sell her and buy a fresh goat." That meant one whose milk production was more recent and whose milk wasn't drying up. The girl must have learned that from her computer research.

As gently as she could, Elizabeth said, "I'm not sure you're even going to get that long if Blossom's diet doesn't improve soon."

Marlee looked stricken. Silence fell between Elizabeth and the teen. She very much feared her words had been a mistake.

Marlee's eyes filled with tears, but she knuckled them away fiercely. "I'm doing my best to change that," she said in a low tone, sounding defensive.

"I know," Elizabeth said evenly, striving to sound sympathetic. "If you don't mind me asking, have you kept track of how much you've spent on her altogether? I'm wondering if it truly is better to keep a goat or just to buy goat's milk, I suppose."

"It might be cheaper to buy it," Marlee admitted. "I didn't think it was going to cost so much to buy her and then to feed her through the winter. I don't mind the clean-up work, but just getting enough straw to help keep her warm has been expensive, and that wasn't even on my first list."

"Did you know we have goats too?" It wasn't an idle question, but to Marlee, it probably seemed like a natural turn for the conversation to take.

"You do? Dairy goats?"

Elizabeth laughed. "We used to when I was your age, but we have nothing so useful anymore. Want to come see them? Their names are Wynken, Blynken, and Nod. My mother rescued them from a small petting zoo before she got sick, and we couldn't bear to get rid of them."

"What happened to your mom?"

Elizabeth drew a deep breath. "She had cancer. She died a little more than a year ago."

"My dad died of an overdose," Marlee said baldly. "Mom thinks I don't know, but I heard somebody talking about it at the funeral." Her lip quivered. "I don't care. Sometimes he wasn't very nice anyway."

Elizabeth could hear the pain in the teenager's voice. "It's hard to lose a parent, especially at your age. Even when sometimes you think they could have done a better job." She fell silent, feeling enormously underequipped for the job God had laid on her to try to help this struggling child. Finally, she said quietly, "I think losing a mom or dad is a terrible thing. You lose the memories they carried, and your own fade as time passes. It can be difficult to know who you are."

"And who you're supposed to be," Marlee said. "I just know I have to try to help my mom."

Elizabeth tried to smile, although she wanted to cry for the child thrust into an adult role too soon. "That's an admirable statement."

As the little goats began to amble across the pasture toward them, Marlee's attention was diverted. "Wow. They're little."

"They're full-grown Pygmy goats."

"But you don't milk them? Or eat them?"

Elizabeth choked on a laugh that bubbled up out of nowhere. "No. We just take care of them. I guess they're pets, although really Blynken is the only one who comes willingly to be handled."

"I'm glad you don't eat them. But..." She looked puzzled as she called for Timmy to come see the goats with them. "They don't do anything?"

"They entertain us." Elizabeth shrugged helplessly. "That's about it."

"Like your dogs," Marlee said. "I always wanted a dog, but Mom said we couldn't afford an animal that didn't do anything."

Elizabeth thought of everything intangible their dogs gave them. She thought of the copious tears she'd shed into Pal's thick coat after her mother died, and of how desperately she'd needed the simple routines of caring for her mother's animals to get her through the darkest days until her sisters had arrived for good. "Dogs and other pets give us love and companionship," she said. "They make us laugh. They need us. They teach us what it means to be responsible for another life that is dependent on us. All those things are important."

"But dogs cost money," Marlee said gloomily.

"They do," Elizabeth admitted.

"Sorta sounds like Timmy," the girl observed, a grin lighting her face unexpectedly. "He makes us laugh. He needs us, and he's dependent on us to care for him. And he totally costs money."

Elizabeth chuckled. "The only difference between Timmy and Pal is that Timmy will grow out of it."

"I hope," Marlee said, and they both laughed.

They arrived at the spacious pen where the goats were kept when no one was home. Blynken came over to the fence and stuck his nose through the upper space between the bars of the fence. Her mother had learned the hard way several years earlier that the smaller goats needed wire lining the lower bars to keep them from strolling about the lawn and decimating her flower beds.

Wynken and Nod followed, although they appeared far less enthusiastic about the squealing Timmy and maintained their distance from his little reaching hands.

Elizabeth kept the fence between them, since Blynken liked to jump up on visitors, and Timmy was a bit small even for a Pygmy goat that was slightly bigger than the border collie who'd walked along with them.

Timmy climbed up a rung and leaned through the fence to pet him, giggling when the wether licked his face with his long tongue. "Yuckeeeeeee!" he said.

"These goats don't smell so bad," Marlee said. "Why not?"

"Blossom smells?" Elizabeth asked, concerned. A healthy doe shouldn't smell bad, and she had assumed the girl was used to the normal odors any animal emitted from time to time.

"No, Mrs. Fischer's goats smelled," Marlee explained. "Really bad."

"Oh." Elizabeth had to suppress a smile. "Mrs. Fischer has male goats, called billies or bucks, that she keeps for breeding. They usually do have quite an odor. Blynken and Nod are wethers. That means they've been fixed so they can't reproduce, and that's why they don't smell."

"I have a lot to learn about goats, don't I?" Marlee asked. "Some of it's not in books. Like the smell."

Elizabeth laughed. "Hands-on experience is always a good follow-up even if you do start with books or Google research." Then, as if the thought had just occurred to her, she said, "I have an idea." She held her breath, waiting for the girl to respond. Would Marlee balk at allowing anyone to help her family, or would she accept assistance from the Classens and perhaps, eventually, others?

"What's your idea?" Marlee asked, when Elizabeth hesitated.

Elizabeth pointed to the fields beyond the little paddock. "Your house is only about a mile or so that way. Did you realize that?"

"Really?" Marlee climbed up the fence and craned her neck to stare into the distance. "I think I can see our roof! That's not so far."

"I was thinking that poor Blossom must be very lonely all by herself. I know you were thinking of getting a second goat"— although she hoped the girl was seeing the economic impracticability of that—"but it might be better for her to have company in the meantime."

Elizabeth saw the flare of hope in Marlee's eyes as understanding dawned, although the teen quickly schooled her expression to careful nonchalance. "But how would I feed and milk her?"

"You wouldn't need to worry about feed," Elizabeth said. "We've got plenty of browse and we feed alfalfa and other grain or pellets every day. One more goat isn't going to make much of a difference. Milking might be a problem. You'd have to hike over here every morning, and evening too, if you're still milking twice a day, and care for her. Mary usually starts morning chores around six thirty."

"I could do that!" Marlee said. "And I could give you money for feed once I start getting jobs."

Elizabeth appreciated Marlee's work ethic. The girl was not assuming this would be a charitable offer. "You could." Although she imagined Marlee's contribution wouldn't begin to pay for the feed and care she intended to lavish on the pitiful little doe. "This way, you'll be able to keep Blossom healthy and well fed until you decide whether you want to continue with your goat-raising or just begin buying milk."

Marlee nodded. "I have to look at all my costs first. But you might be right. If I can get work, it would be a lot easier to just buy milk."

"And you'd make some money from the sale of the goat if you decide to sell," Elizabeth reminded her. Striving to present all the options and not make the decision for the child, she added, "Or you might be able to make a deal with Rachel to breed her when she comes into heat again. Give Rachel one of the kids as payment, and if there are more, and there usually are twins or triplets, then you could sell the others or add to your herd."

Marlee wrinkled her nose. "I don't really want to get into goat breeding. I don't like the idea of selling animals. Plus I don't have enough space for more."

Elizabeth smiled, relieved that the teenager was cognizant of that reality. "Then perhaps it's better to sell your doe now before you have to deal with all of that."

The sound of a car coming up the lane interrupted their conversation. Elizabeth shaded her eyes from the bright sunshine. It was a big, dark sedan. She was pretty sure the pastor and his wife drove compact cars. It was probably John.

CHAPTER SIXTEEN

W e'd better head back to the house," she told the children. "I see more company coming."

Reluctantly, the children said farewell to Blynken and his siblings. As they headed past the other outbuildings along the path back to the yard and house, they could hear the little goat emitting funny bleating sounds that made Marlee giggle. It did Elizabeth good to see the girl smiling and acting her age. She'd been so reserved when they'd first met.

John was just walking up to the porch when they reached him. He wore pressed khaki pants and a blue window-pane checked shirt that made his eyes look as blue as the spring sky. "Hello, Elizabeth," he said. "Thanks for inviting me to dinner. Who are your friends?"

Elizabeth smiled, wondering if he could possibly look any more handsome. Then, recalling his question and realizing she was staring like she was Marlee's age, she blushed and introduced the two children. Surprisingly, the gregarious little boy clung to Marlee's legs and acted very shy all of a sudden.

"Our dad was big and tall like you," Marlee said to John. "My brother doesn't really remember him, and he's not much used to men."

John grinned. "That's okay. My son is grown up now, so I'm not much used to little boys. Maybe we can get used to each other together."

Elizabeth was fascinated. John was usually slightly reserved, but when he winked at Timmy, her heart melted. Oh, how she wished John didn't feel so threatened by her faith...no, *threatened* wasn't the right word. It was more as if he was indifferent. He certainly didn't have the relationship with Christ that she did. And he did not appear to need it or understand why she did. She wondered, not for the first time, how on earth he had coped with his wife's illness and passing. Did he not need faith to lean on during those dark days?

Her thoughts were interrupted by Pal, always alert to an opportunity to chase his beloved ball. The border collie came trotting over with a tennis ball in his mouth and dropped it at John's feet. John picked it up and threw it. "There you go, Pal."

For Timmy, it was as if the sun had shone down and revealed John as a friend with a capital *F*. Shyness melted like ice in summer.

"Pal wikes da baw," he said, coming out from behind his sister's legs. "You fwow 'gain?"

John looked momentarily puzzled by the garbled speech, but then his brow cleared, and he smiled. "Sure. I'll throw it again. I know Pal likes to play ball."

As he threw another one for Pal, and Timmy shrieked with glee at the way the dog raced after the ball, the kitchen door opened. Mary emerged, with Bill close behind.

"We've been dismissed," she announced. "The table is set, everything that could be done early is done, and Martha kicked us out. We'll eat as soon as the pastor and Mrs. Nagle arrive. They were planning to take communion to some of the church members at Morningside Nursing Home after church."

As Bill and Mary walked up the path toward the chicken coop, talking about a few more things that still needed to be done before they could move the birds after the meal, Marlee touched Elizabeth's arm. "Miss Elizabeth, if I wanted to move Blossom over here to your place, how would I do that? Should I walk her along the roads or across the fields?"

"Oh my, Marlee, you don't need to walk her anywhere," Elizabeth said, startled by the very idea. "We have an old livestock trailer we can hitch up." She raised her voice. "Bill?"

Halfway up the slope, Bill stopped and turned. "Yeah?"

"If we needed you to, could you help us hitch the stock trailer up?"

"Sure thing." He raised a hand and gave her a thumbs-up. "What are you planning?"

"Marlee may want to bring her goat over here." She imagined that Mary had explained much of the children's story to him.

"No problem. I'll drive it over and back if you like," he offered.

Elizabeth appreciated the offer. The stock trailer was a bit of a pain if you weren't used to it. Her mother had been much more adept at backing up and turning wide enough with the trailer attached than Elizabeth was, and she was pretty sure neither Martha nor Mary had ever handled the old thing. "Thanks," she called.

"I'm not going to be able to repay you, you know." Marlee was looking at the ground, stubbing a toe in the dirt.

"Oh, honey, we don't expect you to," Elizabeth said. She dared to put an arm over the girl's shoulders, and when the rigidity faded and Marlee leaned against her, she almost felt her heart clench. "Friends help each other out, and I feel like you and I are going to be famous friends."

It was just the right thing to say. Marlee chuckled. "Famous friends," she repeated. "I like that."

They watched John teach Timmy how to throw for a few minutes.

"That's really good for him," Marlee said. "I don't have much time to play with him like that."

Another car came up the driveway a few minutes later. The driver parked under a tree near the driveway beside John's sedan, and the Nagles climbed out of their black Toyota.

"Hello, friends," Maida Nagle called. She was a tiny, cheery woman perfectly suited for the life of a minister's wife. Her husband was tall and burly and could have lifted her in one hand, Elizabeth thought whimsically.

Martha had heard the car and come out on the porch. "Welcome to our home," she called. "Elizabeth, do you want to round up everyone for the meal?"

"I'll go get Miss Mary and her friend," Marlee said. She whirled and ran up the hill.

John and Timmy gave the ball one final toss and came toward them.

"Hi," Timmy said. "We was pwayin' baw."

"I see that," Mrs. Nagle said.

"This is Timmy," Elizabeth said. "As you can see, he lacks the shy gene. His sister Marlee just went up the hill to get Mary and Bill."

"Oh, I saw her with you in church this morning," Maida said. "Are you related?"

John said, "Come on, Tim, why don't we go wash our hands?" and took the little boy on ahead into the house, freeing Elizabeth to explain the children's story to the Nagles.

When she had finished, the pastor said, "Perhaps we can call on them and see if there are any needs the church could help with. Why don't you and I discuss it further next week?"

"That would be wonderful," Elizabeth said gratefully. She would be glad to have the support of the church community to assist in creating a safety net for the family.

Mary, Marlee, and Bill came into view then, and they all went into the house together.

Everyone took turns washing their hands. Elizabeth and Mary filled water glasses and helped Martha set the food on trivets on the table. Martha had outdone herself with a ham baked in a brown sugar mustard glaze, four-cheese scalloped potatoes, peas with pancetta and shallots, broiled asparagus spears with lemon, deviled eggs, macaroni and cheese, and a traditional Paska bread.

Martha looked at Pastor Nagle. "Pastor, would you please return thanks?"

Pastor Nagle nodded and said, "Let's join hands."

Timmy looked wide-eyed around the table as they all clasped each other's hands. "This is fun!" he announced, to a general ripple of laughter.

"Let us pray," the pastor said. "Dear Lord, we thank You for the bounty before us and the skillful hands of our sister Martha who prepared it. We thank You that all of us were able to come together here to share Easter dinner, where we celebrate the miracle of the resurrection. Christ's rebirth is what creates our hope for eternal life..."

As he went on, Elizabeth listened to the prayer through the ears of John, who might not share her amazement at the true miracle of Christ's death for each person present, and through the ears of the children, who may never have experienced the comfort of prayer before. As the minister concluded and most of them murmured "Amen," she tacked on a hasty prayer request of her own: *Let me be a human example of Your grace and mercy, Father. Amen.*

The ham, macaroni, and scalloped potatoes were too hot to pass, so Martha dished portions onto plates and passed those, while they sent the other dishes around the table to be served.

Elizabeth looked around as bowls and platters moved from hand to hand and the chatter of multiple conversations grew in volume, and she realized that during the past few days, something had changed.

She had changed.

She had forged a connection with Marlee, one she was enjoying, and she even thought she'd started at least a distant friendship with Sheila Canner. She loved the conversations she and Marlee had shared, and how interested the girl was in soaking up goat care knowledge. She wondered if Marlee was too old to join a 4-H group. Surely there were some for middle-school-aged kids. Maybe, she thought, they could look into something like that.

She remembered the longing in the girl's voice when she had talked about wishing she could have a dog. Maybe they could look into puppy raising for a service organization. There were groups that used kids for that. And if Elizabeth was willing to partner with her and assume any costs, if there were any, perhaps that would be a possibility.

She could imagine herself working with Marlee, or other young people for that matter, through a mentoring or even a tutoring program. It would be a whole new avenue for her, but she found herself excited by the possibilities.

On her left side, John leaned over and murmured, "You look like you're cooking up an idea."

Elizabeth turned and smiled at him. "Maybe I am."

"You're thinking of ways to help these kids, aren't you?"

"Perhaps. Why do you think that?"

John's smile grew wider. "Because that's who you are."

As she turned to take the Paska bread from Marlee, his words reverberated in her head. *Yes,* she thought, *one who serves others: that is definitely who I am.*

It felt like a very good thing.

A NOTE FROM THE AUTHOR

Hello, friends!

Writing an Easter-themed story for this series brought back all kinds of wonderful memories from my own life. When I was a child, my brother, cousins, and I waved palms with other children in our church during a Palm Sunday processional. My childhood piano teacher was also our choir director, and I think all of us were a little afraid she might use the palms on us if we didn't perform to her satisfaction! But to this day, hearing "The Palms" by Jean Baptiste Faure brings tears to my eyes as I relive that solemn procession.

Fast-forward several decades later, when my younger daughter became the piano accompanist for the high school concert choir, the same group in which I once sang. For months prior to the spring concert, the magnificent piano accompaniment to Handel's "The Hallelujah Chorus" reverberated through our home. On the day of the concert, I invariably felt sick to my stomach, primal terror gripping me as I prayed for her flying fingers to successfully manage the intricate piece of music. I could only relax when it ended. I'm happy to report that she never made any detectable errors, although she assures me there were a few glitches.

As you travel through the Lenten season toward the cross and the promise of the Resurrection, I hope you enjoy the Classen sisters' Easter story.

Warmly,
Anne Marie

ABOUT THE AUTHOR

Anne Marie Rodgers has written over twenty inspirational and inspirational mystery novels for Guideposts Books and over five dozen books in her publishing career, including a number of bestsellers and award winners. Anne Marie is deeply committed to giving a voice to the world's animals who cannot speak for themselves. She has worked in emergency veterinary care and volunteered with wildlife rehabilitation, canine training and foster care, service dog puppy raising, and neonatal orphaned kitten rescue. She currently works in administration for a day veterinary practice. Anne Marie and her husband delight in their family, which includes three grandchildren, another on the way, and a varying number of furry family members. In 2019, they adopted a blind, diabetic Labrador retriever who refuses to believe he is handicapped.

BARN FINDS

Vintage Italian Spelter
Clock with Fauns

You walk into the barn and stroll around, looking for something special for your grandmother's milestone birthday. She collects clocks. Elizabeth hurries over to greet you, a warm smile on her face. "May I help you find something?"

Just then, you see it. It's a mantel clock—and what an unforgettable item it is!

"What can you tell me about this clock?" you ask.

Elizabeth's blue eyes warm. "Isn't this a lovely piece? An elaborate old clock like this might not be to everyone's taste, but in the right setting, it would be a fascinating conversation starter on your mantel or it might command a position of interest on a side table. I believe it's twenty-four inches high, and as you can see, it stands on four feet on a solid marble base." She touches the base with a slender finger. "It was made in Italy, according to the original owner, and is covered in the gilt you see here. On either side of the clock face, you see these hoofed fauns posing." She paused to draw a breath. "The clock face itself features Roman numerals and is glass covered. It is topped with four gilt spires and a taller central gilt and enamel spire."

"Does it tell time?" you ask.

Elizabeth shakes her head regretfully. "The clock does not work although it comes with the original key. A clever tradesperson skilled in restoring old clocks might be able to restore this to working condition for you, and I know someone locally I would trust with a restoration process. We're asking six hundred and fifty dollars for it."

You suck in a deep breath. This would be a perfect gift for your grandmother, but that's a little more than you were prepared to spend, even though she's the most special woman in the world and deserves every penny of that and more. Plus, you've still got to get it repaired. "Would you take four hundred?"

A gleam enters Elizabeth's eye, and the two of you prepare to bargain.

FRESH FROM MARTHA'S KITCHEN

Martha's Strawberry Bread

Ingredients

4 cups fresh strawberries, 2 sliced and 2 pureed

3⅛ cups all-purpose flour

2 cups white sugar

1 tablespoon ground cinnamon

1 teaspoon salt

1 teaspoon baking soda

1 teaspoon vanilla

¾ cup vegetable oil

4 eggs, beaten

1¼ cups chopped pecans

Instructions

Preheat oven to 350 degrees F (175 degrees C).

Butter and flour two 9 × 5-inch loaf pans.

Place sliced strawberries in medium-sized bowl. Sprinkle lightly with sugar and set aside.

Combine flour, sugar, cinnamon, salt, and baking soda in large bowl; mix well. Blend vanilla, oil, eggs, and strawberry puree into sliced strawberries. Add strawberry mixture to flour mixture, blending until dry ingredients are just moistened. Stir in pecans. Divide batter into pans.

Bake in preheated oven until a tester inserted in center comes out clean, 45 to 50 minutes (test each loaf separately).

Let cool in pans on wire rack for 10 minutes. Turn loaves out of pans. Allow to cool completely before slicing.

Notes:

- One Bundt pan may be used for presentation purposes.
- If berries are very ripe, cut sugar back to 1½ cups.
- Slice and serve with a dollop of whipped cream and a strawberry garnish for a pretty dessert.

Read on for a sneak peek of another exciting book
in the Mysteries of Lancaster County series!

Lilacs, Lavender, and Lies
by Leslie Gould

Mary Classen Baxter stopped at the window on the landing of the home she shared with her two older sisters, Elizabeth and Martha. Outside, rain fell on the emerald-green fields of Lancaster County. It was the last day of April, and she could only hope that meant the rain would end. She longed for May flowers more than anything.

The smell of bacon and toast made her stomach growl, and she started down the stairs. Sure enough, she was the last one up, which wasn't unusual. Martha stood at the stove, and Elizabeth was pulling the blender out of the cupboard.

"Good morning." Mary tried to use her cheeriest voice. "Smells good."

Martha continued to turn the bacon. "Would you set the table? We'll eat in just a moment."

"I'm making myself a green smoothie." Elizabeth had started a new health kick a few days ago. She turned toward Mary. "Want one?"

Mary shook her head. "Not today." Honestly, she wouldn't ever want a green smoothie although she might drink a fruit one.

Elizabeth winced as she placed the blender on the counter.

"Are you all right?" Mary asked.

She nodded. "I think I just tweaked my back." Elizabeth had back pain the evening before too. "Probably from moving that hutch yesterday."

Mary felt a twinge of guilt. It had been her idea to move the heavy piece of furniture to the front section of the shop to display Mother's Day gifts. "I'm sorry," she said. "I should have called Bill to help me."

"It's not your fault," Elizabeth answered. "I could have said no."

"Well, we all should probably be more careful about what we move. None of us are getting any younger." Martha pulled a tray of muffins for the quilting circle from the oven and then made eye contact with Elizabeth. "You should get that checked out though. The sooner the better."

"I'm fine." Elizabeth chuckled. "Like you said, none of us are getting younger—which means we're getting older. Starting with me."

Mary set the table as Elizabeth filled the blender and then turned it on. The loud whir ended any conversation. Finally Elizabeth turned it off as Mary put the last of the forks on the table.

As Mary poured herself a cup of coffee, she said, "After the quilting circle, I think I'll buy some flowers." Maybe that would cheer her up on this dreary day.

"Where?" Elizabeth poured her smoothie into a glass.

"Franz Farms." Mary wrapped her hands around the mug.

"I've heard good things about the owner," Martha said.

"Oh?" Mary hadn't heard a thing about the owner.

"He's a widower." Elizabeth put the blender pitcher in the sink and filled it with water. "A handsome one," she teased.

Mary grinned. "Believe me, I'm going to go look at the flowers. And nothing else."

Two hours later, after the sisters readied their business, Secondhand Blessings, for the day, Martha put out the lemon poppy seed muffins she'd made that morning while Mary set up the quilting frame. Elizabeth carried a folding chair but stopped abruptly, her hand going to the small of her back again.

"You probably should go to the doctor." Mary took the chair.

Elizabeth shook her head. "I'll see how I feel tomorrow."

Rachel Fischer, who led the quilting circle, and her daughter Phoebe came through the front door, putting an end to the conversation.

"*Guten morgen!*" Rachel called out.

After a round of greetings, Mary said, "Phoebe, we're so excited to have you work for us for a couple of hours this afternoon." Rachel was their usual extra hand, but it was the first time for Phoebe. "Thank you for being willing to help us out."

The young woman's face lit up with joy. Everyone—no matter how young or old—wanted to be acknowledged. But no one showed their appreciation for it as clearly as Phoebe. The young woman had Down syndrome, had recently turned twenty-one, and was the heart of her family.

She hurried to Mary to receive her welcome hug. Mary knew most Amish weren't very affectionate, but Phoebe was. As Mary hugged her, she said, "I'll go over your tasks for you to do after the quilting circle."

"Great!" she answered as she hugged Mary back. "I will do everything you tell me."

Mary chuckled. She would, including crossing every *t* and dotting every *i*.

"Luke started a new job today too," Phoebe said.

"Oh?"

Phoebe turned toward her mother. "Where is Luke working?"

"Franz Farms."

Martha nudged Mary, who ignored her sister and asked, "Is he working in the nursery?"

"They have started some sort of living history section," Rachel said. "He will be working there and probably in the nursery too."

The historical section sounded fascinating. Mary would check it out when she stopped by the farm.

Mary and Martha waited on customers while Elizabeth joined the quilters, although Elizabeth spent some of her time standing. A couple of times Mary saw her rubbing her side and once her abdomen.

At noon Rachel ended the quilting session, and everyone said their goodbyes. Phoebe had brought her lunch, and once she finished, Mary showed Phoebe her tasks. Rehanging the vintage clothes. Dusting the items in the housewares section. Tidying the books. They were all tasks that Phoebe could do by herself, tasks that she took seriously. Tasks that freed Mary, Martha, and Elizabeth to do other things.

Business slowed, and Elizabeth and Martha went to the house for lunch while Mary waited on the few customers who came in. One was a tourist who was looking for "anything" that came from an Amish home. "Any kind of item," she said. "Whatever you have."

"We have quilted pot holders made by Amish women, and aprons and tea towels."

"I already have those items. I'd really like something different."

Mary walked her over to the pie plates and pointed to a glass one. "This came from an Amish yard sale."

The woman wrinkled her nose. "I have one just like that at home."

"All right." Mary stepped over to the measuring cups and picked up a metal one. "This came from the same sale."

The woman laughed. "My mother had one just like it."

"How about this wooden rolling pin?" Mary held it up.

The woman reached for it. "I'll take it."

Soon after, Martha returned. "Elizabeth's resting," she said.

"Should I check on her?" Mary asked.

Martha shook her head. "Why would you? She's resting."

Mary crossed her arms. "Are you sure she's all right?"

"She's fine." Martha sighed. "Look, we're all getting older. We're apt to have more bad days than we used to."

"All right." Mary didn't feel as if she was getting older, but she didn't say so.

"Go get something to eat," Martha said.

"I think I'll run over to Franz Farms now instead," Mary said. She told Phoebe goodbye and grabbed her purse. She hoped her sweater would be warm enough.

The rain had stopped. Perhaps the April showers were finally coming to an end. "I'll be back soon," she called as she dashed out the door.

Mary was happy it was the last day of April. May had always been her favorite month. True, the number-one reason was that her birthday was May 9, but there were lots of other reasons too. She loved making May Day baskets as a child and when her children were young too. And then there was Mother's Day, which her birthday sometimes fell on. She never minded sharing the day with her mom—in fact, it made her feel special. And then, when she became a mother, Mother's Day was extra special. This year would be her first as a grandmother.

There was also the end of the school year when she was growing up, filled with field trips during her elementary school years and outings with friends when she was in high school. She enjoyed it for the same reason when her kids were growing up. May was filled with special school events—and then the last day of school. She loved having her children, Michael and Jennifer, home for the summer and spending time at the swimming pool or park or going on hikes and bike rides.

But what truly made the month her favorite, even more so than all of the important dates and events, were the flowers. Often, as had happened this year, tulips were still in bloom along with the lilacs. And the dogwood trees too. Next, the azaleas and clematis and rhododendron and tree peonies showed their glory.

By the end of the month, the lavender came on, along with daylilies, delphinium, and poppies.

Mary loved flowers. Loved, loved, loved them. They were what initially inspired her to learn how to paint. Flowers were the Lord's artwork, along with all of creation. But flowers were the showstoppers. She found them absolutely essential to her spiritual and mental and emotional well-being, along with her creativity.

Which was exactly why she was headed to Franz Farms. As she turned off the highway toward the farm, Mary expected it to be quiet on a Thursday afternoon. But when she eased her car around the corner to the parking lot, she was shocked to see it nearly full. And not just with cars and buggies. There was a panel truck and three yellow school buses parked lengthwise, taking up multiple parking spaces each.

She finally found a place to park in the very last row. She grabbed her purse, climbed out, closed her door, and pressed her key fob to lock it. Then she started toward the sign that read ENTRANCE. She was soon on an asphalt pathway lined with trees and shrubs. She felt as if she were entering a hidden world. She passed under an arbor with clematis growing over the top and then, ahead, was a sign that read FRANZ FARMS, EST. 1717.

Wow! There was a lot more history to the place than she'd expected. As she continued on the path, a customer came toward her, pushing a cart of plants.

Soon, wild rosebushes lined the path, and to the left she could see fields and buildings in the distance. To the right there was also a wood.

Ahead, where the pathway forked, was a sign that read Nursery with an arrow that pointed to the right and another one that read Living History and pointed to the left. She glanced up the trail toward the nursery and saw a young woman with auburn hair tucked under a prayer *kapp* and wearing an old-fashioned outfit chatting with a young man, maybe in his midtwenties, pulling a wagon with big rubber tires and several shelves that were all packed with plants. The paved pathway was so well maintained that it was easy to maneuver the wagon on it.

Someone from the history side yelled, "We're ready!" And then Luke Fischer stepped into view, yelling, "Alison!" Luke disappeared without seeing Mary—or at least without acknowledging her.

The young woman giggled and said, "Gotta go."

The young man, who had dark hair and eyes, gave the woman a dazzling grin. "See you soon."

She waved and hurried away, disappearing behind a lilac tree, the white blossoms just starting to bloom, much to Mary's delight. She followed the young man to the right, breathing in the earthy scent of rich soil and the wet woods as she walked.

Ahead was the nursery building, with walls of windows. She stepped inside. A woman at the counter, about her own age, wearing a floral cape dress and a kapp, smiled as she entered.

Mary smiled back and then turned her attention to the vegetable plants lining one side of the structure and the flower plants, both annual and perennial, lining the other. There was a small gift shop area near the counter, where seeds, pots, trowels, gloves, and those sorts of things were sold.

The young man with the wagon approached an older man, probably in his early fifties, who was dressed Plain with a straw hat, black suspenders, a forest-green shirt, and black pants. He had on a good pair of leather boots that appeared expensive.

"Ward, it took you a lot longer to haul your second load up here than your first." The older man seemed to be teasing.

The young man was as serious as could be. "Hi, Gabriel. I was talking with Alison," he said. "But just for a minute, I promise. She was on her break."

"No worries," Gabriel said, smiling at him. "Does Alison seem to like her job?"

Ward smiled back. "As a matter of fact, she does."

"Good," Gabriel said. Mary wondered if he was the owner Elizabeth and Martha had joked about. He had sandy-colored hair, streaked with gray, and a trimmed beard, which most likely meant he was Mennonite and not Amish. "What do you have for me?"

Ward answered, "Vegetables. Peppers, tomatoes, and corn. Leafy greens. Cantaloupe and watermelon." He lifted the top flat. "Here's a sampling."

The older man examined the plants. "Are they out of your greenhouses?"

Ward nodded.

"All right," the man said. "I'll take them." He gestured toward a cleared table. "We'll put them over here."

Mary realized she'd been staring and quickly started walking toward the annuals. She'd already sown lettuce and spinach seeds, but she hadn't planted tomatoes or peppers. Perhaps she could get some here. She'd look after Ward had displayed his plants.

She stopped at the snapdragons. They always made her think of her mother, who used to line the walkway with them. She picked up a couple of plants and continued on to the Sweet William.

"Need a cart?" It was the older man. He was just a few feet from her, pushing a cart her way.

"Thank you." She smiled.

He turned the cart around so it was positioned right for her, bumping it against her hip as he did. His face reddened, and he said, "Excuse me."

"No worries." Mary put the snapdragons into the cart.

He extended his hand. "Gabriel Franz."

She took his hand. "Mary Baxter."

As he released her hand, he asked, "Are you new to the area?"

"No." She grasped the handle of the cart. "I'm rather old to the area, although I've just recently returned." She explained that she was a Classen sister and had moved back to Lancaster County to help run Secondhand Blessings.

"I know exactly where that is," Gabriel said. "I've been in there a few times, although not recently. Welcome back."

"Thank you." She didn't recognize him from high school, but chances were he went to one of the Mennonite schools in the area. "This is a lovely farm," she said. "I've seen the sign on the highway but had no idea you were hiding such a gem back here."

"I've really been working on it this last year, as far as the living history side of it," Gabriel said. "I hope others find it appealing too."

"I'm impressed that it goes back all the way to 1717." Mary brushed her hands on her jeans. "Your ancestors came over really early."

He nodded. "And none of them, in the last three hundred years, threw anything away." He laughed. "I'm beginning to think that all of them were certifiable hoarders."

Mary laughed with him. "You must have some amazing antiques then."

"I do," he said. "Lots of furniture, kitchen items, and other home furnishings—like butter churns and molds and irons and crockery. And tools and farm equipment too. And books and hymnals and Bibles."

"Any original buildings?"

He shook his head. "But the cabin and outbuildings were all built from lumber milled on the property in the early 1800s. I had so many items, I was able to recreate a general store and blacksmith shop too, plus there's an open market area. It really adds to the 'living history.'"

"Goodness," Mary said. "I'll have to take a look."

"Please do," he answered. "But you might want to wait until two thirty. That's when the school children leave."

"Perfect." Mary grinned. "I'll get my plants and then mosey on over there."

Gabriel returned the grin and then headed back over to the table where Ward was setting up plants.

"Gabriel Franz!"

Startled, Mary turned toward the entrance of the greenhouse. A mountain of a man, who looked to be in his sixties with a shaved head and bulging muscles practically bursting out of the sleeves of his T-shirt, stood with his arms crossed over his chest.

"Franz," the man bellowed, "your land wasn't intended for this kind of business."

"Terry." Gabriel stepped toward the man, his hand extended. "It's been a while. Good to see you. What can I do for you?"

"Stop attracting all of these people to your farm. Tourists and now schoolchildren. Buses full!" The man's dark eyes were livid. "Selling plants is one thing, but begging people to come visit your living history museum is another venture entirely. I've called the county and reported you."

"I have all of the necessary permits," Gabriel responded. "It's legal."

"Well, it's not neighborly!" Terry shouted. "You're going to pay for this." He reminded Mary of Shrek, defending his swamp.

Gabriel was a foot away from the man. Mary wondered if Terry might attack him, and for a moment she considered stepping between the two.

But before she could, she heard a buzzing sound, and then Gabriel pulled a radio from his belt.

"*Ja,*" he said.

A fuzzy voice, rather high pitched, yelled, "There's been an accident by the cabin. A child fell into a deep hole!"

A NOTE FROM THE EDITORS

We hope you enjoyed this volume of the Mysteries of Lancaster County series, created by the Books and Inspirational Media Division of Guideposts. We are a nonprofit organization that touches millions of lives every day through products and services that inspire, encourage, help you grow in your faith, and celebrate God's love in every aspect of your daily life.

Thank you for making a difference with your purchase of this book, which helps fund our many outreach programs to military personnel, prisons, hospitals, nursing homes, and educational institutions. To learn more, visit GuidepostsFoundation.org.

We also maintain many useful and uplifting online resources. Visit Guideposts.org to read true stories of hope and inspiration, access OurPrayer network, sign up for free newsletters, download free e-books, join our Facebook community, and follow our stimulating blogs.

To learn about other Guideposts publications, including the bestselling devotional *Daily Guideposts*, go to ShopGuideposts .org, call (800) 932-2145, or write to Guideposts, PO Box 5815, Harlan, Iowa 51593.

Find more inspiring fiction in these best-loved Guideposts series!

Secrets of Wayfarers Inn

Fall back in history with three retired schoolteachers who find themselves owners of an old warehouse-turned-inn that is filled with hidden passages, buried secrets and stunning surprises that will set them on a course to puzzling mysteries from the Underground Railroad.

Sugarcreek Amish Mysteries

Be intrigued by the suspense and joyful "aha" moments in these delightful stories. Each book in the series brings together two women of vastly different backgrounds and traditions, who realize there's much more to the "simple life" than meets the eye.

Mysteries of Martha's Vineyard

Come to the shores of this quaint and historic island and dig into a cozy mystery. When a recent widow inherits a lighthouse just off the coast of Massachusetts, she finds exciting adventures, new friends, and renewed hope.

Patchwork Mysteries

Discover that life's little mysteries often have a common thread in a series where every novel contains an intriguing mystery centered around a quilt located in a beautiful New England town.

Mysteries of Silver Peak

Escape to the historic mining town of Silver Peak, Colorado, and discover how one woman's love of antiques helps her solve mysteries buried deep in the town's checkered past.

**To learn more about these books,
visit Guideposts.org/Shop**

Sign up for the
Guideposts Fiction Newsletter
and stay up to date on the books you love!

You'll get sneak peeks of new releases, recommendations from other Guideposts readers, and special offers just for you . . .
and it's FREE!

Just go to Guideposts.org/Newsletters today to sign up.

Guideposts®

**Visit Guideposts.org/Shop
or call (800) 932-2145**